ANOTHER
DAY GONE

ALSO BY ELIZA GRAHAM

Playing with the Moon

Restitution

Jubilee

The History Room

Blitz Kid

The One I Was

ANOTHER DAY GONE

ELIZA GRAHAM

LAKE UNION
PUBLISHING

Text copyright © 2016 Eliza Graham
All rights reserved.

Published by Lake Union Publishing, Seattle

www.apub.com

Amazon, the Amazon logo, and Lake Union Publishing are trademarks of Amazon.com, Inc., or its affiliates.

ISBN-13: 9781503940031
ISBN-10: 1503940039

Cover design by Debbie Clement

Printed in the United States of America

For Sally Atcherley-Symes

PROLOGUE

Coventry and Warwickshire Hospital, 6 p.m., 25 August 1939

The girl with the cut face sitting up in the hospital bed closed her eyes for a moment. Probably hoping the ward might disappear and she'd find herself back on Broadgate, shopping for frocks or stockings. The sergeant watched fear and confusion sweep her young face as she opened her eyes and looked at her plastered left wrist. From the corner of the side-room a distressed sigh came from the girl's mother.

'Did you see anything before the bomb went off, miss?' the sergeant asked. 'Anything at all out of the usual?'

'Just the pavement sweeper and the shoppers.'

'You didn't notice a bicycle on Broadgate?'

'Oh.' She sat up, grimacing with the effort. 'I saw a man with a tradesman's bike.'

'And this man you saw left the bicycle outside Burton's store?'

She closed her eyes again, replaying the scene perhaps. The sergeant liked a thoughtful witness. 'Yes. He propped it up against the kerb.'

He closed his notepad. 'There'll be an inquest. And police investigations, of course. We'll need to talk to you again.' There were so many people they had to interview. But this girl did seem to have been very close to the explosion this afternoon.

Excitement seemed to overcome the girl, bringing some colour into her wan cheeks. 'I can draw him for you. The bomber, I saw his face.'

'Draw him, miss?'

'I sketch people. I want to study art.'

This girl, who must be just out of school and barely trusted to choose her own frocks, thought she could show the police what the suspect, the terrorist, looked like?

'My pad and pencil are in my bag.' She pointed at her leather satchel, which someone must have retrieved from the pavement.

Her right hand was only lightly scratched. The sergeant pulled the hospital table over her legs and she placed the pad on it, sketching the man, her plastered left wrist holding the paper in place. She didn't seem to fluster herself with detail, working quickly and assuredly.

'Shame I haven't got coloured pencils.'

Did she think this was a school art lesson?

'For his hair,' she added.

'His hair?'

'It was a reddish colour. Quite unusual.' She dotted a few freckles on his nose and added more detail to the pattern on his wool cap. 'That's him.' With a look of satisfaction, she pushed the pad towards the officer, who examined her sketch with surprise. He'd expected some crude approximation to a male, with possibly some useful distinguishing features: bushy moustache, bulbous nose, missing teeth. But this man she'd drawn, well, he was a living human being. Bit of a looker, truth be told. She'd drawn expression in his eyes, which shone with intelligence and something else. Friendliness. Warmth.

'He actually seemed like quite a normal person,' the girl said, seeming to read the sergeant's mind. 'I wouldn't have imagined him as an IRA man.'

The police couldn't say for certain that it was an IRA bomb that had gone off on the busy Coventry shopping street, but the chances were high. Those terrorists had been busy with their damned bombs for most of the year, blowing up hotels, left luggage departments and post offices across Great Britain.

'And the man you saw definitely had the bicycle with him?' the sergeant asked.

The girl sighed and went through it all again, how the young man had propped it up against the kerb outside Burton's store on Broadgate. This was Coventry, home of the bicycle, and like most Coventrians, the girl had an eye for a bike. It was a Halford, a black delivery type, with a large basket on the front.

'Well done, miss. This will be very helpful indeed.'

Seemingly exhausted by the effort, the girl sank back on the pillows. 'Did . . . ?'

'Darling.' From behind the sergeant the girl's mother spoke for the first time. 'Probably best we tell you before you read about it in the newspapers. I'm afraid people died this afternoon and many others were injured.' She approached the bed and took the girl's hand, while the sergeant told her quickly about the casualties – at least, what was known about them. A fifteen-year-old boy. A girl of twenty or so, due to be married. And several others. Scores injured, too, some probably maimed for life.

'Someone was watching over you.' The mother's voice sounded shaky. They'd probably only gone shopping for autumn clothes or new shoes, probably only been at that spot on Broadgate because the mother wanted a tie or shirt from Burton's for the girl's father. Lucky she'd been right at the back of the store when the bomb had gone off, or she too would have landed in a hospital bed or even the mortuary. A mundane lunchtime errand had turned into something terrible for the pair of them.

'I saw a flash reflected in Burton's windows, then they shattered. Everything just unravelled into fragments. Glass, brick and timber – blown to bits.' The girl sounded dreamy now, the shock of it all catching up with her. Or perhaps they'd given her something for her broken wrist. The sergeant stood up.

'Like an impressionist painting, but spikier,' she went on. 'Pavement slabs flying. Then a rumble. This car, it just unfurled into flames. And the people . . .'

Some people said that talking about a terrible experience helped. As he thanked the girl again, wishing her a speedy recovery, the sergeant could see that she wasn't really listening to him. She was running through the explosion again, feeling the blast as it smashed her against the pavement, winding her. Feeling the muscles in her chest relax, so she could gasp in air, dust laden, metallic tasting. Nothing hurting just yet. Opening her eyes, blinking out grit, hearing nothing but a high-pitched ringing in her ears.

The sergeant hadn't been on Broadgate that afternoon, but he'd been in a trench in northern France in 1916 when a shell had exploded, killing his companions. He'd never really talked about it. The girl in the hospital bed was, what, seventeen, eighteen? He'd been that age, too. He wanted to tell her that he knew what it was like, that sometimes he could still taste the burnt metal, blood and earth, smell the roasted flesh, hear the screams.

But that would be highly inappropriate.

ONE

SEVERANCE
SARA

Thames End House, Oxfordshire, 24 July 1992

Young Joe was just a boy a few years younger than I was. He could barely even talk because of a head injury he'd suffered when a lorry had run him over. But what he'd told me had been enough to fill me with a white rage. As I tore back from the ferry mooring to Thames End House, it was a wonder the heels of my pumps didn't throw up sparks as they struck the pavement.

'Hi.' Polly barely glanced up as I came into the kitchen. She looked as relaxed as always. My sister sat at the kitchen table, still laid for two, with crumb-covered plates and empty tea mugs on it. Her response was casual, but I could tell she knew that I was unhappy.

'All very cosy.' I nodded at the table. Bridie's brown earthenware teapot was on the table, too, and somehow this infuriated me. 'He was here today, wasn't he? While I was at school.'

She knew what I meant and didn't try to pretend otherwise. 'So what? Michael's been here before.'

'When he was a child.' When he'd been visiting his Aunt Bridie, our housekeeper, childhood nanny and so much more. 'You've betrayed me.'

'Don't be so melodramatic.' She stood up to put the sugar bowl in the cupboard. Polly had always been tidy. 'You weren't exactly going out with him.'

'No, but we . . .' There'd been something between us. There had been for years, an unspoken mutual awareness. He'd asked me out a few times recently; I'd gone up on the train to London to meet him and once or twice he'd come down to Oxford and we'd hung around together. Nothing much had happened yet – we'd gone to the cinema, walked along the Cherwell. His father had died a few months ago, and sometimes we talked about that.

'Perhaps you made more of it than Michael did?'

My face must have shown my rage. Polly's eyes widened and for a second she looked off-balance.

'I don't think so.' I was trying to salvage my dignity. *Don't let Polly see you care.* But I couldn't keep my cool. 'You always want to spoil things for me.'

'What?' Polly had regained her poise, wiping the table with her usual casual elegance.

'Even my First Holy Communion.'

'I don't know what you're talking about.'

'You spilled Ribena on my dress, remember?' I heard my voice rise.

'Can't believe you're still brooding about something that happened, what, nine years ago?' She shook the crumbs out of the cloth over the sink. 'God, Sara.' She hadn't denied spilling the drink on purpose, though.

'I want to know why you've started seeing him,' I said. Now it all made sense. Michael hadn't sent me one of his postcards this week. Usually there was a card he'd picked up from some obscure museum or gallery, a funny picture on the front and a few cryptic words on the back. He sent them to me care of Young Joe so that it could be our secret.

'How did you find out?' she asked.

'Young Joe saw you together.'

'Oh.' She didn't sound surprised. How could she be so cold? The years of hurt swelled up in me, hurt for the times she'd taken my love and thrown it back at me, taken my trust, and now stolen Michael from me. 'Is that what this is about?' she said.

'I sometimes wish you weren't in my life.' I thought how it would be if I didn't have a sister like Polly, if teachers weren't always comparing us, if Bridie didn't use my sister as the constant, perfect exemplar of every single virtue. *Neat Polly, clever Polly, athletic Polly, beautiful Polly.*

'Do you really think you'd be happier without me, Sara?' She sounded almost sad for a second. Part of me wanted to tell her I didn't mean it, but the other part, the proud part, wanted to hurt her, show her she was nothing to me.

'Sometimes.' I didn't tell her that I'd sometimes fantasised about how life would be when Polly went to university and it was just Grandad, Bridie and me living at Thames End House, how I would be freed from that constant feeling of being compared. I didn't say any of this, but she must have read it on my face.

'OK.' She sounded resigned. 'I was going to go away soon, anyway. It's all planned.'

'You mean university?'

'I don't need a degree.'

'What?'

'University isn't for me.'

'Of course it is.'

Polly was clever. She was supposed to be going to Bristol in September to read English, if she got her grades, and of course she would. If she did even better than expected she might even change her plans and take a year out to apply to Cambridge.

'I don't need to be stuck in some library or lecture theatre. I read a lot anyway,' she said. I'd seen her in her bedroom at night. A lot of the books she read were history volumes she'd borrowed from Grandad. I'd noticed that quite a few were books about Ireland. Michael's influence, I realised now. He'd never talked about politics to me. When we were together we didn't seem to talk about much in particular: just music we liked, or films we'd seen. But perhaps with Polly he preferred more serious conversation. Maybe conversation wasn't all they'd got up to. I pictured his hands on her body, her hands on his.

'I don't fit in here like you do,' she said, suddenly.

'What the hell are you on about?'

'You can be a bit dense, Sara.'

I stared at her.

'Yeah, yeah, you don't know what I'm talking about.' White patches appeared on her cheeks. I'd rarely seen my sister angry.

'I don't.'

She looked at me for five full seconds. 'Seriously?'

I shrugged. The white patches faded. The fury in her eyes turned to disbelief and then a kind of puzzled acceptance.

'Work it out for yourself, Sara. And have a think about how it felt for me to find out.'

'Find out what? You sound paranoid.'

She turned her attention to the table, fetching the dishcloth and wiping up more crumbs as carefully as Bridie herself would have done. 'You used to think that Bridie was harder on you than me, didn't you?'

'Of course she was.' I had simply never been like my sister. Things that Polly found easy eluded me. That I'd managed any kind of competence in life at all was down to Bridie: chiding, scolding, not letting me get away with second best. Watching my diet with unblinking scrutiny when it had become clear that particular foods, bread particularly, made me ill. 'I needed her on my back,' I told Polly. Bridie had pushed me to study hard, to work on my daydreaming, my absent-mindedness, my physical weakness.

Polly laughed at that. 'You really haven't a clue.' Her voice trembled on the last word, which was enough to make me step towards her, to believe that I could still connect with her as we had done as young girls, bring her back. 'I really thought you must know.'

'Know what?'

She shook her head, shaking out the dishcloth and then looking at her watch. 'I can catch the 5.20 p.m. I wasn't planning to leave this soon, but Michael and I were due to go next week anyway.'

Michael and I.

I closed my eyes, thinking back to the last time I'd seen Michael, a fortnight ago. We'd gone to the Phoenix Picturehouse in Oxford to see an old French film. He'd been quiet, I remembered. Hadn't wanted to buy anything to eat or drink because he said he was saving his money. We'd been supposed to meet up again, two days after Polly's birthday, for another film, but he'd sent me a card the day before saying he'd have to cancel, he was going to Leamington Spa. It had sounded like a respectable old person's kind of town, and I couldn't imagine Michael there. It had hurt me.

Had my sister been away at the same time? Of course, there'd been the day she'd claimed she was going to London with a friend from school.

'Where are you and Michael going?'

I felt Polly hesitate, felt the longing in her for our old companionship: the three of us females in the kitchen each evening – Bridie preparing a meal, Polly and me doing our homework – and Grandad coming in with a pile of typed papers for Bridie to look over when she'd finished peeling the potatoes and helping me with my Latin. She didn't answer.

'Is it just for a holiday?'

'I'm not sure how long we'll be away. I'll let you all know.'

'How will you afford it?'

'Savings. And Michael's earned quite a bit in his holiday job.' He worked on construction sites in London during university holidays.

'You can't just go off,' I said, 'not without telling them. I'll ring Grandad now, tell him. And Bridie.'

'By the time they get here I'll be gone.'

'The police—'

'I'm eighteen, Sara.'

I thought of the little birthday party Bridie, Grandad and I had organised just five days ago: the cake, the presents carefully chosen and wrapped. Polly had seemed to enjoy it, putting on the silver necklace with its little silver eternity ring pendant that I'd bought her, and thanking Grandad with real warmth for the large cheque he'd given her. No wonder, I thought now: she needed the funds for running away. She'd sat at the kitchen table with her birthday cake in front of her looking so expectant, as though she were waiting for something big to happen now that she was officially an adult. Had the arrival at adulthood disappointed her? Or was it us? Me? Perhaps I'd always been a disappointment to my newly grown-up sister?

She was wearing the necklace I'd given her today, I noticed. 'You'll break their hearts,' I told her. I meant that she'd break mine, even though I'd hated her and wished her gone just a minute earlier.

A flash of something like pain passed over her features and I thought I'd pulled her back to me. 'That's not what I want,' she said. 'It's for the best. Michael and I—'

Someone shouted out from a pleasure craft chugging past the end of our garden and she jumped. Laughter rang out. Polly's face hardened. 'Look at the photographs, Sara,' she said. 'Have a good look at all the faces, the Sheehans and the Stantons.' The Sheehans were Michael's family; Polly and I were Stantons. Our father had been the first-born of Grandad's twin boys.

'Why? I've seen them a thousand times.'

'You're very pale.' There was concern in her voice.

'I'm always pale. Even in summer.' And my eyes were always shadowed and my legs and arms skinny, untoned.

'I don't get tired like you do, Sara.'

'Thanks for the interest in my health, just as you steal my boyfriend.'

'But he wasn't ever really your boyfriend, was he?' Again, she didn't sound unkind, but that made the words even harder to hear. I felt my eyes prickle. 'I wish you'd go back to the doctor.'

'Don't try and divert me. What did you mean about looking at the photos?'

She shrugged, starting to walk out. I grabbed her arm. 'What did you mean, Polly?'

She tried to wriggle free. Polly was stronger than I was, but emotion made my grip tight.

'Look at the documents in the filing cabinet too,' she said. 'In the file where Grandad keeps our passports.'

Polly pulled her arm free and left the kitchen without looking back at me. 'I've left them a note,' she called as she ran upstairs. 'On Grandad's desk.' I heard her taking clothes out of cupboards and opening drawers. Minutes later, the front door closed. I wanted to run after her.

I stayed where I was. I could hear music tinkling down the stairs: Polly's musical box. She must have wound it up as a kind of tuneful farewell. Or to taunt me with memories of our lost childhood closeness. Or perhaps she'd just wanted to hear the Brahms Lullaby and watch the little ballerina dance one last time. I ran up to her room and closed the lid to shut it up. Then I went down to the drawing room to look at the photographs, as she'd suggested. There were two in silver frames on the piano: Polly and me as teenagers. Grandad with his twin sons – Mark, our father, and Uncle Quentin – as toddlers. I picked them up. In a photo album there were wedding photos showing our American mother, Jenny, on Mark's arm. Jenny had died in the same car crash as Mark and Quentin. Grandad had employed Bridie to look after Polly and me when we were tiny, and she'd stayed on at Thames End House ever since. Polly and I had looked at the wedding pictures of our dead parents on several occasions, but she hadn't directed me towards Mum and Dad today.

Again I went upstairs, this time to Bridie's room, immaculate as it always was, the old-fashioned dark-green candlewick quilt – Bridie didn't like modern duvets – pulled tightly up over sheets and blankets. On the bedside table stood a small black-and-white photograph of a woman in forties dress with two little girls: a baby, who must have been

Bridie's half-sister, Kathleen, and a girl of around four, who must have been Bridie herself. On the mantelpiece was a picture of Kathleen with Michael and his younger sister, Nuala.

I took the photographs I'd collected into my own room and laid them out on the carpet. Green-gold light from the garden fell on the images: Grandad and his two sons. Bridie and Kathleen. Kathleen and her children. Polly. Me. Round and round went the thoughts in my mind. When I entered Grandad's study my legs were shaking. Bridie had been with me when I'd last needed to go into the filing cabinet, a year ago; she'd always been so good with paperwork. She'd taken the key out of the top drawer of Grandad's desk and quickly helped me find the passport I needed for my French exchange trip, which she'd apparently already applied for weeks before I even realised I would need it.

I tried to ignore the white envelope on the top of the desk with Polly's handwriting on it. I trawled through the drawers of the cabinet until I found what I needed in an unlabelled, dun-coloured cardboard sleeve. I pushed aside Polly's letter and sat at Grandad's desk, checking the last details on the two documents in an orderly, almost distanced manner.

So now I knew. It seemed to be taking me time to process the information.

I finished and tidied all the papers neatly away – I was Grandad's granddaughter, after all, trained to know the importance of an orderly approach to research. A couple of old newspaper clippings had inserted themselves into the personal documents file. I placed them in the top drawer of Grandad's desk. Probably something he'd used for research into post-Second-World-War terrorism. My feelings towards him, Bridie and Polly were churning themselves up into a mess inside me, but I couldn't bear to leave the clippings misfiled in the personal filing cabinet.

I lined up Polly's letter in the centre of the desk again.

All my attention to neatness and order was a mask. I needed to shield myself from my anger. Emotion burned and bubbled inside me. Even when I went and sat on the jetty by the river, the rage would not let me go.

TWO

TWO

A HAUNTED
MUSICAL BOX
SARA

8 July 2005

I clung to sleep, resisting the sensation trying to tug me into wakeful-
ness. I wanted to stay in blissful numbness. The sensation divided itself
into discomfort verging on pain, and curiosity about something outside
myself. For a few more minutes I floated before half-opening my eyes.
Something was different, something in the quality of the light in this
room: watery, soft and fluid. I heard birdsong: blackbirds and thrushes
as well as ducks quacking and the chug-chug of a motorboat, its wake
lapping against a wooden jetty. Water. The river. The Thames. I was at
Thames End House, my grandfather's house.

Yesterday I'd returned here blindly, instinctively, rather than going
home to Battersea. The key must still have been in my handbag. The
tube hadn't been running when I left London, so I'd walked the short

distance to Paddington. Images of myself stumbling through streets, trying to get a mobile signal, flashed through my mind. Of how I'd hung around in Paddington in a coffee bar until the mainline trains were running again. Of how a little girl on the train had stared at me and I'd eventually realised it was because my face had a bloody cut on it, which I tried to wipe with a crumpled tissue I found in my trouser pocket. I hadn't even checked that I still had the old key to this house in the zipped pocket of my handbag. Luckily for me, the key had been there.

Something in this room wasn't right. I closed my eyes, trying to work it out. It was the positioning of the wardrobe and the chest of drawers. Bridie had never ever changed the layout of the rooms. The chest ought to be in the corner by the door and the wardrobe opposite the bed, but their positions were reversed. And on the bedside table sat a lacquered wooden musical box. It was not mine.

And this was not my bedroom. Like Goldilocks I'd crawled into someone else's bed. This was Polly's bedroom. As a small girl I'd often crept into Polly's bed when bad dreams had disturbed me, longing for the comfort of her warmth and smell. Without waking, Polly would fling an arm around me, her steady breathing calming me. Bridie would find us together in the morning. *You should have come to me, Sara,* she'd say.

But for all I'd loved Bridie, I'd only ever wanted my big sister when nightmares racked me. The habit had continued until we were adolescents. We'd both become more secretive then, more guarded.

And then, thirteen years ago, she'd left this house, placing a short letter on Grandad's desk, explaining that she and Michael needed to take some time out, a kind of sabbatical, that she would be in touch. All we'd had after that were occasional postcards. A letter, when Grandad had died.

Phone. I needed to phone Ben. I reminded myself that he was probably still out of coverage.

I needed Polly. But I didn't know where she was. The thirteen-year-long loss of my big sister hit me again and I longed for her just as I almost hated her for not being here.

I could ring Nuala – she would actually be appalled if I didn't, but Bridie's niece, close to me since childhood, had just finished more of her gruelling accountancy exams and deserved a break. Would she even remember that I'd been taking a few days out to visit a private collection of letters north of the city? I'd been on that tube train heading back to Oxford Circus to do some clothes shopping before I returned to my flat in Battersea, but why should Nuala know this?

In an emergency I still instinctively thought of Grandad. He would have known what to do, how to deal with this. His class and generation of man was bred to handle what he would have called *incidents*. But even Grandad couldn't manage events from beyond the grave, couldn't tell me that I was all right, that I had merely seen things, bad things.

Bridie. Would she even understand? How many times had I come home from school as a girl of thirteen or fourteen, finding the transition into adolescence confusing and complicated, to sit in her kitchen with a cup of strong tea and piece of tea loaf and have her tell me I'd be just grand? She was never physically demonstrative, but her words were like props.

I reached for my handbag. Her number was in my mobile's memory. My finger paused as I went to push the green dial button. What to say? But I made the call. 'It's me, Bridie,' I said when the now elderly sounding voice answered. 'It's Sara. Are you all right?'

Silence.

'Have you watched the television news, Bridie?'

'Like before,' she said. Was she thinking of the IRA mainland campaign of last century?

'Yes. But I'm fine, Bridie. And I'll be up to see you in the next few days.' I paused. I wanted to tell Bridie that I'd been so scared I'd shot back here, to the old sanctuary on the Thames, that I missed her and loved her, that it was weird to be in her kitchen and not see her standing at the sink, peeling the potatoes or filling her earthenware teapot from the kettle. But Bridie had already hung up. I rang the care-home reception and asked to speak to the manager.

'I'm not sure she's really taken in what happened yesterday, but in case she's upset, could you keep an eye on her?'

The manager promised to speak to Bridie's main carer. I must have sounded shaky because she asked me if I was all right. I told her I was fine.

I could try again to call Ben. Perhaps he would have moved back into a part of the Peruvian Amazon that had satellite connection. My mobile still had enough battery to make the call. God knows how much it would cost if I did manage to get through. When I dialled I went straight to his voicemail. I pushed the red button to end the call.

My heart was pounding again. To calm myself I looked around Polly's bedroom. I picked up her musical box, but was unwilling to open the lid and hear Brahms' Lullaby. I went on to the landing and looked downstairs into the black-and-white-tiled entrance hall. At first glance the house appeared almost unchanged, but I smelled the slight scent of neglect: rooms not regularly aired or dusted enough since Bridie had gone into the care home. *I promise the house will be looked after*, I'd told her, when we'd explained about the care home. *Make sure they use bees-wax on the mahogany*, she'd urged. *Those aerosol polishes don't do the job.*

I made a note to myself to ask the cleaner to come in more frequently than once a month. But the neglect wasn't just because of the dust; the house seemed to lack the spark of personality it had once possessed. It lacked Bridie standing at the front door telling the postman that he needed to get the doctor to look at that chest of his. It lacked Polly and me playing indoor tennis in the hall when Bridie was safely out shopping. Thames End House should be sold so that a family could live in it again. But because the lawyers still couldn't locate Polly, who shared ownership with me, the house could not be put on the market.

I needed to return to London, to reclaim the city as my home, my workplace. And to see Bridie in her care home in Putney, a location chosen so Nuala and I could visit her more often. I needed to clean myself up and get on a train. I went back into Polly's bedroom and drew the curtains, standing at the window, which I must have opened before I'd thrown myself into her bed last night. I breathed in the scent of the garden and the river. The Thames was a sheet of soft silver this morning. Another fine July morning. Commuters all across the Home Counties would make for the station, cracking jokes to try to hide their nervousness about the train journey, staring at dark-skinned, bearded men if they boarded carriages carrying rucksacks or wearing unseasonal coats.

The waft of fresh air did not blow away the slight reek of burning metal and smoke. I realised the odour was coming from me: I smelled of what had happened yesterday. Last night I had washed quickly in the basin and it hadn't been enough to remove the stench.

I looked at my watch. Half an hour to shower and find something to wear. Old clothes of mine might still hang in my wardrobe. Failing that, I could borrow some of Polly's clothes, something she'd rarely allowed when we were teenagers. I laughed at the cheek of me, as Polly herself would have put it, but it was a jerky, painful kind of laughter that risked turning into tears.

Bottles of shower gel and shampoo still stood on the shelf in the shower. The water was so cold it made me gasp. I'd forgotten to turn on the boiler last night. But when I got out I felt reinvigorated, ready to examine myself. The cut above my right eyebrow looked sore but not infected.

In the bathroom cabinet I discovered antiseptic cream and plasters, and once I'd dried myself on an old, stiff towel hanging behind the door I treated the cut. In my handbag I found concealer, which I dabbed on the red mark, along with some paracetamol, which I took for my headache.

In Polly's room I pulled the old-fashioned eiderdown into a neat rectangle over the duvet, puffing up the pillow so the bed might almost have passed muster with Bridie. I felt I should change the sheets, but nobody ever came to Thames End House any more.

In my own bedroom the oak wardrobe opened without a squeak to show me folded shirts on the shelves on one side, still smelling of the washing powder Bridie had always used. An old pair of jeans, the cotton washed to smooth, fine softness, hung solitarily from the rail. I could dress in a respectable enough fashion to make it back to my own house without people staring. I rolled up the dress I'd been wearing the previous day. There'd be a plastic bag downstairs I could wrap it in to transport it home.

The kitchen, which Polly used to refer to as Bridie's command station, smelled fusty, though everything looked neat enough, a folded dishcloth still hanging from the taps as though awaiting Bridie's return. Bridie had kept old carrier bags in a drawer beside the sink and they were still there. I stuffed the dress into an orange supermarket bag. She wouldn't have approved: *Plastic bags are only suitable for carrying food home from supermarkets.*

I just had time to look at the rest of the house. The furniture in the drawing room was covered in dust sheets. The silver frames around the photos of Polly and me and Grandad's twin sons in toddlerhood had tarnished.

In the study Grandad's last manuscript still sat neatly on his desk, bound by two rubber bands, one north to south, and the other east to west. Dust veiled the top sheet. We'd never had the heart to move the manuscript. I pulled off the bands and leafed through the pages to the end. Under the very last paragraph, he'd typed *11 September 2001*: the date he'd finished the book. He would have printed off the very last amended pages and bound the manuscript carefully with the rubber bands so that Bridie could take it to the post office, according to the long-established routine, which this last time had also involved a special lunch of steak and kidney pie, runner beans from the garden and a glass each of claret. Bridie would have bought a new roll of brown paper and carefully wrapped the manuscript, creases folded sharply and precisely, without using sticky tape, because that was for lazy people who couldn't use a ball of string. They ate lunch. She was preparing to take the parcel to the post office as a plane smashed into the North Tower of the World Trade Center.

Grandad and Bridie thought it was an accident, she'd told me. And she'd still been intending to take the parcel to the post office when a second plane had hit the South Tower. And then Grandad had known that it was no accident, that his thesis was wrong. The twenty-first century world hadn't metamorphosed into a safer place after all.

He'd unwrapped his manuscript, replacing it on the desk, wondering how he could revise it. But his imagination and knowledge of historical precedent had failed him. *I was too caught up in Europe,* he'd told me. *I should have looked east, seen all that was being fomented in the Middle East and Africa.*

There was no answer for what he and Bridie had witnessed on television that September day. Or if there was, he was too tired and old to find it, he'd said. He'd never written another word of this or any other book. There was no solution to the eternal, infernal problem of man's violence. *I couldn't help him*, Bridie had told me, sorrowfully.

Yesterday's events in London had proved Grandad right.

I closed my eyes, willing calmness on myself, making myself think of more cheerful memories. The river at the bottom of the garden. I would go out and stand on the jetty for a few minutes. It would clear my mind. I was aware that I was pushing what had happened yesterday out of my consciousness, probably unwisely.

I found the back-door key in the old pottery bowl Polly had made. The Thames sparkled as I walked outside. A family of ducks swam past, and across the river a swan arched its wings into an ivory fan. I felt my breathing slow down. I might have stood on this spot at any time in the last thirty years and seen the same things.

Back indoors, I was replacing the key in the pottery bowl when a sound from upstairs made me freeze. My heart pounded. From Polly's room came the sound of the musical box. The tinkling notes of the lullaby made me shiver. Sometimes a vibration from a passing heavy vehicle or from the old timbers in the house contracting or expanding could set off the internal spring mechanism, Grandad had once explained; that was why the music played. It was nothing supernatural, even if was unsettling. Sometimes, in the weeks after Polly's disappearance, the box had played its tune and I had rushed into the bedroom, hoping that my sister would be sitting up in her bed, giving me her slow smile. Bridie never followed me into the room, but I felt her eyes on me as I tore upstairs, felt her hurting for me. If Grandad were in the house, he would bow his head onto his hand. I knew he'd be thinking that there must be someone else he could ring, someone else who might be able to help track Polly down.

We had only slowly come to the conclusion that she'd gone to Ireland. At first, Grandad thought that the pair might have taken the classic middle-class dropout route to India, or Thailand. It was Nuala who'd pointed out that both Michael and Polly had shown considerable interest in Ireland and its history, and that Michael knew the country well as a result of all the summer holidays spent in Cork.

Hopeful that it might be easier to find Polly if she were only hundreds, not thousands, of miles away, Grandad had flown to the Republic on several occasions, but nobody had been able to tell him anything. Michael's mother, Kathleen, had travelled back to her birth country too, asking cousins and family friends if they had seen the pair. They'd gleaned nothing more than rumours of an attractive young couple appearing here and there, sometimes in a small seaside town in Cork or County Clare, occasionally even in Dublin itself. But they had always vanished before they could be located, and the Garda would always tell them the same thing: Polly and Michael were adults, not children, and they had left their homes of their own free will. They sent postcards from time to time, and some of them had Irish landscapes on them, but sometimes the postmarks had been French or Dutch. At first I'd felt anger towards Grandad and Bridie for their seeming impotence, but our mutual despair at Polly's disappearance had driven that anger away. Despair had given way to fear when we'd heard rumours about the kind of people Polly and Michael had been talking to.

Time to go. I slammed the front door behind me, striding towards the railway station and a fast train to Paddington, away from my childhood home, which now felt like a house of mirrors, each one reflecting yet another unsettling image from my past.

I needed coffee. The trains went frequently enough for me to tell myself it didn't matter if I missed the next one. I found a pavement cafe by the station and sat outside with a double espresso, trying to ignore the newspapers open around me. I couldn't help noticing that a bomb had also gone off on a bus in Tavistock Square, something I had not known yesterday. Whether you were on wheels above ground or in a metal tube beneath it, a fanatic might look you in the eye and pull on a wire to blast you into eternal oblivion.

I drank my coffee and ordered another one. Only the shakiness of my hands prevented me from going on to a third cup. I wanted a croissant. I knew I had to resist as I couldn't eat foods containing gluten, and asked instead for a yoghurt and a bottle of water. Train after train departed. Still sitting out on the pavement, I watched as they crossed the bridge over the river. I knew I should be in a library or an archive in London, or even buying the summer clothes I'd planned to shop for in Oxford Street, but I couldn't seem to make myself move towards the station. I couldn't get on a train today. I could still smell burning metal. And blood.

And if I didn't force myself to push it out of my mind, I could see the teenage girl's face. *Will they be all right?* Her English was good and she was trying hard not to shake as she glanced towards the shattered tube carriage. I'd told her the medics in London were some of the best in the world. Once we were off the train I'd stayed with her at Edgware Road station until the woman hosting her exchange visit came to collect her. They'd wanted to take me to get some first aid for my cut, but I'd managed to escape.

The waiter was asking me something, trying not stare at my forehead. I nodded and let him remove the empty yoghurt pot and water bottle. When he'd gone, I left a tip and found myself walking along the towpath out of town, studying geese and ducks and the ripples on the water's surface. My eyes made out the familiar shape of Young Joe on the opposite bank of the river. No passengers for him yet; he was applying some kind of oil to the oars of his boat.

After an hour I turned and found myself walking back into town, but instead of turning up the High Street to the station I walked back towards Thames End House. Perhaps I didn't have to go back to London right now. Ben was still away. I had my laptop with me. I could work from here, take a week, perhaps longer, travelling to archives and libraries in London as needed.

I could stay. I felt the blood in my veins pulse less fiercely; my heart slowed. This was where I needed to be.

THE PAST'S A
RAGGED STORY

SARA

14 July 2005

I found myself adopting a new rhythm in the week I spent alone at Thames End House. The tube train still flashed through my mind when I woke in the mornings. My mouth filled with the taste of burning metal. I trembled in my bed, but every day the memory hit me later and I seemed able to push it away sooner.

I'd get up and shower and then walk to have a coffee and a bowl of yoghurt and fruit at the cafe by the station. From there, I'd walk along the river, stopping to talk to Young Joe as he polished his boat and oars. The first time I spoke to him, he'd greeted me as casually as if I'd seen him the previous day, but pointed at the cut on my face in silent interrogation. I told him I'd been caught up in the London bombings. He nodded, offering no words in response and absolving me from talking about it.

This morning Joe gazed at the shimmering water. 'Polly likes it when it's all shiny,' he said, uttering one of the longest sentences I could remember him saying.

'Yes.' On summer holiday mornings in our childhood, my sister would run out to the jetty to dangle her hands in the water, begging to be allowed to take the boat out. Bridie would never let her do this until after breakfast. I wondered if Joe still missed Polly and Bridie. He rarely mentioned them. Perhaps people who were out of sight were out of mind for Young Joe. But I saw him staring at an empty stretch of water with a deep look of concentration. No, Joe and I shared a sense of loss, one which we would probably never manage to express to one another, but which flickered between us, creating a momentary sense of kinship.

I checked my mobile in case Ben had managed to text me. A missed call from Nuala. She'd tried to get me earlier in the week and I'd meant to call her back, but had been lulled into torpor by my new routine. I walked on.

As I returned to Thames End House, I noted that the cars in the street had changed. I had come to recognise the town's daily pattern. The commuters drove off to work and the shoppers parked up for a morning's activity. I'd found reassurance in this daily rhythm: the quiet period just after the morning rush; the sense of build-up after three o'clock; the relaxed, light evenings when people sat laughing and chatting in riverside pubs.

Soon the schools would break up for the summer and it would be quieter first thing. Even more pleasure crafts would run up and down the river and the swans would hiss their displeasure at their lost tranquillity. I would be back in London by then, I told myself. Staying at Thames End House was only temporary, to help me recover from what had happened in the underground. The fact that I'd slightly changed my routine today in order to replenish my supply of clothes and was returning to the house with several large bags of sandals, dresses, shirts, trousers and shorts bought on the high street here meant nothing. I'd been planning the overdue shopping trip in any case.

I remembered how Polly and I would stagger home on Saturday afternoons, laden with purchases, pulling out clothes on the kitchen table for Bridie's judgement, which usually amounted to a shake of the head and a sigh. We never dressed quite as she thought Grandad's granddaughters ought to. I sometimes went clothes shopping with Nuala, and that was fun, but not the same as it had been with my sister.

I hadn't double-locked the front door this morning when I left for the cafe, an omission that annoyed me. I went into the drawing room and sat on the sofa, which I had finally stripped of its dust sheet, taking a moment to sort out my shopping bags before I went into the study to open my laptop. My work was going well. *Too well*, a little voice inside me insisted. I'd been using it as distraction from what had happened to me, in the same way as I had avoided news reports on the radio and newspaper headlines. At night I reread my way through Grandad's ancient but elegantly bound collection of Anthony Trollope. The rural world of heart-torn young women, hunting clergymen and career-minded bishops clothed me like a protective blanket, blocking out the frightening images of twenty-first-century London. As I walked to and from the town, I could almost hear the swish of long skirts, imagining myself on the way to visit the rector's wife or the daughter of the local squire.

I thought about Bridie a lot, too, missing her presence in the house. Until now, I'd not been here for any period of time since she went into the home. Seeing her few remaining possessions in her bedroom made me wish again that I'd asked her questions about herself earlier on. So much of her childhood was now lost to us. Her sister was dead, so a whole generational link was missing.

I heard it again: the unmistakable sounds of the lullaby coming from Polly's musical box, breaking into my reverie. I'd once adored the tinkling melody, but now I was starting to hate it. I wanted to sprint upstairs to see if she was back, to scream at her, to ask her what she'd been thinking, putting us all through this for so many years, Grandad dying without seeing her again, Kathleen dying too, Bridie descending into her mental prison. Just Nuala and me left now, thrown together as survivors. Until Ben had come along, Nuala had been the only person to whom I'd felt a sense of family closeness. We saw each other, though not as often as we would perhaps have liked: she had her friends and her accountancy exams and I had Ben and my writing. Nuala knew everything I did about my family and its dark and secret places.

Footsteps outside the room made me forget my rage with my sister. I stood up, fists clenching, heart pounding. I'd never had to face an intruder before.

'I'm just ringing 999 and I am not alone.' The voice in the entrance hall was female, angry.

A woman in her mid-twenties was coming into the drawing room. Nuala herself.

'Sara?' She sounded uncertain, amazed. 'That was quick. I only left the message on your answerphone first thing this morning. I couldn't get you on your mobile.'

'Message?' I'd already reached her, wrapped my arms around her. She was still tiny; she'd been elfin as a child, and adulthood hadn't added much to her frame. 'It's so good to see you.'

It always was. We met up for meals, visited Bridie together, sometimes drove to the cemetery in west London where Nuala's parents were buried to put flowers on their graves.

'How did you know I was here?' I realised as I asked the question that she hadn't expected to find me at Thames End House, had actually thought I was a burglar.

'I didn't. I meant to leave a message on your mobile as well, but things . . . Well, they all got very complicated very fast.'

'Things?'

'She's been asking for you.'

My face must have betrayed my confusion.

'It's Polly.'

My arms fell from Nuala's waist. 'Polly?' A rush of emotion hit me. I couldn't even make out what it was: excitement and shock and something else. 'You . . .' My brain was whirring and wouldn't seem to connect with my mouth. 'What are you saying? You've heard from her?'

'She came back to London.'

'Polly's back?' I was saying words I never believed I'd ever hear.

'She went to your flat last week, but you weren't there.'

Because I'd been here. And Polly wouldn't have had my mobile telephone number because mobiles hadn't really been around when she'd left this house all those years ago.

'How does Polly even know where I live?' I asked.

'She said she tracked you down via directory enquiries and the electoral register.' Nuala was speaking slowly now. 'Polly couldn't get you to answer your door or landline, so she took a taxi to my flat. She'd located me too, in the same way.'

She tugged at my sleeve. 'Sit down for a moment, Sara, you're terribly pale.'

I felt as though all the blood in my veins had turned to water.

'What've you done to your face?'

'Just a scratch.' I couldn't go into it all now. 'Where's Polly now? Can we go to London to see her? Now?'

'Sit down first.' She pulled me onto the sofa.

'Where's she staying? Has she seen Bridie yet?'

'There's more you need to know, Sara.' Nuala sucked her lips in. I knew that expression from our childhood. It meant she had something to say she knew I wouldn't like to hear.

Polly still hated me. She hadn't really wanted to see me again, at all. She'd sent Nuala as her emissary to tell me that she was all right, but that was as far as it went.

'Polly's very ill.'

'Ill?' Polly was never ill. As a child she'd almost radiated health.

'Breast cancer. It seemed to have gone away a few years ago, she said, but then they found secondaries. She came back to London from France a week ago, to see one last specialist. It wasn't good news.' Nuala paused. She was trying to give me time for all this to sink in. I was shaking my head, as though the news were a burr to be flicked off. 'She had to decide whether to go back to France or to see whether a hospice over here would take her in for the . . . end.'

Polly hadn't even wanted me to look after her.

'I don't think she felt she could, in her own words, roll up after so many years very ill and expect you to drop everything and look after her,' Nuala said, eyes on my face as if she had read my mind. 'But when I saw her last week I realised how much she just wanted to come home for the last bit.' Nuala's voice was tender, mournful. My brain was starting to catch up. *Hospice. Last bit.*

'She's not going to get better?' I stared at the fireplace, at the poker and brush that needed polishing.

'No.' Nuala's eyes brimmed. 'I'm so sorry we've only found you today. I assumed you were overseas or buried somewhere deep in the country. Or even that you'd decided on a whim to fly out to South America to see Ben. I had no idea you were here.'

'Polly really wanted to come back home?' How long we'd been waiting for her to feel like this. But I'd never dreamt the circumstances would be these. 'After so long?'

'She's here now.' And now Nuala was smiling. 'Upstairs. In her old bedroom.'

My mouth was opening and closing. Polly, here at Thames End House?

'Bridie,' I said. 'I need to go and get her straight away. She needs to see Polly.'

'I wanted to bring her down with us, but I didn't think I'd be able to manage.'

Moving Bridie anywhere these days took some preparation, I reminded myself.

'Polly needs to rest. The drive down has exhausted her more than we'd thought it would.'

'I'll get Bridie.'

'Not now. Wait until later. You just need to go up and see her yourself. That's enough for her for one day.'

My leg muscles stiffened. I was almost frightened to go up those stairs, to see her again. Reunion with Polly was something I had dreamt of for so long, but now part of me wanted to run out of the house. How would she be with me? What would we say? How could I face her after so long, knowing she was dying?

Nuala led me upstairs to Polly's room. My sister lay in the bed I'd taken refuge in on my first night here before moving to my own room. The old-fashioned quilt and eiderdown had already been folded away and the bed remade with a plain duvet cover and pillowcases, white with a subtle sheen, obviously some high-thread-count bed linen. Nuala had only been in the house for a few hours while I had my breakfast, did my shopping and had my riverside stroll and chat with Young Joe, but she'd already filled a glass vase with delphiniums, stocks and sweet peas, which filled the room with their scent. Young as she was, she'd always managed houses, along with a busy career as an accountant, with aplomb, taking after her mother and Bridie, sisters who were natural homemakers, competent at any domestic task.

Polly lay in bed, propped up with cushions, a pale blue turban on her head. Her face was a little fuller than I remembered. Probably the drugs. Her eyes were slightly lined, but she didn't look her age – five days off thirty-one, just a year older than me. I thought Polly had a tan before I realised her skin was yellowed and slightly sallow, though not unattractive. From a distance, at least, it made her look as though she'd been on holiday. The turban matched the colour of her blue eyes.

'Polly.' I don't know how the thirteen lost years melted away, but we found one another in a tight embrace. She smelled of Chanel Cristalle, which I remembered her wearing as a teenager – usually when she'd pinched a bottle of it from some unfortunate store.

'I'm so glad you're here.' Her voice sounded the same, but quieter. 'I should have told you before. I'm sorry. I kept hoping I'd get better and I wouldn't have to. I was a fool. I thought I could prove the doctors wrong. I thought I still had ages yet.' In her eyes I could see the horror of the end racing too quickly towards her.

'Why did you take so long to come back?'

'It's a complicated story. I'm going to tell you everything,' she said, her breath still falling on my neck as I held her. 'Why I was so messed up. Why I did what I did with Michael.' She closed her eyes, looking drained.

'Don't say anything now.' I let her rest against the pillows. I couldn't remember ever looking after my sister when we'd been children. It had been Polly who'd brought me glasses of lemon barley water when I had a sore throat and who'd smuggled up copies of *Jackie* magazine with its enticing problem pages, a publication that didn't meet Bridie's approval.

'You look really well,' she said approvingly after a moment. 'Not so thin. Lovely glow to your skin. Did you get yourself checked out?'

'Yup. Coeliac disease. I should thank you, really, for telling me I should go to a doctor and ask for a check-up. What put the idea into your head?'

'It only occurred to me when we spoke to—' She stopped herself, smiling. 'I'll come to all that. As long as you're all right now?'

'I have got lots of energy and my brain isn't full of fog. I even wrote a thesis and I'm researching a book.'

'Nuala was telling me about your work. I'm so proud.' She sat up straighter. 'She also said you'd got some lovely man? Someone called Ben, who's really, really good news but isn't around at the moment?'

'He's looking for Peruvian woolly monkeys in the jungle.'

She grinned. 'I like the sound of this Ben. Is he good to you?'

'Very.' I couldn't help smiling at the thought of Ben. 'When he's not thousands of miles away. When we met, we were both working in London.'

She squinted at me. 'What's wrong with your face, Sara?'

'Someone was . . . in a bit of a state, upset. They lost balance and accidentally scratched me as they fell.'

'Drunk?' Her eyes narrowed. For a moment, we were little girls again and she was about to launch herself, furious, at anyone who'd pushed me over in the playground.

'Yes.' It seemed easier than explaining about the tube bombs. Her attention already seemed to have switched to another subject.

'So you looked in the filing cabinet like I told you to?'

'Yes.' I remembered how I'd extracted the dun-coloured cardboard file and looked inside, how I'd sat on the jetty watching the water flow by, making sense of what I'd discovered.

A silence fell between us that seemed to express it all: the sadness, the missed opportunities. She took my hand and squeezed it. Her palm felt warm and dry, like it had when she'd been a teenager.

'I didn't think you'd just vanish without good reason,' I said. 'Even if you and I were going through a . . .'

'Love–hate crisis?'

'We were teenage girls.' Time had caused me to reflect at length on my relationship with my sister. 'I suppose it was natural for it to feel so visceral.'

'Hormones played a part, no doubt. But what Michael and I found in the filing cabinet really . . . well, it was a blow. We weren't expecting to find that file. We were just nosy, bored teenagers on a rainy summer-holiday afternoon.' She paused. I could see that she was back in the past, a girl of fourteen or fifteen or so, emboldened by the presence of Michael Sheehan, liberated temporarily from the presence of the ever vigilant Bridie, seizing the opportunity to unlock the filing cabinet and open files she was not supposed to see. 'We just wanted stationery from his desk, but then I saw the filing cabinet key.'

'But then you waited for, what, three or four years before you went off?'

'If you run away from home when you're a child, they send the police after you. Michael told me to wait, to see if Grandad and Bridie would explain. I thought it might happen on my eighteenth. But it didn't. It made me sad and angry that they still didn't trust me – us – with the truth.'

Her eyelids flickered over her eyes again.

'By then, I'd finished my A levels. I was legally an adult and could do what I wanted. Michael wanted to drop out of university; he didn't like his degree course at King's. At first I thought he was suffering some kind of reaction to his father's death, but he insisted it was more that he didn't want to be in education any more. If we were going to go away, it seemed like a good time. He was very interested, obsessed, really, with finding out more about Bridie's early childhood and family.'

I'd never asked Bridie questions until it had been too late. Her stroke and the onset of dementia made it hard for her to relate much about herself. Occasionally small details of her early life growing up during the air raids of the Second World War dropped out, but they were snippets only: jumbled and fragmented. And the one thing I really needed to know was still locked up in Bridie's mind.

'I knew about Bridie's dementia.' A shadow passed over Polly's sallow features. 'I'm good at keeping tabs on people. I actually rang the care home once and spoke to the manager.'

'She didn't tell me you'd rung.'

Polly looked down, mouth pulled into a wry grin.

'You pretended you were me, didn't you?'

'Sorry.' Polly had always been good at pulling one over on people. 'For the last few months I've been burning to come back here and tell you everything.'

Only for that long? I wanted to ask.

'I tried to come back before, Sara. But they . . . I was warned it wouldn't be a good idea.'

'Who warned you?'

'I'll tell you about it later. Then, when I could easily have returned, the cancer changed everything. It held me up, getting diagnosed and treated.' Her face twitched; she looked uncomfortable. 'I need more morphine. I need Nuala to come and help me.'

I was her sister but she needed Nuala, not me. Nuala had been there when she'd come back to London last week and I hadn't, so she'd probably sat in while nurses and doctors briefed Polly on the care she needed now.

I turned my face to hide my pain. 'I'll go and get her.' In the kitchen Nuala pulled medicine from a white pharmacy paper bag. 'She'll sleep for the next few hours after she's had the morphine. Have a rest Sara.' She frowned at my face. 'You haven't told me how you came by that, yet. Let's talk when I come back down from Polly.'

'I'll take the boat out,' I said. 'The exercise will be better than a rest. We need to get Bridie, too.'

'Yes,' she said. 'Tomorrow. After Polly's had a night's sleep.'

Polly woke while Nuala and I were making soup. 'She might take a few spoonfuls,' Nuala said, ladling a little into a bowl.

She was awake when we brought the soup up to her. 'Smells lovely.' She sounded stronger. Nuala sat her up, placing a cushion behind her head. Polly managed to eat the soup unaided, but from a glance the two of them exchanged I wondered whether they were acknowledging that

Nuala might soon need to feed her. Did I make my sister so uncomfortable that she couldn't ask me to help her eat? My eyes pricked. I busied myself folding some of Polly's clothes that were already neatly arranged on the back of a chair.

She managed half a bowl and a bite of the soda bread Nuala had baked for her. 'As good as Bridie's,' she said.

'It was the recipe Mum gave Bridie. She always said it was an old family one, but I don't see how as our grandmother died before Mum and Bridie were old enough to have a recipe handed on.'

'It looks authentically Irish, all the same,' Polly said. 'I can almost smell the shamrock.'

Nuala laughed. 'I don't think Bridie ever went to Ireland.' I remembered this puzzling me. 'But Mum passed on enough of her views about what was proper food to her,' Nuala added.

'Bridie wouldn't buy us ice creams from the ice-cream van,' I remembered, 'because she said it wasn't proper stuff, made with cream and butter, like it was in Ireland.'

'Even the crisps were better in Ireland, too.'

'True fact,' Polly said.

Nuala placed Polly's half-empty bowl on the tray. 'For all that, Bridie always seemed almost like a proper Englishwoman to me. She loved this house and the river and tea in proper china cups.' She tutted. 'Listen to me. She still loves all those things.'

Especially this house and the river. Which we had banished her from because she couldn't cope alone.

'Bridie's best off where she is,' Polly said, the telepathy between us functioning as it had when we'd been children. 'You did the right thing, choosing that home for her.'

I felt a lump in my throat.

'Nuala told me about Bridie wandering off in the night, being found by Young Joe standing in the river in her nightdress.' She frowned. 'I wondered whether she was thinking about . . .'

'What?'

'The river gods. You remember the stories Grandad used to tell us about people sacrificing themselves in ancient Egypt or Africa or somewhere? Letting the river take them for the good of the tribe or community?'

I remembered.

'Whatever was on her mind,' Polly said, 'it was dangerous for her to live here alone.'

'I'll take this down.' Nuala left with the tray. I knew she was giving me another chance to have Polly to myself.

Polly took a sip of water. 'All the booze I used to drink. And now cold tap water and the occasional ice lolly are the most delicious things ever. Can't even drink tea. Even if Bridie made it for me herself in that old earthenware teapot, I wouldn't be able to drink it.' Her lashless eyes blinked away tears.

'Do you remember the cider?' I asked, giving her time to recover. 'How we used to take it with us in the boat?' I gave myself a mental kick. Perhaps Polly had needed to express emotion and I'd distracted her from it.

She brightened. 'And the fags. God, Bridie would have died if she'd known what we got up to.' She placed the glass on the side table, suddenly serious. 'When Michael and I found that file and opened it, I didn't want it to be true.' She looked at me with a fierce protectiveness. I remembered how she'd looked after me at school, thrown those balls at me on the netball court to teach me to catch well enough to have a chance for the team, allowed me to join in with her group, even though they were all in the year above. Polly had loved me. Despite the times she'd sneered at me or nudged me or tripped me over when nobody'd been looking, she'd loved me.

'I tried to forget what I'd found in that file, but I couldn't. As time went on it started to hurt more.'

'You hated me, sometimes, didn't you?' I asked.

'Sometimes, even before I knew. I suppose I must have picked up on something subconsciously. I had to have someone to blame. And you know what they say about those closest to you being the ones that you strike out at. As I grew up, I started blaming everything else. The system, the Establishment, the authorities – whatever you call it. Perhaps even people like Grandad and what he stood for: the British Army and what happened in Northern Ireland.'

'Grandad never served over there.'

'No, but Uncle—' she stopped.

She'd been going to say Uncle Quentin. Our father's twin had been a serving officer in Belfast until he'd received a head wound.

'It's never just one individual. It's the system, Sara.'

'We heard rumours that Michael had fallen in with gunmen while you were in Northern Ireland.' We'd picked up occasional fragments of information from Kathleen's family across the Irish Sea.

She nodded. 'I thought you would want to talk about that. You probably don't remember, but Michael and Nuala had a cousin on their father's side with special needs: Down's syndrome.'

I vaguely remembered Kathleen talking about the cousin.

'He disappeared from Belfast.' She placed a slight emphasis on the word *disappeared*.

'The IRA took him?'

'A few weeks earlier they'd accused him of passing information on to the British Army. I doubt he did. Kieran was just a very sweet, simple young man.'

'Why did they think he had?'

'Kieran took his dog out on a very cold day. It ran out on to a frozen pond and got into difficulty. An army patrol happened to be in the area, and a young squaddie helped pull the dog out. Kieran forgot he wasn't supposed to be friends with soldiers and chatted to him briefly. By chance, that same week some IRA men were shopped to the security services by people who lived on the same street as Kieran.' She had slowed down, sounding weary. 'The dog limped back a day or two later. It had been burnt with cigarette ends.' Polly shuddered. 'Kieran didn't come back until the following day. At least he did actually come back. In that respect, it wasn't a real Disappearance. He couldn't say where he'd been or what had happened. He was in shock. Bruised. Missing a tooth. They must have realised they'd made a mistake. Bad PR.'

Her words had been emerging more and more slowly. 'Even if Michael had been at all taken in by them, his blinkers certainly came off then. He knew they were more gangsters than Guevaras.'

'When was this?'

'Late 1992, I think. We'd moved north of the border after a brief break from Ireland. A friend of Michael's got us a few weeks' work packing china in a warehouse in the Netherlands. We needed to earn some cash.'

Grandad had gone to Ireland in November of that year. No wonder he hadn't picked up their trail. 'Where did you go when you came back from the Netherlands?'

'Near Carlingford Lough. You mightn't know it, Sara, but it's a beautiful sea inlet, a fjord, really, with mountains alongside.' She told me of the walks she and Michael had taken, how they'd talked of perhaps getting a dog. 'Sometimes I could just pretend we were in some novel, a pair of lovers who'd run away together. But the violence felt . . . closer. There'd been awful things happening there back in the seventies. There had been an IRA ambush and eighteen British soldiers were killed. It happened close to this ruined castle right on the water's edge. That's what was so shocking, really, all this beauty and violence existing together.'

I didn't know Ireland, north or south, and was curious, needing to imagine her somewhere all those years she'd been missing.

'Even though I loved the lough and the mountains, I started to wish that we'd stayed in the Republic. I liked Cork and Kerry, though we had to keep our heads down there, in case anyone tipped off Kathleen.'

'The Sheehans had family in the south and south-west.' She gave a little smile, perhaps picturing herself and Michael playing at cloak-and-dagger in bars along the coast. Then she looked at me and the sallowness of her face turned to red. 'We were arrogant – callous, really – not to understand the consequences of our absence for other people. That changed, Sara, it really did.'

I nodded.

'Apart from anything, Special Branch were on to us almost as soon as we crossed the border. The local police must have told them about us. They made it clear that we were a nuisance and causing a lot of anxiety to people. But then it turned out they wanted us to keep on doing what we were doing, striking up conversations, making connections, getting closer to the men in black balaclavas.'

Why? I wondered. *What exactly were Polly and Michael doing out there?*

'Special Branch wanted us, or really Michael, to act as their eyes and ears. It was dangerous, they warned us.'

I shivered.

'By spring of 1993 I'd got myself some freelance marketing and copy-writing work. I was only nineteen, but I could act older, look more experienced. I wrote bits and pieces of brochure copy for local firms. They didn't take me seriously at first, but I worked for cheap rates, pretty well for free, to start with. Eventually I got some decent projects. Michael was able to pick up odd bits of manual labour.' Her lips gave a little twitch. Clever Michael, who'd never had the chance to take up the glittering career his parents would have predicted for him. 'We sensed that everyone bar the paramilitaries was sick of the violence. By then Michael had made contact with men who'd known his family years back in the thirties and forties. It started with him just knowing the right words to the right songs. Then he started talking about . . . more serious things.'

'They accepted him?' I thought of Michael trying to persuade gunmen that he wanted to play their bloody games with them and felt sick.

'They took him off for a few nights. I never found out where he'd been. When he came back he was pale and shaking, but somehow full of excitement. He said they'd interrogated him for hours and hours, threatened him. They were still wary, though. Especially because of me. I ended up staying in the cottage, not even going out for walks, for weeks.'

'Why didn't you come back?'

'I couldn't leave Michael. They wanted him to plant a bomb in a coach station to show them they could rely on him.' Her voice indicated dark amusement at this. 'Don't look so disapproving, Sara. We were given a dud to substitute. On the news the bomb disposal experts claimed it had been defused.'

I didn't know what to say. Bombs. Paramilitaries. Intelligence services. *Why had she involved herself in all this?*

'By the autumn Special Branch were asking us to do other things.' She must have seen the horror on my face. 'I won't go into all that now. It was around then that I first tried to get home. It was Grandad's seventy-fifth birthday. Sending you those postcards wasn't enough. I had to see you. But the intelligence people told me it was dangerous – October '93 had been a murderous month with a bombing by the IRA and a mass-shooting by the Ulster Freedom Fighters. They said Grandad was an establishment figure and I shouldn't do anything to draw paramilitary attention to the three of you.' She sounded wistful. 'Now I wish I'd just taken the risk, instead of you thinking I just didn't care about you all. But back then I was scared at the thought of them finding out about you. I'd been so discreet about who I was in Ireland, using Mum's maiden name.'

I wondered whether Grandad had ever thought to search for her under that surname. I hadn't, on the occasions I'd tried to find information about her on the internet.

'Why didn't you come back for Grandad's funeral?' I asked. The question had to be put, as brutal as it was.

'In 2002 I was in Jordan,' she said. 'I first noticed the lump in my breast about then and I had surgery. They said it was a rare but aggressive type of cancer. Not caused by one particular gene.' She looked at me and gulped. 'When I saw the obituary I was still in hospital. I should have tried to explain all that when I wrote.'

Her letter had been brief. Now I understood why.

'They thought they'd caught it early enough,' she said, quietly.

I couldn't answer. It took a moment before I could speak again. 'I still don't fully understand why you got involved in the first place, why you felt you had to go off. Leaving aside Michael, what was Ireland and the Troubles to you? You're not Irish.'

'Michael would have been a lot to leave aside.' Grief darkened Polly's features. 'We still don't know what happened to him, Sara. He just went out to buy a newspaper.'

Michael had always been a news addict. I could close my eyes now and see him in this very house, downstairs in Grandad's study, reading a pile of history periodicals on a rainy summer-holiday afternoon.

'Michael was only twenty-two,' Polly said. 'And Kathleen had to die not knowing where he was, whether his body would ever be dug up in some peat bog. Or whether he'd simply had a fatal accident somewhere and never been found. And Bridie will probably never know, either.'

Bridie had been so proud of her handsome and clever nephew.

'I just hope that Nuala finds out the truth about what happened to him one day.'

I found myself incapable of speech. Polly seemed to be forcing herself to make even more effort with her account of what had happened to her and Michael.

'You still don't really understand why I went to Northern Ireland, do you? I should have written you a letter too, when I left, but I couldn't find a way of doing it. Anything I tried to write just looked petty. Or over-heroic, somehow.'

It had hurt that the letter she had left on Grandad's desk had been addressed just to him and Bridie.

'I really thought you'd read the newspaper cuttings in the file with the birth certificates,' she said.

'Cuttings?'

'It would have explained why we left.' Her voice sounded as though it were coming from someone decades older than she was. 'I should have been clearer when I told you to look. But perhaps even then you wouldn't have spotted it.'

'You need to rest.' I covered her with the duvet as gently as I could. Even in the few hours I'd spent with her, she seemed to have grown frailer. I had the sense that she might shatter if she told me too much too soon.

I went down to talk to Nuala, who was writing a shopping list. 'I don't know how much food to get.' For a moment her usually confident expression faltered. She didn't know how long we were all going to stay at Thames End House, how long Polly would live for.

'I wish I'd made more effort to search her out before. I should have thought she might change her surname like that.'

'Polly's Polly. If she didn't want to be found, no way you'd have found her.' Nuala rolled her eyes and might almost have been her mother expressing half annoyance, half frustration. 'I think she was scared, too, of how it would be between you two when she reappeared. She might have thought you'd be angry. Justifiably so, perhaps.'

I couldn't deny it. Perhaps only the news of the cancer cells metastasising had been enough for her to overcome her fear of reappearing.

'It should be me looking after her,' I said. 'You have your job.'

'So do you. I'm between exams now, and I have holiday owing me.'

'I can write my book from here. Grandad was productive enough in this house.'

'She's your sister. I don't want to get in the way.'

'You're not.' It wasn't a case of three being a crowd. Seeing Polly again was such an intense experience that having Nuala here too felt like a much-needed emotional cushion.

'I'll help as much as I can,' she continued. 'I hope you don't mind, but I organised for the district nurses to come out tomorrow. I registered Polly with a GP practice here as it was her last permanent UK address. I was also looking into getting nursing cover for the nights from one of the charities, if we need it.' She looked at me more closely. 'What really happened to you, Sara?'

I put a hand to my eye. I'd forgotten about my injuries, caught up in Polly. I told Nuala briefly what had happened. 'I was on a train going the opposite way to one of the trains where the bombers blew themselves up a week ago. It was near Edgware Road. We heard . . . I saw this . . .' I couldn't really describe what I'd seen. 'We didn't even know what it was at first. Some kind of collision. A power outage, perhaps. But then . . .' Then I'd seen other people. People who had been hurt, irreparably damaged. A man with bloodied face and hands had waved desperately at me through the windows of our carriages. I hadn't known what to do, hadn't been able to smash the windows. In the end I'd stayed where I was, trying to comfort the young exchange girl, dragging fragments of French from my memory. When we'd been let out of the rear of our train, a woman who'd been on the stricken neighbouring train had lurched at us from the dark: shaking, clutching at me, catching my face with a jagged nail that she must have torn as she escaped her carriage. I'd fallen then and banged my head on the side of the tunnel.

I hadn't allowed myself to think of this today. Polly's reappearance had pushed it all out of my mind. Was grief for a loved one's imminent death an appropriate way to get over disturbing flashbacks?

'So you're probably suffering from some kind of shock. Have you spoken to Ben?'

'He's out of coverage. He'll ring me when he can, though.' I felt my eyes prick. *Oh Ben, why did you have to be right in the middle of a rainforest just at this moment? Polly dying, the suicide bombers . . .*

Nuala went on, her voice gentle. 'You shouldn't have been alone. You should have called me.'

'I know. I suppose I felt, I don't know, almost ashamed about scuttling back here. I wasn't even in the train that was blown up.'

'You don't like showing weakness, do you, Sara?'

'Me?' I smiled. 'No.' I never had done, not since Polly had gone. Perhaps I'd decided then that nobody was going to make me feel so vulnerable again.

'Seeing you is doing me good, Nuala.' I realised how much it was true as I said it. Polly had almost overwhelmed me emotionally, but seeing Nuala was simply refreshing, as it always had been since she'd been a little girl: simple, uncomplicated.

'I'll be keeping an eye on you,' Nuala said. She might have been her mother, half chiding, half affectionate. She seemed to fall into a reverie. Eventually she spoke again, 'Mum and I barely dared talk about our fears and suspicions over the years. But she always said Michael wouldn't be involved in any of the violence, that he was too clever to fall for their lies and promises. But I think it broke Mum. I'm sure that's why she had the heart attack. She wasn't that old.'

Polly had sent a letter to Kathleen, telling her that Michael had vanished, that the police on both sides of the border were looking for him, that she herself was talking to anyone she could think of, going through his computer to find clues, walking the routes they regularly took in case there was some sign of him.

'Did Kathleen think the IRA had taken him?'

'It seemed a possibility. Though the Disappearances had pretty well stopped by the nineties.'

'Polly told me they were actually passing on bits and pieces of information to the security services. I should have known Polly and Michael wouldn't have had anything to do with those people.'

'Don't go blaming yourself. Polly's always been a dark horse. And that brother of mine, too.' She sounded tired now. Looking after Polly must have worn her out. 'They were such a golden pair as teenagers, weren't they? So good-looking. I used to sit at this table wondering why some people got it all: looks, brains, charm.'

'You and me both.'

'Funny how things turn out.' She looked at me directly. 'Of course, both of us had something very important that Polly didn't have.'

'Yes.' I knew what she meant, but couldn't bring myself to name it. The silence, heavy with its unspoken truth, hung between us for a few seconds. We'd both had a gift that Polly, for all her beauty and poise, had not possessed. Something that the fairy godmothers had neglected to provide her with when they'd lavished her with all the other blessings.

'Talk to Polly again when she's woken up and had something to eat,' Nuala said.

I looked over at her upside-down list, trying to decipher the words, giving myself time.

'Sometimes I think I see my brother on the street,' Nuala said, dreamily. 'I imagine that if I turn round quickly Michael will be right behind me, making sure I'm all right.'

'I used to feel like that too,' I told her. 'With Polly. She'd be coming out of a pub, or sitting outside my flat, or standing on the riverbank, watching me row.'

'Because Michael was quite a bit older than me – I think Mum had miscarriages in between our births – we didn't do that much together, but he was just *there*. My big brother. He wasn't outwardly affectionate, but once, when I had some trouble with some older kids at school, he sorted them out for me. Then he just went away, just rang us saying he'd decided not to finish his degree, that he was going travelling with Polly. He used to send us postcards, but the postmarks never matched the pictures on the front.'

'Same as Polly's postcards. They must have got other people to post them.'

Nuala doodled at the bottom of the shopping list. 'Michael wasn't even there for Mum's funeral. Perhaps he was dead himself by then.' I saw that Nuala's doodle was a small cross.

I remembered how Bridie and I had stood with Nuala at her mother's committal. We'd seemed such a small group of mourners, Gerard having died before Polly and Michael had even left home. How grateful we'd been for the family group from Cork who'd come over and insisted on a proper wake.

I found myself pulling her into an embrace. She'd lost everyone in her immediate family. I still had Bridie. And Polly, for what was left of her life. 'You're not alone,' I told her. She pulled me tighter in response. 'Can you forgive Polly?' I asked.

'There'll be a reason for what she did. And she knows she's got so much to explain. When she couldn't get hold of you in London, she was distraught.'

Until now I could hardly have imagined my sister ever being distraught.

'At least she tried to come back home,' I said, telling Nuala what Polly had mentioned about being warned off a return to Thames End House. 'It makes me feel better knowing that she wanted to be with us.'

Nuala didn't appear surprised.

'Polly told me she'd tried to come back on at least one other occasion, a year or so later. The flight from Belfast was cancelled.' Nuala laughed bitterly. 'Bomb hoax, would you believe.' She hesitated for a few moments. 'Go up to her in about an hour,' she said 'She might be less sleepy then.'

Communication between me and my sister was now going to be restricted by her pain and her varying degrees of fatigue, I reflected, trying not to remember the healthy girl throwing the ball across the netball court or running the last leg of the relay race to bring victory to her school house.

While I waited for Polly to wake up I chatted to Nuala about her accountancy exams, the holiday she was planning in the early autumn, the man she'd been out to dinner with and thought she liked. When the time had passed and we thought Polly might be stirring, Nuala went up alone first, carrying a small plastic basket full of drugs, telling me that there were things Polly needed her to help with. Perhaps Polly would feel comfortable enough to let me help her in due course. Or perhaps the old relationship between us, in which she was the helper and I the helped, would continue to prevent her from allowing me to nurse her.

Nuala returned with the plastic basket. 'All done.' She looked at me anxiously. 'I'm not trying to push you out of doing things for her, you know, Sara. It's just that the nurses showed me what to do before we left London.'

'I don't mind,' I said. It was nearly the truth.

Polly was listening to an audiobook CD on her laptop when I came in, something bloodthirsty about vampires. 'Hope I don't die before I reach the end.' She switched it off. I raised an eyebrow. 'Not the worthiest deathbed story,' she said, drily. 'No great moral to it, or deep truth. That's why I like it. Remember how Bridie used to bribe us into good behaviour by threatening not to finish stories we liked?'

'More blackmail than bribery,' I said. She grinned. 'You need to tell me your story,' I told her. 'Beginning, middle and end.'

'You're a historian. You know the past isn't always as easily tidied up as that.' She let her eyelids drop over her eyes.

'What are you thinking about?' I asked gently.

'You. You and Michael.'

I laughed. 'Not much to think about there.'

'Oh, you're wrong. He really liked you, you know. I think he found you more attractive than you realised. And it was only because we found out . . .' She opened her eyes. 'Even then, he couldn't keep away from you, could he? Started seeing you again when you were older, before he and I left. We weren't romantically involved then, you know. We only really . . . became a couple . . .'

Slept together, she meant.

'. . . just before we left for Ireland. After he stopped seeing you.' She looked directly at me. 'If he'd stayed in England he would have wanted to be with you, for definite. There was something about you that he found, I don't know, familiar. Like being at home, he once said, being with someone he belonged to.'

The complexity of Michael's feelings for me would have taken a long time to describe, I realised. They would have been a whole conversation in their own right, and Polly was looking tired again.

'Apart from you turning eighteen, what made Michael decide that then was the time to go off?' I asked. 'He seemed to like his university course at first.'

'He read a newspaper article about old IRA men who'd been involved in the original campaigns between the First and Second World Wars dying with their secrets.' She let out a sigh. 'Of course, without seeing the newspaper cuttings I was talking about, that won't mean much to you. I'll explain why it mattered, why we had to make a move then.' She stretched her neck, appearing uncomfortable. 'I think he tried persuading authorities at King's to let him take a year off and come back to finish his economics degree, but they wouldn't do it.'

'Here, let me.' I helped her sit up on the pillows. 'Why was Michael so bothered about IRA men? I know he was very concerned about the Troubles, of course. But his parents came from the south, didn't they?'

'There's so little time to explain,' she said, sounding almost panicky. 'And we need to go right back to the beginning, to Coventry.'

'Coventry?' This mention of a random city in the Midlands seemed so jarring. But in my mind a bell tinkled gently. Someone had mentioned Coventry once before in my hearing.

'I'm going to tell you. But my mind . . .' she put a hand to her head. 'Everything's starting to get muddled, Sara. And if I can't tell you, what's the point of me coming back now?'

I took her hand. 'Even if you can't tell me anything more, coming back now is the best, the *only*, thing you could have done.'

She squeezed my hand back. 'I *can* do this, Sara.' Her grip on my hand was almost painful. 'If I keep it all in the right order. But I need Bridie.' She looked distressed.

'We'll get her.'

I could see her trying to take command of her failing body. 'She's part of this. It all started in a busy Coventry street when an IRA bomb detonated.'

'In the seventies?' I was too young in that decade to remember much of the television news, but I remembered Grandad talking about the mainland IRA bombing campaign.

'Decades earlier. Just before the Second World War.' She let my hand go.

I'd had no idea that the IRA had been bombing the mainland back then.

'What has Coventry got to do with Bridie? With us, Polly?'

She took a sip of water, eyes closed, concentrating. 'A girl sketches a man for the police. Remembers him so clearly, every detail. His name is Jack.' She replaced the glass, looking tired. 'Things weren't as they seemed, though. It took the air raid for the truth to come back to her.' I could barely hear the mumbled words.

'Air raid?'

'In Coventry. Then another one in Walthamstow.'

I knew very little about Walthamstow, except that it was near Epping Forest. I couldn't remember ever visiting that part of the world, with or without Polly.

'The mind fills in the gaps,' she said. 'Sometimes wrongly.' I knew this from my own academic research: misinterpreted letters; connections between people and ideas, misconstrued or ignored. 'That's what happened to Dorothy when she saw Jack. She was the witness that lunchtime in Coventry.' Her words were slurred now, coming more slowly. 'Can't finish it now,' she said. 'Sorry.' She seemed to have dropped off, but then opened her eyes again. 'When can I see Bridie?' she asked.

'Tomorrow. I'll go and get her. First thing.'

She murmured something else about bombs in Coventry and someone being hit on the head. 'Anna,' I thought she said. Her eyes closed. I walked to the window and drew the curtains so that the light wouldn't disturb her sleep.

A GREY, WIDE PRESENCE

SARA

15 July 2005

'I'll go to Putney for Bridie,' I told Nuala, the morning after she and Polly had arrived at Thames End House. We sat in the kitchen with a pot of tea. I'd gone in to see my sister very early. As the light got brighter she had spoken, lucidly to start with, about our childhood. But this talk of our old life in this house had made her longing to see Bridie more intense. I hadn't had the heart to press her more about her life away from us and the reasons for her departure.

'Does Polly sound confused to you?' Nuala asked, pouring me a strong cup of tea.

'I'm worried that her . . .' I wasn't sure how to say it.

'That the cancer's affecting her brain,' Nuala said quietly. We let the implications of that sink in for a moment.

'She's talking about being with people in Walthamstow in an air raid, and then we're in Coventry in another air raid. There's a girl called

Dorothy who saw something, but I can't work out what. And she was murmuring about someone called Anna or Hannah.'

'Hannah?' Nuala shrugged. 'Doesn't ring any bells. A friend?'

'I don't think so. What about a man called Jack?'

Nuala shook her head. Her eyes were shadowed, sorrowful.

'Sorry. You're probably right. Bridie may well remember things that happened years ago, even if her short-term memory's pretty well gone.'

Between them, Polly and Bridie might be able to construct a piece of patchwork out of the scraps and tatters of family history. And Bridie needed to be with Polly now.

'I'll drive down to Putney for Bridie,' Nuala said. 'You stay with your sister.' She opened the fridge to get out the milk, and I saw the stacks of neatly labelled plastic containers containing soups and purees: food that Polly could eat. Nuala seemed to know exactly what my sister needed: like her mother and aunt, she instinctively understood how to cook for people when they were sick. Polly would allow Nuala to feed her, and would let her help with even more personal tasks until the nurses arrived.

'No. You're . . . Polly needs you. And I should be the one to break this to Bridie, to try and make her understand what's happening to Polly.'

It was better this way round; we both understood this. Nuala nodded, picking up her handbag. 'Bridie's going to be so shocked by what's happened to Polly.'

And Polly would be shocked by Bridie's dementia.

'I'll drive you to the station. Polly will be all right for twenty minutes.' She took out her car keys. 'And I'll organise a hire car to be delivered to the care home. You won't want to take Bridie back on the train.'

Sitting on the mainline train didn't feel as difficult as I'd feared. But once I'd arrived at Paddington, I had to get back onto the tube: the District Line was the easiest way to reach Bridie's care home in Putney.

I half hoped some minor incident would have closed the Underground, but the entrance was open. I stood at a turnstile, sweat beading on my forehead.

A man in London Underground uniform was watching me. 'You'll be safe, my sweet,' he said, approaching slowly. 'There are undercover police everywhere.' I'd already seen clusters of armed officers standing around Paddington. They wouldn't let it happen again. *Why not?* a voice inside me whispered. *They can't check everyone.*

'How did you know?' I asked him. 'That I . . . ?'

'Seen it in many people in the last week.'

The train wasn't crowded. Was that a good or bad thing? If a bomb went off, would extra bodies absorb the blast? Was I actually wishing that other people would risk their own flesh to keep me safe? My skin felt clammy. I sat with empty seats beside me, staring at the crossword in the *Evening Standard* I'd picked up, feeling myself shiver and perspire at the same time, flinching at every jolt of the tube, expecting to smell that burning metal stink from last week. If it hadn't been for the fact that I really needed to see Bridie, and that Polly was waiting for us with apparently so little time left, I would have got off at Earl's Court and found a taxi. But I couldn't waste time. I made myself stay in my seat until we reached East Putney.

When I got off the tube I felt as though I had undergone some rite of passage, that I had completed some archetypal challenge: Demeter struggling through the underworld. Or did I mean Persephone? It was a five-minute walk to the home. I found Bridie cheerful in her room, watching a television programme about a couple renovating a mill in the Dordogne.

'Very neat work.' She nodded at the closing shots of newly plastered and white-painted walls. Neatness was Bridie's highest virtue. 'You need to wash your face, Sara.' She frowned at my cut. 'You'll let your grandfather down if you wander round with dirt on it.' I wondered about telling her that it wasn't dirt but a scab, but couldn't face explaining.

I switched off the television with an apology and told her as quickly and simply as I could that Polly had returned, was very ill, and had only a week at most to live, using words I'd rehearsed all the way down from Oxfordshire. Bridie watched me, expressionless. 'Do you want to come back to Thames End House with me and see her?' I asked.

Bridie had always adored the house, but it had defeated her after she'd had the stroke. Nuala and I had chosen this home in an attempt to recreate as much as we could of familiar surroundings: the Thames, trees, ducks.

'Polly.' Bridie went to the window, looking out at the river, which was separated from her by a discreet but tall wrought-iron fence. The Thames was a grey, wide presence, yet it seemed to retain some of its youthful upstream energy.

'Polly's at home.' I took her by the arm, trying to lead her back to the chair. 'Shall we pack you a bag?'

'Polly,' she said again, pulling away from me to return to the window.

'She's in her old bed at home. We've hired a car to drive you down to her.' I looked at my watch. The car should be arriving in about half an hour.

I needed to ask Bridie so many questions. Would it be easier when we were on the road? Perhaps the motion would soothe her confused mind and make it easier for the connections between past and present to refire themselves.

'Goodbye, Polly.' Bridie was still watching the river. 'Goodbye, my darling girl.'

Polly had always been Bridie's pride and joy. I'd seen her look at my sister when she'd been a little girl, leaving the house for school, making the drab uniform look like something fresh and bright, or standing up at prize-giving to receive yet another award. How would Bridie cope with seeing her so ill, her hair fallen out, that beautiful golden mane that Bridie had brushed and plaited for her so often when Polly was a child? Would she understand what was happening? Perhaps we were being cruel even to have told her that Polly was back. She'd be expecting to see a vibrant girl, not a cancer-riddled woman. Bridie's short-term memory was indeed very poor. Perhaps she'd already have forgotten what I'd just told her and I could pretend this was just one of my usual visits. I stood still, undecided.

But Polly would be waiting for Bridie.

Bridie had closed her eyes. I started packing her case. I'd give her five minutes to rest and then move her into reception while we waited for the car to arrive. Something about Bridie's peacefulness puzzled me. But then the relationship between Polly and her had long been complicated. *Polly does you credit*, I'd heard Grandad tell Bridie more than once. *Her own mother couldn't have brought her up with more care.* And Polly had cared deeply for Bridie in return, bursting into the kitchen when we came home from school each evening to find her, spending hours as a small child making her Christmas and birthday cards. Stealing silk scarves for her.

The bonds between us all hadn't been all they seemed, I reflected, as I packed. They'd seemed straightforward and strong until Polly and I had grown old enough to see the things in our upbringing that were unusual and strange.

Then it had all started to unravel.

THREE

THE OLD HOUSE
ON THE RIVER
SARA

My earliest childhood memories are of light bouncing off the river and flickering over the walls of my bedroom, dancing as the trees and clouds outside played with it. Bridie told me I'd lie silent in my cot for long periods as a baby, watching the reflections on the ceiling.

Our grandfather had owned the old house on the Thames, about seventy miles upstream from Westminster, since the fifties, living there by himself after his wife died and his twin sons left home. The house was a narrow white Regency terraced villa with lawns sloping down to the river. Window cleaners must have hated it for its many panes of glass. In early summer wisteria climbed up the back wall and insects murmured sleepily around it. When the windows were open you could hear the Thames lapping against the jetty.

Polly was barely a toddler and I a small baby when we took up residence at Thames End House with Bridie, whom Grandad had employed following the crash that had killed our parents and Uncle Quentin.

For the first years of our lives we regarded our domestic set-up as ordinary. The four of us – Grandad, Bridie, Polly and I – all belonged to Thames End House in the same way as the piano, the wisteria and the river at the end of the garden. It was only as we approached the ages of eight and nine that Polly and I began to notice the differences between ourselves and other girls our age.

'People think we're weird,' Polly said. 'They all live with parents.'

By *people* my sister meant the girls at our school, a small Roman Catholic convent a mile away, to which we walked or cycled each day, Bridie striding beside us until she regarded us as being of a suitable age to risk the traffic and undefined potentially harmful people on our own. Our classmates were the daughters of local Catholics and a number of Anglican girls whose parents sent them to the convent because it was considered to be good at turning out tidy, quiet girls who didn't run in the corridors and wrote in a neat hand. Our classmates observed our family's make-up with interest, and sometimes downright curiosity: a Protestant grandfather with one Protestant granddaughter and one Catholic.

'It was easier to have you Catholic, Sara,' Bridie explained to me once, in a rare burst of openness. 'I had to organise your baptism, see? There was nobody else left after the accident, and your grandfather . . . well, he wasn't up to making the arrangements.'

Grief-stricken, she meant.

Our mother had been the only child of parents who'd died before the time of the crash and there was no more family in America, so there was nobody else to interest themselves in arranging the service.

'Why didn't you do Polly at the same time?'

'She'd already been baptised C of E.' She made it sound as though Polly were a wall that had been painted a regrettable but irreversible colour.

'Why couldn't I have been redone with Sara?' Polly asked. It mattered to us that we were both the same, or in some way marked out as belonging together. If Polly had a particular shirt in green, I had to have the same shirt in blue. We liked to do our hair the same way: in two bunches. Hers was blonde and mine brown, but the hair bands were always the same.

'Once a baptism's done, it's done,' Bridie said. 'Though I suppose you could convert when you're grown up, Polly.'

'I am what I am.' Polly sounded resigned. Nonetheless, she accompanied us to Mass on Sunday mornings until she was eight and would have been left out when the children her age started Communion classes. She switched to attending Sunday school at the old Anglican church that Grandad occasionally attended. It didn't seem important to Protestants to go to church every single week, something which seemed very unfair to me, as Bridie and I rose early on Sundays to attend the 8.30 service. Bridie despised the family service at 11, claiming that it was for mothers who could not control their own children.

She had few problems controlling me, tapping me on the arm if I fidgeted, and scowling at me if I was tardy in my standing or kneeling. During the homily, Bridie stared fixedly at the priest, barely blinking, her hair covered in a black mantilla, even though only very old women still wore them to Mass. At least at this hour the service was shorter, with no hymns.

Sometimes I'd glimpse Bridie's face and sense she had found herself somewhere beyond the distraction of coughing elderly parishioners, no longer feeling the alternating stuffiness and draughtiness of the modern yet ill-constructed church. Bridie never spoke about her deepest religious feelings, and I felt shy about asking her.

The first Sunday after Polly stopped attending Mass, instead of walking me briskly home, Bridie stopped outside Lehman's baker's and confectioner's, a shop I'd never entered and from which I'd only ever sampled one product: a cake for Grandad's seventieth birthday, which had been delivered in a white box and duly served up on the best Spode cake plate.

'Would you like a cake?' Bridie pulled her battered purse from the black handbag she carried on every excursion regardless of season.

'Cake?'

She prodded me. 'No need to stand there with your mouth open, Sara. One of those pink fondant fancies? A Chelsea bun?'

I chose a slice of *millefeuille*, not knowing what it was but liking the shape of the name on the little card on the tray. I thought Bridie would insist on the slice being wrapped and borne home to share with Polly, but she told the shop assistant that we'd be eating in, ordering a cup of Earl Grey, not her usual strong brew, for herself. We sat at a metal-topped table, like normal people, as Polly would have said.

'I hope that's real cream, not artificial.' She eyed the oozing layers between the puff pastry on my plate.

'It's wonderful.' I ate slowly, making it last. 'Thank you for treating me, Bridie,' I added when I'd finished.

For a second her features softened. She liked it when I remembered my manners. Polly was good at knowing what to say; it always seemed that I needed a reminder. 'Sit up straight,' she urged, as though worried she was weakening. 'Your sister has perfect posture.'

I obeyed, but emboldened by the expression I had seen in her face, I pointed at the grey scarf around her head, which had replaced the mantilla as we left the church. 'Do you always wear that when we're out?'

'Don't point. And yes, I do.'

'Why?'

'It keeps my hair neat.' The flint had returned to her expression. She replaced her cup on the saucer without a sound. All Bridie's movements were silent, measured. If she opened or closed a door, you never heard her. Milk bottles never clinked when she put them out on the door-step. By the time we reached our front door I was feeling light-headed.

It happened sometimes, even though I ate well. 'You need a rest after lunch,' Bridie told me.

'I can't need more sleep.'

'Some need more than others.'

The Lehman's stop became a regular Sunday fixture. I switched to meringues, which seemed to suit my digestion better. We never brought anything back for Polly. 'She gains a lie-in,' Bridie said.

When I was eight I was enrolled in First Holy Communion classes and duly made my first confession, listing a not-very-exciting collection of sins. Bridie sat up each night making me a dress from white georgette organza, tacking the pieces carefully and fitting it round me before sewing it up on the old manual Singer she refused to let Grandad replace with an electric sewing machine.

'I've borrowed a veil for you from my sister, Kathleen,' she told me. We hadn't met Kathleen, but she sometimes came down for lunch with Bridie during term. Bridie unknotted the string around a brown paper parcel and undid the tissue paper beneath to reveal the veil: the light from the river picked out the little embroidered crosses on the transparent white, gauzy fabric. She undid a second tissue parcel to reveal the little silver comb that held the veil in place.

'Was it your mother's?' Polly asked.

'My grandmother's. Kathleen will need it for little Nuala in due course, so don't go getting it torn or dirty, Sara.' If it had been Polly borrowing the veil, Bridie wouldn't have been as anxious because my sister was so neat.

'Polly would be much better at all this, wouldn't she?' I asked when Bridie made her fourth practice attempt at ringlets in my hair, using a set of Carmen rollers borrowed from the next-door neighbour.

Polly's hair was thicker than mine and could be curled easily. It would also hold a silver comb more securely. I knew that Bridie was worried the veil would slide off my hair, probably at the moment I took the Host on my tongue, letting us both down. The ringlets Bridie produced in my hair lasted for half an hour at the most, even with all the hair spray she pumped onto them.

I looked at the new white ankle socks Bridie had bought for me. 'And these won't stay perfect for long if it's me wearing them.' Bridie's hands tightened on the pack of socks. 'I will try my best, I really will.'

She pulled me into her thin chest and held me for a moment. 'You're a credit to me, Sara.'

I thought I'd misheard for a moment. I was surely no credit to her. Dirt seemed to seek me out. Polly did all the same things I did, climbed trees, splashed around in the boat, cycled through mud, but she never looked as grubby as I did.

'You'll be fine.' Bridie released me. 'I've something for you. To wear with your dress.' She pulled a small jeweller's box out of her handbag, looking shy. I opened the box. A small silver crucifix sat on the green velvet cushion.

We didn't usually receive presents outside of Christmas or birthdays, unless they were books.

I fastened the crucifix over my school shirt. 'Does Polly have one, too?'

'No, just you.'

I must have looked uneasy.

'She understands. Wearing crosses is a Catholic thing and most girls have them on their First Holy Communion day.'

'Thank you,' I said. 'I really, really like it.' It was the first piece of jewellery I'd ever had.

'Let's have it off you so you don't break the chain before the day.'

First Holy Communion day did not dawn fair, which seemed strange as you'd imagine God would want you to have celebratory weather.

'A soft morning.' From the kitchen window Bridie observed the drizzle falling onto the grey Thames. 'But the BBC says it'll clear later. You'll need to watch your white shoes in the puddles, Sara.'

Her brow creased. I knew she was wondering whether she should ask Grandad to drive us to the church. But that would mean I would not be seen on the streets in my finery. Normally Bridie scorned any signs of showing off, but today I sensed she wanted me to be seen in my white organza. Bridie tied back her hair with a silk scarf I hadn't seen before, with a soft silver and green print on it.

'I bought it for her,' Grandad said, seeing me admire it. 'That mantilla is too funereal for today.'

Bridie looked as though she was going to disagree, but smiled. The drizzle blew over as we left the house, a tentative sun shining through the clouds, steam rising from damp pavements. I felt my cheeks burn as curious passers-by stared at us, and I wished we'd gone by car.

I sat with the other children in the pew in front of the lily-covered altar, remembering to stand and sit and pray hard before taking the Host on to my tongue. It was disappointing that nothing dramatic seemed to happen after I'd dissolved the cardboard-textured circle. Did I feel closer to Jesus? There was the tiniest warmth in my heart that perhaps hadn't been there before, but that might have been because Bridie had made me wear my summer vest under my dress.

I opened my eyes and turned to look at my family, sitting two pews behind me. Bridie's eyes were fixed on me. She blinked and nodded at me. I took this to signify approval. Polly caught my eye and grinned. I wondered whether she was regretting her non-Catholicism. Grandad appeared lost in contemplation. Perhaps he was praying. Protestants must pray too, mustn't they? They must do something in those services of theirs which didn't even have Communion each week.

'It went well,' Grandad said as we walked home after the sandwiches and iced cake in the church hall. 'You looked beautiful, my dear. Your father would have been proud.' Grandad didn't often mention our parents or the car crash that had killed them. It made him sad, Bridie said.

'And our mother,' I said.

'I wasn't forgetting her,' he said, with a smile. Bridie let out a slight intake of breath.

'Mind your gloves on that wall.' She snatched my hand from a stone boundary that I hadn't even thought of touching. She'd turned back from the softer Bridie into her more brittle personality. When we reached home she went off to the kitchen to boil the kettle and bring in the special tea.

'I don't know if I can eat any more.' Polly groaned and flopped into a chair.

'You must,' I said. 'She'll be upset.'

Bridie returned with the laden tea tray: smoked salmon sandwiches on brown bread, Hula Hoops and fairy cakes. I wasn't sure I could eat more, either. The church hall refreshments were sending little ripples of discomfort through my stomach.

'I have something for you, Sara.' Grandad handed me a small white paper bag. Inside was a set of silver and quartz rosary beads.

'I hope it's all right. The lady in the shop in Westminster Cathedral told me it was appropriate.'

'It's wonderful. Thank you.' Two presents in one day. 'I'll use it every day.' Bridie kept a rosary on her bedside table, though I had never seen her hold it while she prayed.

'Do that, sweetheart.' His smile made him look simultaneously more and less like an elderly man. 'And remember your parents in your prayers. And Uncle Quentin.'

'I'll pray for them all.' I kissed his bay-scented cheek. How awful for him to have lost both his children in that crash. I wondered if now was a time when asking questions might be appropriate. We seldom talked about Mark, Quentin and Jenny. Bridie moved the tea tray and the teaspoons rattled together, and the moment was lost.

Polly watched us, expressionless.

'I bought something for you too, my dear.' Grandad disappeared briefly into his office, reappearing with another white paper bag. When Polly opened it she pulled out a wooden box, polished and lacquered. 'It's from Bridie and me,' Grandad told her. When she lifted the lid a little ballerina in a tutu pirouetted around to a tune. 'Brahms,' he said.

Polly touched the rotating tutu gently. 'I love it,' she said softly. 'So pretty.'

I had the sense that a test had been passed, that Grandad and Bridie had been holding their breaths and could now relax. It had been weird, having all the attention focused on me, as though the normal world order had been reversed. It was Polly who ordinarily received all the notice: the child that passers-by smiled at, that teachers chose for plays, that everyone wanted to sit next to in class.

'I'll get changed now.' I must have sounded abrupt. 'Don't want to spill something on my dress.' It seemed sad to put the dress away for ever.

'I was going to pack it away for Nuala,' Bridie said, 'but we could dye it for you to wear to parties.'

'We don't go to parties,' Polly said. 'And Sara will grow out of the dress.' She placed her half-drunk glass of Ribena on the tray. We only had Ribena on special days because Bridie said it was bad for our teeth. As I stood up, my leg seemed to catch the side of the tray, which tipped, spilling the Ribena over my dress. I gasped. Bridie hated carelessness, and what had I done? Ruined this special dress she'd spent so long making for me, after I'd managed even to keep the mud off it walking to and from the church.

'The stain'll come out,' Bridie said. Her tone was not harsh. 'Run upstairs quickly with me. We'll soak the dress in Milton.' She almost dragged me out of the room.

I knew I was clumsy, but how had I managed to collide with that tray? It had seemed to glide towards me as I stood up.

While I changed, Bridie took the dress down to the kitchen sink to soak, her face set. I suspected the stain would not come out.

'Don't worry.' Polly came into my room and put an arm around my shoulders. 'I'll get changed into my shorts, too. Don't let it spoil your special day. Grandad says we can take the boat out. Alone.'

This would be the first time we'd been trusted to do this. Polly unlocked the shed where the oars and rowlocks were kept. We knew how to fit them onto the boat. We pushed off, sitting side by side, me on the port side, Polly on starboard – Grandad had taught us the proper terms. 'I wish I could row as well as Old Joe,' Polly said, watching the ferryman downstream from us as he silently rowed a party of tourists across, hood down across his face. His son sat on the jetty on the opposite bank waiting for his return. Young Joe never said much either: his brain had stopped developing when he'd been younger than us, Bridie had told me, as a result of a road crash. She sometimes took the boy slices of cake and sandwiches, handing them over without a word and receiving no verbal thanks, only a brief moment of eye contact, something he gave nobody else but his father. I wondered whether Bridie would pack him up the remains of our celebration tea.

Bridie came out of the kitchen and sat on the jetty with her feet dangling over the water, watching us as we set off. She had taken off her scarf, unpinning her hair and shaking it out. She smiled as we rowed past and I could hear her singing quietly to herself. Perhaps she was pleased with how the day had gone, after all. Perhaps the Ribena was coming out of my dress. For the first time, I had a sense of Bridie as a person in her own right. I'd thought of her as being a grown-up in the same way Grandad was. Now I realised she was much younger.

'Bridie looks pretty with her hair down,' Polly said, following my gaze. 'She looks . . .' She stopped, frowning.

'Looks what?'

'Nothing.' She dipped her oar into the water and splashed me gently. I returned the gesture with interest. I thought Bridie would shout a reprimand from the jetty, but her gaze was on a glass bottle bobbing in the water close to the bank. Bridie loathed litter and fished it out of the river with distaste whenever she spotted it in the proximity of our garden, but this afternoon she continued to watch the bottle as it floated, occasionally catching on the root of a tree, but working its way determinedly downstream. I wondered what would happen when it reached the weir, and farther down, all the locks between here and Teddington, where Grandad told me the Thames became tidal. If it got that far, the bottle would drift under all the bridges of London, past all those places Grandad had taken us to see – Big Ben and St Paul's and the Tower – then out to sea.

'Daydreaming?' Polly sprinkled me again. We rowed away from the lawn. She was stronger than I was. I was her sister, ate the same things as she did, slept for as long as she did, but my limbs were thin. I sometimes had stomach pains, and I could never pull as much water.

'Bridie looks happy,' I said. 'Was that what you meant?'

Polly considered the question. 'Yes. Happy.' But she frowned again.

'It was a good day,' I said. Apart from the accident with the Ribena, nothing bad had happened. The griping pains in my abdomen had died away now.

'Enjoy being the centre of attention?' my sister asked softly. 'Make you feel good being everyone's little darling?' Her blue eyes were narrow and appraising.

I stared at her, dumbstruck.

Her eyes regained their usual expression and she gave me her most brilliant smile. 'Let's see how fast we can row.'

BOAT

SARA

Four years later – 1987

'You can take the other children out in the boat,' Bridie said, 'if you're sensible and stay in sight of the kitchen window. I'm not sure how strong Kathleen's two are at swimming. Nuala's only little.'

Thames End House shone with even greater brilliance: from the white stone steps on to the street, to the kitchen window. Even the dish-cloth hanging over the kitchen taps seemed more dazzlingly white than normal. A tea loaf had been baked and, as a special treat, two packets of Wagon Wheel biscuits had been purchased, along with a bottle of orange squash and some crisps. Bridie fiddled with the cuff of her navy cardigan. She turned her head. 'That's them now.'

'How can you tell?' Polly asked. The footsteps coming down the street could have been anyone's.

'Kathleen has one leg a little longer than the other and when she walks it sounds uneven. She was injured when she was a baby.' Bridie seldom talked about her childhood, and Polly and I pounced on any scraps of information she broadcast, but today we were distracted by the approach of the visitors. Bridie had long wanted her sister to visit with the children, but Kathleen's husband, Gerard, had been poorly for some years now.

Bridie was right: one of the visitors coming up to the front door walked with a just perceptible clunk-swish, clunk-swish. We could hear Kathleen's children, too, a boy saying something. His mother was telling him to mind himself.

Bridie went to let them in before Kathleen even had time to knock on the door, greeting them in a low voice, Kathleen responding equally quietly.

'Why is she whispering like that?' I asked Polly. 'Grandad's not even here.'

'Part of Bridie believes she's just a servant. She probably thinks she should take her sister into the kitchen for tea.' Polly helped herself to one of the crisps in the bowl and smiled at my shocked expression. The confession I now made at church once a fortnight had made me attentive of my sins – and those of others.

Bridie brought the visitors in. Kathleen looked nothing like Bridie, was my first thought. I looked again and saw in the softer curves of Kathleen's face and figure something that might have been Bridie in a different life. Her boy and girl peered at the room and us with curiosity.

Kathleen smiled at my sister. 'You must be Polly.' Her gaze stayed on Polly. My sister was used to the effect she had on people and smiled back. Kathleen turned to me. 'And Sara.' Her focus sharpened. She'd be marking the differences between us.

'Sit down, won't you, while I wet the tea.' Bridie disappeared into the kitchen.

'This is Michael and Fionnuala,' Kathleen told us. We smiled at the other two and they nodded back.

'Thank you for lending me the veil,' I told Kathleen.

'You've a good memory. You looked grand, Sara. Bridie did a decent job on that dress of yours.'

'Shame the Ribena never came out,' Polly said.

Kathleen was looking at us again. I knew she was noting our clothes. Bridie bought us unfussy clothes that didn't look expensive until you looked closely – or saw the shop receipts.

Michael was looking around. 'Where's your Grandad?'

'Why would an important writer like him want to see you?' his sister asked.

Polly blinked. I knew she was feeling surprise, like me. We knew that Grandad was sometimes on BBC Radio talking about history and wars, but we'd never had someone our own age show an interest in him.

Bridie returned with the tea tray. She'd brewed the tea in the old earthenware pot she preferred. Michael pulled a Wagon Wheel off the plate. His mother snatched it back before he could unwrap it, giving him a light clip around the ear. 'Tea loaf first.'

He rubbed his ear, looking untroubled. We ate the food in the pre-scribed order. I saw Kathleen watching me as I pecked my way through the tea loaf. Bridie had sliced a thin piece for me, but I ate it slowly.

When we'd finished, Bridie suggested that we go out in the boat. 'But mind the currents,' she urged.

'Like raisins?' Michael asked, in a mock-innocent tone.

His mother gave him a sharp smack on the arm. 'Don't get your clothes muddy.'

'Come on.' Polly led us through the house to the back garden. I could see Michael and Nuala looking at the rooms and furniture.

Nuala had barely spoken, but when we came out onto the lawn she gave a little whoop. 'It's like being on holiday.'

Michael rolled his eyes at her, but something inside me warmed to Nuala's open enthusiasm. 'Can I row?' she asked me.

'Polly and I will row to start with,' I said. 'Then you can have a go, too.'

She beamed.

Polly and I had already prepared the boat, fitting the rowlocks and leaving the oars on the jetty. I jumped in, holding a hand out to Nuala.

Polly took the oars, Michael opposite her in the stern, watching her, appraising her command of the boat. After a while I took over. Grandad had coached us for hours. Even I could row well.

'Can I have a go now?' Nuala begged.

Polly instructed her on how to swap places with her.

'Do what Polly says.' Michael was suddenly very much the older brother. Nuala managed to row us for a few minutes without too much splashing or colliding with the bank. After a few minutes of zigzag progress, I asked Michael whether he wanted a go.

He shook his head. 'I'm fine here.' He and Polly had still not exchanged a word. Michael trailed a hand in the water, while Polly folded her arms, apparently staring at the river bank.

'Mum says your Grandad's just finished another book,' he said, addressing me.

'He's going through the copy edits.'

'What's that?' Nuala asked. Polly explained how the copy editor ensured the details made sense, querying anything that needed checking. It was Grandad's favourite bit of the process, and we'd hear him humming as he flicked through the marked-up pages.

'The last bit's the proofs. Bridie helps with that.' I told them how Grandad went through the very last version of the book, word by word, relying on Bridie to confirm that the text was really perfect. Her eyes, so attentive to specks of dust or dirty fingernails, picked out mistyped characters and incorrect spacing. When she spotted a mistake, she emitted a half-sigh.

'It's like the sound angels would make,' Polly added, 'when humans fail to meet heavenly standards.'

Michael laughed. It was the first time I'd heard him sound approving. 'Mum makes the same sound if I get a bad school report.'

Polly rowed us back to the jetty. I hopped off to sneak into the house for more of the Wagon Wheel biscuits, which I knew Bridie would have tidied away into the larder. But Kathleen and Bridie were still in the kitchen, putting away cups and saucers.

'. . . not sure why you're still so worried . . .' Kathleen said.

'It's Coventry,' Bridie told her. 'Always in the background. But let's not worry about that now. Will we sit in the drawing room? I want to know more about Gerard's health.'

'He's much better than he's been for years. But his kidney's never going to be grand, the doctors say.'

'Looking after him has been hard on you.'

'Ah, you know me, strong as they come. But it was a shame it meant we couldn't get the children together when they were younger.'

I lingered outside until I heard the drawing-room door close and then I dashed in to liberate the Wagon Wheels. I was keen to get back to the others and didn't have time to wonder what Coventry was all about. Bridie would kill us for taking the biscuits without permission, but that would be something to worry about later.

I found the other three sitting on the jetty, legs dangling over the water. 'Chuck one here,' Michael said, holding out a hand for the biscuit.

'You've had two already,' his sister complained.

'Who's counting?'

I gave one Wagon Wheel to Nuala and hesitated, looking from Polly to Michael.

'We could halve it,' Polly offered. Nobody seemed to have noticed that I'd left myself without a Wagon Wheel. I didn't actually mind as much as I might have: I liked the thought of Wagon Wheels more than the reality. They were yet another food that made me feel nauseous and tired.

'You probably have them all the time. Mum doesn't often buy us treats. Our dad was ill for ages and wasn't earning much.' He took the biscuit from me, looking at Polly with a challenge in his eyes. She blushed.

'Give it back.' I pulled it from him. We teetered on the edge of the jetty. I knew I was going to fall and tossed the biscuit to my sister as I went in. The water was shallow and I managed to regain my balance enough to land on my feet, knees bent.

Polly watched me clamber out.

'Sara, your shorts are all wet,' Nuala told me. 'You look . . . as though you've wet yourself.' She said it with horror and without malice.

Polly and Michael looked at one another. He smiled. Polly's lips trembled. She was going to laugh.

'You should have just let him have the stupid Wagon Wheel,' she said.

'I thought you wanted it?'

She shrugged. I was searching for a barb to throw at her when Bridie called us in from the house because it was time for the Sheehans to go home.

'Michael and Polly were mean,' Nuala whispered, throwing her arms around me into an unexpected hug. She released me and scowled at her brother. 'You're a pig, Michael.'

'And you're a brat.'

Kathleen gave him a cuff around the ear. 'Stop giving out to each other.'

I didn't know what to say to Polly, so I changed my shorts, sandals and socks, hoping that Bridie wouldn't give me a telling-off. I went into the kitchen and picked up a drying-up cloth, drying the teacups in the hope that this might let me off the harshest telling-off.

'Do you miss Ireland?' I asked Bridie.

She pulled the plug. 'I've never been to Ireland.'

'But how come Kathleen's from there?'

'The war split us up.'

I'd seen the old film coverage and photographs of young children being sent away to avoid the bombs.

Polly came into the kitchen. She was wearing a faraway expression and didn't look at me. I decided not to speak to her until bed time. I couldn't bear not saying goodnight to my sister, but she needed to know I was angry with her.

'Did you get on with Kathleen's two?' Bridie asked, sounding almost keen that we should have done so.

'I didn't mind Nuala,' I told her. 'Michael's a bit of—' I'd been going to say he was a show-off, but I stopped myself in time. He was Bridie's nephew, after all, son of her beloved sister. I thought of the look Michael and Polly had exchanged when I'd emerged from the river in my soaked shorts.

'Michael does well in school, though, Kathleen says. He's a good head on him.'

Polly studied the floor, but I could tell she was listening intently. I wondered if she felt sorry for having shared that conspiratorial look with Michael. I wasn't going to speak to her for a bit.

'Michael was interested in Grandad's writing,' I told Bridie.

'Ah, that lad loves reading.'

'Would you like to go to Ireland for a holiday?' I asked Bridie.

'Me? What would I do in Ireland?' She rinsed out the sink.

'Be with your family?'

She gave me a long look. 'I've got enough to be getting on with here.' She looked out of the window towards the river. 'You two go and make sure the boat's properly tied up and the oars neatly stored away or your Grandad will have something to say. I've got supper to prepare now. If we don't get on it'll be another day gone.'

'I'll do it,' I said, before Polly could come with me. I didn't want to face her alone now. I checked the knots on the rope and stood on the jetty looking out at the river. Grandad's firm, precise footsteps down the garden path made me turn round.

'You're back.' I let him kiss me and he came to stand beside me, asking me how the afternoon with the Sheehans had gone and seeming pleased when I said it had been fun. I didn't mention the bit about me falling into the river, which wouldn't have surprised him as everyone in the family knew how clumsy I was.

'Strange to think this little river becomes such a great, grey body of water by Westminster,' he said.

'I remember when you took us down to see Big Ben and we stood on the bridge. I couldn't believe it was the same Thames.'

'One day we should make an expedition up to the source,' he said. 'It's a tiny little stream up there.' He straightened one side of the tarpaulin on the boat. 'I've seen you rowing, Sara. I know you're in an old rowing boat rather than something a proper competitive rower would use, but I think you've got some of your father's love of being out on the river.'

Grandad made a small choked-sounding noise as he said the last bit. Perhaps thinking about his dead sons was making him sad. Again, I wanted to ask him about my father and mother. We knew so little about them. 'I'll go in,' he said. 'I feel the chill from the river. I'm becoming a feeble old man.'

'You're not.'

He touched the top of my head lightly before he turned. 'One of these days we'll try you in a scull.'

The current was running quite strongly now. I pulled a leaf off a rose bush and threw it in for the current to take.

I watched my leaf disappear into the watery distance.

NEW ALLIANCES;
OLD LOYALTIES
SARA

Two years later – July 1989

Though Bridie had never been a loud presence in the house, Polly and I had noticed her increased quietness. One evening, after she'd given us our supper, she retired to her room instead of sitting as she usually did in the kitchen, door open, while I practised the piano in the drawing room. I was fourteen now and had been playing for a few years. Polly had not been given lessons. I suspected that Bridie had wanted to encourage me in an area outside my sister's ambit. When – occasionally – I played my scales smoothly, I could almost feel Bridie vibrating with approval.

Practising without Bridie's presence meant I could amuse myself by playing parts of pieces I could already perform fluently, neglecting the trickier bars. It felt like eating the cake before the sandwiches.

When I'd finished, Grandad called us into his study. 'Bridie saw a doctor today. She needs a minor operation,' he said. 'Nothing too serious, but she'll need to be in hospital up in London and there'll be a convalescence afterwards.'

'What's wrong with her?' I burst out. Polly shook her head at me. 'Sorry,' I muttered.

Grandad patted my hand across his desk. 'It's routine, don't worry. But we'll need someone here to look after you two. I can't cook, unfortunately, and I have few other domestic skills.'

I'd never seen my grandfather prepare as much as a piece of toast.

'Sara and I can cook,' Polly offered. I tried to think of any one dish that we could reliably prepare.

'A wonderful offer. But this is a big house, sweetheart. I don't want Bridie rushing to get back on her feet because she thinks we can't cope. So I've arranged for Kathleen to come and stay for three weeks.'

'What about Michael and Nuala?' I asked. 'Or are they in Ireland for the summer?'

'They can go over to Cork later this year, Kathleen says. I'll stay in London during the weeks that Bridie's away so that I can keep an eye on her in hospital and have easy access to the libraries.'

Michael and Nuala here for weeks? I glanced at Polly. She gave a little shrug. We hadn't seen the Sheehans since they'd come to tea two years earlier. Michael was a year or so older than Polly, which must make him sixteen or seventeen. Nuala was just a kid of ten or eleven.

Bridie came downstairs, ashen, but smiling. 'Did he tell you?'

'Yes. Do you know where my tennis racket is?' I knew that Polly wasn't meaning to sound callous; it was fear that meant she couldn't discuss Bridie's illness.

'Are you going to be all right?' I asked Bridie.

'I'm going to be just grand.' Her green eyes looked soft for a moment and she touched my cheek. 'I didn't hear you play your scales, Sara. Do them now or it'll be another day gone.' The rest of the evening passed with her listening to me play and scolding me because my hem had come down and I hadn't told her. 'Your sister would never walk around looking scruffy like that,' she said.

It was true. Although if Polly's skirt had come down it would have looked as though it were meant to be that way.

Bridie timed her departure to the private hospital in London for the very last day of term. She and Grandad had left for London and Kathleen and the children were in the house by the time we returned at lunchtime. Old Joe had rowed us across the river, according to the usual end-of-term custom. Polly had managed to open the envelope containing her school report, scanning her near-perfect marks in all subjects. She'd resealed the envelope without leaving a mark by the time we reached the opposite bank. I sat quite still, my own white envelope unopened in my bag. Given Bridie's absence, there was a chance that my almost certainly poorer report might be overlooked. I listened to the smooth, even rhythm of Old Joe's oars in the water. Young Joe had remained on the jetty this time, going through the cash box and lining up piles of ten- and fifty-pence pieces on a wooden plank. Bridie had given me a plastic box of fairy cakes to give him, and those sat beside him.

'We had to miss the whole last week of school,' Nuala said, opening the door to us. 'Mum says private schools have shorter terms. She told our teachers we had a family emergency.'

'So I did.' Kathleen put her hands on her daughter's shoulders and steered her towards the stairs. Behind her lurked Michael, now almost as tall as Grandad. 'Take your bag up to the room and wash your hands.' Nuala and Kathleen were sharing Bridie's room and Michael was to have the spare room. 'If you or your brother leave scuff marks on the paintwork up the stairs you'll feel the back of my hand on your legs.'

Michael laughed. 'I'm taller than you now.'

'I have a belt.' I couldn't tell from her expression whether she meant it or not, but Michael looked unbothered. I wondered whether Kathleen really hit Nuala as well if she misbehaved, or whether she'd smack Polly and me. Surely we were too old for that? She winked at me. 'I have to be stern with that boy of mine, Sara, or he'd push me to the brink.'

She seemed quite at ease in the house. 'Let me have those uniforms when you're changed and I'll put them through the wash.'

Perhaps she'd been down here to have lunch with Bridie while we'd been at school. The thought of the two of them inhabiting their own secret world of which Polly and I knew nothing felt strange. But why shouldn't Bridie have her own sister to visit? When Polly and I were grown up we'd want to see one another, wouldn't we?

When Polly and I had changed we all had lunch. I eyed the steak pie with a mixture of greed and concern: something about pastry tended to send me dashing to the lavatory. Bridie wanted to take me to the doctor, but Grandad had said it could wait until after her operation. 'We could take the boat out?' I suggested, when we'd finished.

Polly looked at Michael. He shrugged. 'Why not?'

She seemed less assured in his presence this time, winding a lock of hair around her fingers, cheeks slightly pink.

'Can I look at your grandfather's books later?' he asked. 'Aunt Bridie said he told me to help myself.'

I saw Polly blink at the way he referred to Bridie. She was Michael and Nuala's aunt. She wasn't a blood relative of ours, I reminded myself.

'Mr Stanton said you could look at anything that was on the study shelves,' Kathleen corrected him. 'No snooping through his desk or filing cabinet, though.'

'There're enough books on the shelves to last you years,' I said.

'Michael's got a great interest in history.' His mother gave him a fond look. 'And current affairs.'

'He and Dad watch the news and they both shout at the politicians,' Nuala piped up. Her face saddened at the mention of her father. 'Shame Dad couldn't get more time off work and come down here with us.'

'He'll join us soon enough in Cork,' her mother said.

Polly stood up. 'Let's go.'

'Does she feel sad about not having a Dad?' Nuala whispered to me as we followed.

Our father, Mark, was someone we had never known. When we looked at family photographs I wasn't always sure which twin was which, though helpfully as they grew older they dressed differently. Our father seemed more arty, dressed in relaxed clothes. Uncle Quentin had been in the army, and even when he had time off he seemed more formal, his clothes more pressed and traditional. His smile wasn't as confident as his twin's, but he had a kind face. I couldn't miss either our father or our mother, Jenny, in the photos a pretty woman with long hair and a warm smile, because I hadn't really known them.

'Grandad and Bridie have been like parents to us,' I told Nuala. 'I know it's not normal, but it's all we've known.'

'You're orphans,' she said knowingly. I'd never really thought of Polly and me as that. Orphanhood suggested abandonment and loneliness, perhaps poverty too, like my namesake character in *The Little Princess*, which I'd read as a younger child. It implied orphanages and children's homes. Thankfully we hadn't had any of that. I still knew very little about the car crash that killed them all, and I wasn't even sure exactly when in my infancy it had happened.

Polly was already attaching the rowlocks to the boat. 'I'll row to start with,' she said. Michael sat in the stern, watching her. Nuala and I sat together in the bow, she chatting about school and her holiday to come. I'd never heard anyone talk as much as Nuala. Bridie wasn't given to chatter, and Polly wasn't garrulous, either.

Michael observed the large houses on the riverside.

'Grandad said wealthy people used to come down here for the summer in the hot weather,' Polly told him.

'Bit different from our place in Ealing.'

He and Nuala had clothes that weren't particularly smart, but seemed well looked after. He was skinny, but then most people our age were. Especially me. Nobody else was as weedy as me.

I wondered about Bridie, how delighted she must have been when Kathleen came to England and raised a family here. The younger sister had gone over to Ireland in the war to avoid the bombs. But why had they left Bridie? She was only four years older than her sister. She'd always been so vague about her life as a girl and young woman, saying only that she'd had experience of domestic service of various kinds.

Polly turned the boat and laid the oars down carefully so that they wouldn't fall into the river. I got up to swap places with her. The boat hardly rocked as we switched positions.

I could feel Michael's eyes on us. 'When we get back I'll look at your grandfather's books.' There was a quiet wonder to his words which made me like him more.

'Not the desk or filing cabinet, though,' Nuala reminded him.

He scowled at his sister, but she was distracted by the little ferry making its smooth progress across the Thames. 'There's Old Joe again.'

'He rowed us across today when school finished,' I told her. 'It's a special treat for the end of term.'

'It must take longer to go by ferry than to cycle over the bridge,' Michael said.

'Yeah.' I felt unable to explain why sitting in the ancient vessel felt like a rite, the ferrying to the holidays. Old Joe's hood was up, covering most of his features in the usual way.

'He must be hot,' Nuala said.

'He never uncovers his head.' Polly spoke for the first time in some minutes. 'Grandad told me he was badly burnt during the war when a ship he was on blew up.' She told them about Old Joe's son, born late in Old Joe's life, and the accident that had arrested the boy's intelligence. 'Young Joe was on his bike. A lorry just folded him up inside itself as it turned left. But he always seems happy, and Bridie says he watches everything.'

I suggested turning for home.

We tied the boat up, Michael watching me intently as I made the knots, as though keen to see exactly how we did things. 'When did your granddad buy this house?' he asked.

We knew this part of the family lore by heart; Bridie had drilled us: *Your grandfather is a very clever man and he wrote a history of the Second World War. It sold lots of copies and so he bought this house in the fifties for your grandmother to bring up their twin boys.*

Michael followed me up the path towards the house. 'What's he working on now?'

'How the Cold War will end and then there'll be a century of peace.'

'Peace?' He looked surprised.

'Apart from more localised conflict, such as Northern Ireland.' I was reciting what Grandad had told me. I remembered Michael's own Irish heritage and decided I didn't want to say more. We didn't tend to comment much on the bombs. They just seemed like part of the everyday news. If Grandad was in the room when the news was on, he'd lower his paper and observe the TV screen with an intense stare that seemed to express sadness and anger.

'Localised conflict? Is that what you call it?'

Michael looked at Polly, and I thought I saw them each raise an eyebrow. I'd probably said something very dense. I jumped out of the boat with the oars, trying to look as though I hadn't noticed. Polly and I rarely stood on different sides when it came to our response to people or events. *Thick as thieves*, was how Bridie described us when, as young children, we refused to admit which one of us had walked muddy shoes onto the hall parquet or left toys lying all over the drawing-room floor. But then Polly would suddenly turn cold – switching, that was what I called it – saying or doing things that made me feel we were not really a pair, after all, not really close sisters, but enemies.

Kathleen was in the kitchen when we came inside. Her sharp eyes flickered between me and Polly and then on to Michael. Kathleen was prettier than her sister; her hair fell loose to her shoulders, with a half fringe. Her clothes were softer and more fashionable, though her figure was not as good as Bridie's. I felt guilty for even thinking these things. It was impossible not to respond to Kathleen's confident cheeriness. Had Bridie ever been as carefree as her sister?

Kathleen certainly didn't have the same anxious view of life that Bridie had. Even the day of Bridie's operation found her looking cheerful. She visited her sister, leaving us alone for the afternoon.

'She's going to be just grand,' she said, on her return from the station, in the taxi Grandad had insisted on. 'Sends her love, says she'll see you both on Sunday.'

On Sunday there was no question of getting up early for the 8.30am service. 'We'll go to the Saturday Vigil Mass,' Kathleen said. 'Have our beauty sleep and go up to town to see Bridie on Sunday.'

'I'm not going to Mass,' Michael said.

She flashed him a look, the like of which I had never seen on Bridie's face even when she reprimanded us. 'You'll come with us, Michael Francis Sheehan.'

He scowled. On Saturday evening, however, he shuffled into the kitchen with Nuala. 'We off?'

Kathleen took her handbag off the table. 'We are.' She gave Polly an amused glance. 'You can put the potatoes on, missy. So tea's ready when we come in. The ham's in the oven already.'

Kathleen was as attentive as Bridie to the requirements of the service to stand and kneel, glaring at her son if he failed to move quickly or quietly. He submitted with only the merest eye-rolling, but refused to go up to Communion.

'I didn't go to confession over Easter, so I can't anyway,' he informed her in a whisper as the rest of us stood up. 'It'd be a mortal sin.'

Kathleen tutted but made no further comment. It seemed that religion was taken more seriously by the female members of the Sheehan family.

Polly was sitting in the kitchen when we returned. 'The potatoes are nearly done,' she told Kathleen. 'I did carrots and peas too.' She'd laid the table as well.

'You're a good girl.' Kathleen sat down with a sigh. 'Bridie told me you would be.'

I wondered whether Bridie had claimed that I would be helpful in the house, too. I wasn't sure I actually knew how to peel carrots. Judging by the thick, jagged scrapings in the colander, Polly hadn't been too sure, either. Michael glanced at the carrots and then at Polly. She gave him a slight smile and looked away, still holding the smile, head tilted.

'Do you ever go to church, Polly?' Nuala asked. 'Do Protestants have to go every week like we do?'

'Grandad likes me to go with him sometimes,' she answered. 'I may go next Sunday.'

Did Polly want to say a prayer for Bridie?

'Can I come with you?' Nuala asked.

Kathleen sat up straighter. 'You're not a Protestant.'

'The vicar told me once that Christians in England are automatically members of the Church of England,' Polly said.

'I'd like to go to the Protestant church too,' Michael said.

His mother stood up and opened the oven door. 'This meat is done.'

'I know you don't approve, Mammy. But what do you think'll happen to me if I go? Extra years in purgatory?'

'None of your cheek now.' She put the roasting tin on the stove and found the carving knife. 'We're Catholics.'

'In a Protestant country,' he said.

'Sara's been to church with us a few times,' Polly said. 'Bridie didn't mind.'

'Did she not?' Kathleen picked up the carving knife and frowned at the ham. The slices she carved were thicker and less regular than Bridie's, but the meat was tasty.

We travelled up to town by train in the morning. Kathleen brought packets of crisps with her, and Nuala and Michael squabbled over which flavour they wanted until Kathleen cuffed Michael and threw Nuala a look of such sharpness that they both fell silent. When we reached Bridie's ward, Polly and I went in first with Kathleen. Michael sat outside and pulled one of Grandad's books about the British Empire out of his rucksack. Nuala had brought comics.

Bridie was sitting up in bed with a knitted bed jacket round her. She looked pale, but her face lit up when she saw us.

'Both girls still alive,' Kathleen told her. 'As you can see.'

Polly kissed Bridie.

'Are you practising your piano?' Bridie asked me as I leant down in turn to her white cheek. 'Even the scales?'

I nodded towards Kathleen. 'I have a witness.'

'She played for half an hour at least last night,' she told Bridie. 'Sounded grand.'

'You're wearing that old shirt, Sara?' Bridie's sharp eyes were running up and down my clothes. 'I thought I'd thrown it out.'

'I took it out of the bag.'

'I looked at your report with your grandfather when he came in to see me.' So Kathleen had posted it and Polly's on to Grandad. I'd been hoping they might have overlooked the reports this year. I tried to decipher Bridie's expression. 'Not bad. But room for improvement in maths. Were you daydreaming in class again?'

'Now don't go always telling off the child first thing when you see her,' Kathleen told her sister. 'Sara's been worrying herself about you.'

I'd thought I'd kept my concern to myself.

Bridie's hand found mine across the hospital blanket and squeezed it. 'Silly girl. It's nothing to worry about. Look at me, taking up this bed but pretty well ready to come home.'

'You'll not be coming home just yet. And you'll go off for that convalescence on the coast, Bridie Br—'

Bridie made a slight sound of discomfort. Perhaps her stitches hurt. I didn't know exactly what the operation had entailed.

I wanted Bridie back. How could Polly seem so calm about her absence? Then I remembered the sidelong smile she'd given Michael in the kitchen. Perhaps Michael was distracting her from missing Bridie.

We chatted on about nothing in particular for ten minutes longer, Bridie's eyes still sweeping me, noting, no doubt, every flaw, every failing. 'The other two would like to say a quick hello,' Kathleen said, 'if you're up to it?'

Polly and I said our farewells and went out into the waiting room so that Kathleen could usher in Michael and Nuala.

A fine drizzle had set in by the time we returned to Thames End House, so the four of us trooped upstairs to Polly's bedroom, the largest of our rooms. Michael picked up Polly's musical box, raising and lowering the lid.

'I try and open it just a tiny bit to see if I can stop it playing,' he said. 'But it always catches me out. It's as though there's a tiny invisible person inside it, watching me lift the lid.'

'Grandad says the mechanism is very delicate,' Polly said, taking it from him. 'Even a tiny vibration sets it off.'

He yawned. 'I may go and read.'

'Mam said I could help her make a cake.' Nuala went down to the kitchen. Polly sat on her bed, rearranging the pieces of jewellery in her musical box. I could tell from the set of her shoulders that she wanted to be left in peace.

To my surprise, Michael came into my bedroom a few minutes later. 'Boat?' he asked. I looked out of the window. It was still drizzling, but in a half-hearted manner.

'The oars will be slippery.'

'Doesn't matter.' He grinned at me. 'Go on, I want to practise so I'm better than Polly.'

We took our anoraks, disregarding Kathleen's disapproval and suggestion that we play a board game instead. Michael insisted on rowing. He was getting better at it, and I told him so, causing a quick flush of pleasure to cover his cheeks before he could hide it.

'It's OK,' I said. 'I know what it's like trying to do something as well as Polly. Sometimes I wish there was something I was number one at. Everyone just thinks she's so wonderful. And she is.'

'But Bridie cares more about you than Polly.'

I sat up straight in amazement. 'Why do you think that?'

'I once heard Mum tell Dad that Bridie worries about you all the time. When she rings Mum on Sunday evenings, she barely mentions Polly, Mum said, it's always about you, what you're eating, whether you had to miss school, how you're doing in lessons.'

'She's always making a fuss of Polly and telling me how I should try to be more like her.'

'Mum said Bridie shouldn't make it so obvious.'

'Perhaps it's because I'm younger than Polly and Bridie thinks I need more worrying over.'

'How much younger than Polly are you exactly?'

'Just under a year.'

He whistled. 'Irish twins, in fact.' He explained what this joke meant.

Almost like real twins, like our father and Uncle Quentin.

'You don't look like Polly.' He studied me. 'Well, maybe just a bit, when you look closely. Same foreheads and chins.'

You could see the resemblance in photos: the wide brows and slightly prominent chin. They came from Grandad.

'And you . . .' Something about me seemed to puzzle him, probably how it was that Polly's sister could look much less pretty.

'What?' I was starting to feel annoyed. 'I don't gawp at you and comment on your looks. Personal comments are rude, Bridie says.'

'Bridie.' He said the name ponderously.

'What about her?'

'Nothing. Can you time me back to the jetty?' He was turning the boat, seeming to lose interest in the conversation. When we went indoors he ran upstairs and I heard him say something to Polly about Bridie, heard Polly say something that sounded mocking in return. Something stirred in my imagination, something someone had said or started to say earlier in the day. But the usual fog was rolling through my mind.

Michael's attention seemed to flicker from me to my sister over the next week. I would look up to see him staring at me, almost puzzled, it seemed. When he looked at Polly there was a completely different expression on his face. The summer holiday weather had resolved itself into a mixture of almost springlike showers and bursts of sunshine. When it rained I was happy to lie on my bed and read. Polly seemed restless, walking from my room to Michael's and chiding us for being boring. 'Can't you finish that project later?' I heard her ask him but couldn't hear the response. 'Plenty of paper in the desk,' I heard Polly say in answer. The two of them walked downstairs.

The muffled sound of their voices from Grandad's study reached me up the stairs. A drawer or cupboard door closed as they pilfered Grandad's perfectly sharpened pencils or thick, creamy writing paper and envelopes. They stopped talking. The study door closed. Perhaps they were reading some of Grandad's book. Michael was a keen reader, wasn't he?

I went downstairs, passing the door and half wanting to knock on it, ask if I could join in whatever it was they were doing, but uncertain of my reception. I went into the kitchen instead and poured myself a glass of water, feeling suddenly lonely, glad when Nuala and Kathleen came up from the utility room and I could help them fold towels.

That evening I came across Michael and Polly sitting close together on the window seat in the kitchen, heads almost touching as he showed her something. It looked like a newspaper cutting. Polly seemed to sense me looking at her and folded the cutting, placing it in the back pocket of her shorts. She didn't say much to me. Had I done something to bug her? I couldn't think of anything. She tucked her knees up and twirled a strand of her hair. Bridie would have told her off.

'I got you this.' I was in my bedroom when Polly pulled a Mars bar out of her bag. I hadn't seen her buy anything. 'Kathleen sent me out to get milk. I didn't have enough money to buy them for the others too.'

She was giving the Mars bar to me to show me that I was still the closest person to her, still her little sister. She might be caught up in Michael's intelligence and the flattery of that intense blue-eyed stare on her, but she and I shared something unique to us. I unwrapped the Mars bar and offered her the first bite, as I always did. She shook her head. 'It's just for you.'

I loved Mars bars. They didn't seem to sit as heavily on my digestive system as the cakes Polly liked. My pleasure must have shown on my face as I bit into it.

Polly's face softened. 'I wish it was just us here,' she said.

'I thought you liked having the Sheehans here?'

'Michael's fun and Nuala's sweet. But it makes me feel . . .' She struggled for the words. 'I don't know.' She lay down on my bed, with her head resting beside my legs, golden hair splaying out over the white quilt. 'It's not like it is when it's just us. It's changed everything . . .' She let her eyelids fall over her eyes. 'I'm happier not thinking, not knowing.' Her arms fell outwards in a gesture of abandonment.

'Knowing what?'

'Oh, you know, more about the world.' She sat up and fingered the candlewick quilt on my bed. 'We get one view, don't we, from Grandad? His view on why wars start, what a good one is, and what a bad one is. Fighting Hitler is good. Sending soldiers to Northern Ireland is OK because it stops the terrorists on each side from doing even worse things. But Michael has a different slant on things. He tells me things I didn't know.'

'What kind of things?'

'Oh, about history. Particularly Ireland.'

'Does he support the IRA?' I heard the astonishment in my voice.

'No. Well, not exactly. He thinks they have a point about Northern Ireland, that it should be part of the Republic.'

'He thinks it's OK to bomb and kill people?'

'He says that today's guerrilla is tomorrow's freedom fighter.'

I looked at her. 'Do you believe that too?'

She shrugged. 'I'm not that interested in Northern Ireland.' She was staring at me. 'But when you hear about some of the miscarriages of justice, for example.'

'What miscarriages of justice?'

'Imprisoning innocent people for bombing pubs in the seventies. The Guildford and Birmingham verdicts were travesties of justice, Michael says.' She quoted his words at me very carefully. 'He's read a lot about the cases.'

And Polly had lapped up all he'd said. I'd heard about the appeals against these sentences on the news. Grandad had always told us that terrorists needed punishing to acknowledge the awfulness of taking human lives. Surely if we put people in prison it was because they were indeed guilty? British justice was supposed to be among the best in the world, wasn't it? I shifted on my bed quilt.

'The IRA do awful things,' I said. 'Last week they put a bomb in a British soldier's car and he wasn't even in Northern Ireland at the time. He was in France or Germany or somewhere.'

'It's just that when you start looking into things . . .' Polly trailed off.

'I heard you two in Grandad's study.' I was careful not to make it sound like an accusation or as if I was jealous.

'We were just looking for paper.' She looked me straight in the eye. The answer sounded a bit too pat to me, as though she'd prepared it. And still she kept her gaze on me. I shifted uncomfortably under it. 'I wish it could always stay like it is when it's just you, me and Bridie, and Grandad pottering away in his study in the background.' She said it almost as a challenge. Perhaps the presence of Michael made Polly feel she had to be fascinating, clever, magnetic Polly all the time. She could never relax completely and be the girl who liked to slump on my bed with me with chocolate bars and magazines.

'Do you wish it was like that too, Sara?' I wished she'd stop staring at me; it felt weird. 'Just the four of us, all one family?' I'd never heard her speak to me so intensely. Normally Polly scoffed at people being too 'heavy', as she put it. 'Would you want to change our set-up if you could?'

'How could we? Grandad, Bridie, you and me are all we have.'

Her features seemed to relax. She looked at the last morsel of Mars bar in my fingers and plucked it from me gently. 'Open up,' she said, feeding it to me.

When she left my room I sat very quietly by myself, feeling unsettled. Had there been a call from the hospital about Bridie? Was that what was troubling Polly? I went down and asked Kathleen if there'd been any news.

'Not a word.' She was peeling potatoes in the sink. 'Not since we saw her yesterday. The ward would only ring you up if there's a problem, infection or bleeding or something.'

I felt myself tense.

'But as they've told us no such thing we can assume all is well. That sister of mine could ring us herself for a quick chat, so she could. They have a portable telephone they wheel around. But she's probably counting pennies again.' With her back to me, she nodded towards the fridge. 'Do me a favour and take out the lamb chops.'

The following afternoon, Michael and I took the boat out on the river. Polly had gone into town to meet a school friend. I'd noticed something that looked like relief in Kathleen's eyes as Polly closed the front door behind her, and I wondered whether she was also worried about the growing closeness between the two of them.

Michael reached inside the rucksack he'd brought with him, removing a bottle of cider and a box of cigarettes. I hadn't smoked before, but Grandad gave us a half-glass of wine at Sunday lunch. We stopped when we were out of sight upstream and lit our cigarettes. The smoke felt like a bonfire searing my throat. I coughed and extinguished the cigarette in the water.

'You'll not make a smoker,' Michael said.

I glared at him.

'Your sister smoke?'

'Probably.' I'd never smelled smoke on her clothes; she'd be too careful for that.

'Bad Polly and good Sara.' He laughed.

'It's usually the other way round. If I do something bad I always get caught. Polly never does.' I thought of the time she'd spilled the Ribena on my First Holy Communion dress.

'She just looks too angelic.'

'And I don't?'

'You'll be stronger than Polly.' He looked at my arm. 'You just need to put on some muscle. You're good at rowing.' He drained the cider bottle and wiped his mouth on his sleeve. 'In our family, Nuala is Little Miss Perfect. Always does what she's told. Sweet. Good.'

'Polly's good at everything.'

'She doesn't play the piano.' I'd noticed him sitting quietly in the drawing room while I practised.

'Only because she wants me to have one thing that I do that she doesn't.'

'Polly can't row as well as you, either.' He took another sip of cider and passed me the bottle.

I felt my cheeks burn, unused to praise. 'I'm not as strong as her. I never seem to build up any muscle.' I felt his gaze on my upper arms.

'You do it with more, dunno, style or something. Like you were meant to be a rower.'

'Perhaps I won't be so weak when I'm older.' We'd let the boat drift. I took the oars and corrected our direction.

He moved swiftly and smoothly to sit next to me, placing an arm around me. He kissed me on the cheek. 'I wish Nuala and I had got to know you earlier on.'

I blinked in surprise.

'I'll write to you when we go back to London. Will you write back, Sara?'

'Yes,' I replied. 'What do you do with Polly when you're together?' Thoughts of Michael and Polly alone could never quite be banished. Was he going to write to her, too?

He shrugged. 'Look at the books in your grandad's study. Polly shows me old photos and things.' He gave me a long, searching look. 'We . . .' He let go of me, sounding suddenly awkward and looking over my shoulder. I hadn't been concentrating and the current had brought us back to the jetty. A shadow fell over us. I looked up, catching sight of Polly's tanned, plimsolled feet. She'd been watching us.

'Kathleen's made a pot of tea, if you'd like some.' I knew by the way she smiled at us that she was furious.

About a week later, when I was bored and fancied taking the boat out again with Michael, I found him gone. 'He's off rowing with Polly,' Nuala told me.

I went downstairs to the kitchen window. Polly and Michael were in the boat, alongside the bank opposite Grandad's lawn. She was leaning back, laughing, the long curve of her neck pearlescent in the watery light. Michael was at the oars, saying something to her, his face looking older than it usually did, but filled with animation. What were they talking about?

He stopped rowing and reached into his pocket for something. The cigarette packet. Without even worrying about the kitchen window overlooking them, the two of them lit cigarettes. Polly smoked like someone who'd been doing it for years, tapping the ash elegantly on the side of the boat. Michael pulled a bottle of cider out of his rucksack. He rubbed the lip of the bottle on his sleeve before passing it over to her. He hadn't bothered doing that for me.

I watched as they finished their cigarettes. Michael patted the seat beside him and Polly moved next to him, taking an oar. With her spare hand, she pulled his face towards hers and fastened her mouth on his, kissing him long and slow, like a film star in a love scene. Michael dropped his oar and grabbed her round the waist. The embrace lasted several minutes. When Polly detached herself she looked directly at the kitchen window. I realised that the light was on behind me. She must have seen me watching them. Michael looked dazed.

When Polly came in for tea I ignored her, addressing all my comments to Michael, Nuala and Kathleen. Polly's eyes held a silent mirth. After we'd cleared the plates, I asked her sweetly if she wanted to play Monopoly.

'OK.' Her eyes narrowed at me.

I treated every square on the board as war bounty, grabbing rows of hotelled and housed streets and extorting rent from my opponents.

'To those who have shall be given more.' She passed me her rent for landing on Park Lane.

'You think I have everything?' I forgot the presence of the other three, staring at her over the cluttered Monopoly board.

She raised an eyebrow.

'You're mad.' I snatched the bank notes from her.

Nuala rolled the dice. 'Mum says Aunt Bridie spoils you two rotten.'

'What?' Polly and I stared at one another, animosity forgotten.

'You never change beds or put on loads of washing like Mum and Aunt Bridie did at your age and you can't do kitchen things I can do, even though I'm younger. Mum says Aunt Bridie's bringing you up to be young ladies who'll have people to do those things for them. You'll be doctors or lawyers with cleaning ladies, so it doesn't matter.'

It was true. I'd seen Nuala sort out piles of laundry and iron pillowcases.

Michael gave a snort of laughter. 'Aunt Bridie treats you both like princesses.'

Polly and I looked at each other. 'She's actually quite strict with us,' Polly said. 'About doing homework and stuff.'

'She dotes on you, Mum says.' Michael looked thoughtful. 'It's funny – I suppose she's really your servant, isn't she?'

'Shut up,' Polly said quietly. 'Don't say that about her.'

I hated hearing him say that word, too. 'Bridie's family,' I said. 'That's how it feels.'

Michael gave me an impenetrable look.

'I heard Mum tell Dad on the phone that it was weird Bridie wasn't stricter with you, seeing how well they taught her to be so keen on everything being perfectly done,' Nuala went on.

'"*They* taught her"?' I asked. 'Who do you mean?'

'Dunno. The children's home, I suppose.'

'Children's home?' I asked.

'Where she went after their mum died in the war,' Michael said. I didn't look at my sister, but I knew we were both trying not to show that we hadn't been aware of this.

'It's odd, isn't it?' Nuala went on. 'That one of them was taken in by family in Ireland and the other went into the home.'

Michael looked at Polly, concern flickering over his features before he turned back to the board. 'Come on, let's finish this capitalist non-sense of a game. I'm getting bored with it.'

Polly held up her hands. 'I've got a headache.'

We split her money and her houses into three, a process which took ages and involved Michael and Nuala throwing bank notes at one another in fury. Polly retired to an armchair at the back of the room, observing the three of us in silence. Beside me, the two dark-haired Sheehans squabbled and swore at one another, seeming to flit from wanting to rip one another to shreds and roaring with laughter. I found myself laughing and squabbling too, telling them that they were mad, that I hated them and then dissolving into fits of laughter when Nuala tickled me. Polly, when I glanced back at her a few moments later, had never looked so blonde, so cool, so *English*. So separate from me in a way she hadn't ever before.

The game finished. I looked around for my sister, but she had gone.

'Let's read a book.' Nuala walked over to the bookshelf and pulled out a large illustrated fairy-tale collection.

'I love that book,' I said.

'Babies' stuff,' Michael scoffed. What was wrong with him? He could be so changeable: sometimes almost ignoring me, then treating me almost like family. And then there'd been that other feeling, that sense that he found me attractive in a completely different way. Yet, he'd kissed Polly in the boat, or let her kiss him, in a way he certainly hadn't kissed me. And all their whispering together, and Polly's sudden interest in Northern Ireland, what was that all about?

Michael murmured something and left the room.

Nuala sat beside me on the comfortable old sofa and we turned the pages. She felt small and warm and uncomplicated.

When Nuala was called up to bed I didn't know what to do with myself. Polly and Michael still hadn't reappeared. The silver Scottie dog from the Monopoly game had rolled under the armchair, unnoticed when we'd packed up the game. I lay on the floor and pulled it out.

The windows on this side of the house overlooked the street. I heard the front door open. Michael and Polly walked outside, talking. Perhaps they'd sneaked out for a cigarette in the street, out of sight of Kathleen. Some of their words reached me through the partially opened window. 'Just wait,' Michael told her. 'Everything will be easier when you're eighteen and can do what the hell you want.'

What was it that Polly wanted to do so badly that she had to be told to wait?

I wished that Nuala was my little sister. I wished that Polly was not such a riddle. And that she and Michael did not share whatever it was they shared, excluding me. It had been Polly and me against the world before the Sheehans had come and spoiled everything.

Grandad drove Bridie home from her convalescence the morning of Kathleen's departure.

'You wouldn't be wanting the two of us together in the same house,' Kathleen told us, after giving her sister a quick hug. 'We'd drive you mad.'

Bridie held Polly and me for longer than she would normally have embraced us, looking us over. I tried to compose my face into complete neutrality but feared, all the same, that Bridie would know that something had happened between Polly and me. We watched Kathleen pack her suitcases into the taxi Grandad had ordered for them.

'Have a good time in County Cork.' He pressed an envelope into Kathleen's hand – the money she'd earned from looking after us and the house. She thanked him with obvious gratitude.

Kathleen kissed Polly and me, her hand lingering on my shoulder. 'See you again soon, Sara.' The words sounded heartfelt, and her sharp eyes seemed gentle as she smiled at me. Her farewell to Polly was brisker. Yet another person feeling sorry for me as the younger, smaller, less gifted sister.

'Bye.' Michael gave Polly a quick pat on the shoulder and nodded at me without meeting my eye. Polly raised an eyebrow at him without a word. Despite the silence, I knew that some kind of communication had been transmitted between them, that there was something only they shared.

Nuala wrapped her arms around my waist. 'Goodbye, Sara. I wish you were coming with me. I want to show you our Grandda's little house and the donkey. And the sea.'

'I wish I could see it too.' I pictured Nuala and me hunting for shells on some wild Atlantic beach.

'One day I'll take you both over there,' Bridie said. 'If your grandfather doesn't mind.' It was the first time she'd ever suggested doing this. I wondered what had happened to make her think a trip to Ireland might be a good plan.

Grandad was paying for the taxi to take them all the way to Heathrow, and from there they'd fly to Cork. Usually they took a ferry.

'No puking this time,' Nuala called as the taxi door closed. 'No horrid, smelly boat.'

'Well.' Bridie folded her arms, letting out a sigh as the taxi turned the corner at the end of the road. Half sorrow at parting with her sister, and half relief to have the house back under her control, I thought. The sheets on the beds pulled into their proper sharp angles, the kitchen worktop cleaned to its sheen. 'I'll see to the rooms.'

'You'll do no such thing.' Grandad spoke firmly. 'Kathleen said they'd stripped the beds.'

'Oh, I'm fit as a fiddle now,' she said. The sea air from her convalescence had brought some pinkness to her normally pale cheeks, and she had put on a little weight. She looked softer, younger. Her hair was tied into its normal bun, but I could almost imagine that while she was on the coast a little of it might have escaped and blown around in the sea air. That she might even have been tempted to throw a pebble into the waves.

Polly stooped down to pick up a flinty stone with a sharp edge from the side of the path and scratched something on the bottom of the front wall, just above ground level. I went to look.

G, B, P, S, she'd written, with a heart around the letters.

'Grandad, Bridie, Polly and Sara,' I said.

She nodded, adding *4ever*.

Grandad stooped to look. 'I should probably tell you off for the graffiti. And the appalling use of English.' He patted her head as though she were a dog. Bridie made a *tsk* noise.

'Us four against the world,' I said.

'*Contra mundum*,' Grandad murmured. 'Some say that's when we're at our best as a country.'

'The Sheehans made the time pass more quickly while you were away, Bridie. But I'm glad us four are back together again.' Polly sounded fierce.

'*We* four,' Bridie said. 'Your grammar is awful. Come and help me load the washing machine, or it'll be another day gone.'

'Don't let her load the machine, Polly,' Grandad called after them. Bridie made a sound denoting disgust.

'She thinks she's as strong as an ox. But look at her, slim as a willow.' He sounded almost sad.

'Kathleen's strong, too,' I said. 'She carries bags of shopping. For miles.'

'A tough pair, those sisters.' Grandad sounded thoughtful. He was treating me as a grown-up, as though my opinion mattered.

'How's your book going, Grandad?'

'I seem to have hit a wall, a literal wall, the fence across Europe. I can't seem to push past that barrier between us and the Soviets. I'd hoped I'd see some chink by now, some end to the Cold War.'

'Things are a bit better over there, aren't they?'

'People in the Eastern Bloc have more refrigerators and televisions, but dissidents still go to prison for saying and writing things they shouldn't.' He let out a long sigh. 'My publisher is getting impatient. I may have to try and reach some kind of conclusion. Even if it's just that the stalemate looks interminable. At least there haven't been tanks moving over the North German Plain. No running for the nuclear shelters. No fear of total—'. He broke off. I knew he meant complete devastation of the planet and the wiping out of the human race but didn't want to scare me.

'Would it be in Europe that a big war would happen?'

'Europe's always been the cockpit.' He said it matter-of-factly.

He closed the door behind us.

When we'd eaten the evening meal Kathleen had left for us, Grandad retired to his study. Bridie washed the plates and looked surprised when Polly and I dried them for her.

'There's something I need to tell you,' she said. 'About me. About where I was before I came here.'

'What do you mean?' I asked. 'You were working in Oxford as a housekeeper, you told us that. It's why you're so good at looking after everyone.' Was she ashamed of her former job? We'd barely given it a thought.

'You're right, Sara.' She gave me her calm smile. 'But I was somewhere before then. I think you're going to find out soon. Kathleen says I should tell you.'

'The children's home,' Polly said. 'Nuala mentioned that.' She said it lightly, but I could tell that it bothered my sister that Bridie had been in a home. She'd be imagining something Dickensian.

'Oh, you know about that.' Bridie was forcing a smile. 'It wasn't what I meant. Though that was a . . . challenging part of my life.'

'Why wasn't Kathleen in the home, too?'

'She was just a baby. She went to Ireland when our mother died.'

'What happened to your father?'

'It was wartime and my father had already died.'

I sat up straight. 'Your father wasn't Kathleen's father?'

'No. Kathleen's father was my mother's second husband.'

Had I known before that Kathleen and Bridie were half-sisters, not the real thing like Polly and me? Did the Sheehan children know this? I scoured my memory for any remarks indicating they'd known yet another thing we did not. Polly frowned. I was watching her face because I wanted her to express all the things that I couldn't articulate myself.

'But couldn't Kathleen's father take you in?'

'I was coming up to school age,' Bridie said. 'Better for me to stay in England.'

I didn't know much about Irish families other than what I had observed with Kathleen and her two children, but it surprised me that a place hadn't been found for Bridie too.

'Anyway,' Bridie continued, 'Nuala told her mother she'd told you about the home, and Kathleen and I thought . . . well, there's something else.'

I remembered what Nuala had said about Bridie having been trained in housework. Did the Sheehan children already know Bridie's secret? Jealousy flooded me.

Polly's face was twisted into a frown. I knew she'd be thinking the same as me, fearing we might be the last to be told.

'Before I worked in Oxford I was somewhere else for a long time. Somewhere . . . unusual. Somewhere that made a great mark on me. I know I'm a bit different from other women, from your friends' mothers, for instance.' She flushed.

Shame filled my soul. At times I had felt abashed about introducing friends to Bridie. Most of our friends didn't have housekeepers. Sometimes I referred to her as our nanny, but that was almost as awkward.

'Don't feel bad if you've been asking yourselves some questions about me. You're clever girls, you notice things.' She gave a little smile that nearly broke my heart. I touched the sleeve of her cardigan and she looked down at my fingers.

'Bridie, were you in prison?' Polly asked the question I couldn't frame, her voice clear but her face pale. If Bridie had been in prison for a long time, she must have done something truly bad. Killed someone, perhaps.

Bridie smiled. 'I was not in prison. I was a sister, in a convent.'

FOUR

REACTION
BRIDIE

The two girls were sitting at the table, staring at her, eyes wide.

'A sister? You mean, a *nun*?' Polly sat back, frowning. 'In a *convent*, Bridie?'

Bridie let out a long breath. *Keep calm*, she told herself. *Don't let them see how anxious you are.* 'I know you'll have a lot of questions for me.' Telling the two of them about her past had pushed her to the very limits of her endurance. Perhaps she was still feeble after the operation. She should have listened to Kathleen, given herself time. She pushed her mouth into a smile.

'Does Grandad know?' Sara asked.

Bridie nodded. If their grandfather knew, this revelation couldn't be that shocking to the girls, could it? She felt herself scanning the kitchen, noting dishes on the dresser that had been incorrectly arranged, a drying-up cloth that needed replacing. She resisted the temptation to stand up and attend to them.

'How long were you in that convent?' Polly wanted to know.

'About fifteen years.'

'But you must have been just a girl when you went in.' Polly sounded shocked.

'Eighteen. I was a probationer first, and then a novice, so I didn't become what you would think of as a proper nun, or, to be accurate, a sister, until I was twenty-one or so.'

'Was it very strict?' Sara whispered. The girl would be imagining rules, prohibitions, denial.

She nodded. 'The other sisters were kind. In the main. But it is a hard life, there's no doubting it.'

'Sister Bridie,' Sara said. 'Or were you Sister Bridget?'

'I was Sister John.' Bridie could see the girl going through the options. There were a number of Johns in the sainthood.

'How could you bear it?' Polly burst out. 'Locked up like that, taking a man's name, wearing those black clothes.'

'We didn't wear the long black habits you've seen in films, at least not by the time I was thinking of leaving—'

'Horrible. Cruel.' Polly interjected. 'How could you let them do it to you, Bridie?' She stood up, pushing her chair back, and stormed out.

'I don't know why she's so upset,' Sara told Bridie. 'I mean, it's a bit weird finding out, but even so.'

Bridie watched the door through which Polly had just exited. 'I've disturbed her impression of what I was,' she said quietly. 'It doesn't match the old image she had of me. Polly thinks of herself, not much younger than I was back then, making that decision, retreating from the world. She can't bear it.' She halted, worried about hearing a tremble in her voice. She mustn't upset Sara. 'Polly will adjust herself to the idea.' Was Sara feeling the same revulsion as Polly?

'I like most of the nuns at school,' Sara said. 'Except for Sister Lucia in the kitchens.' Bridie couldn't resist a smile. The girls had told her about Sister Lucia. She had red, brawny arms like sides of beef and she shouted at the girls in a rough Offaly accent if they asked for smaller portions of liver or cabbage. The only creature Sister Lucia cared for was her large ginger tom, a cat of uncertain temperament who was allowed to walk along the kitchen surfaces.

'In every religious community there is a sister who is harder to love than all the others.'

'Is that why you left, because you didn't like the other nuns?' Sara asked.

Bridie stood up, placing a hand to her head, trying to contain the jumble of images and memories talking about her vocation had churned up. 'I can't rightly pinpoint what it was that made me feel a religious life was no longer for me. Nothing in my past changes the way I feel about you and Polly. You're my life now.' She struggled for self-control. 'This my work, looking after the two of you and keeping you . . .'

Safe, she'd been going to say. Murmuring an excuse about the washing in the machine, she left Sara.

When she returned from unloading the wet sheets and hanging them over the pulley in the utility room, she stood at the kitchen window. Mr Stanton and Sara were in the garden. She saw him approach the girl and touch her head, which was his way of acknowledging that she was struggling with something. They'd agreed Bridie should tell them about the convent this evening.

'The girls know nothing,' Kathleen had said when she'd visited the hospital. 'Tell them that much at least. Perhaps in time you can tell them more.'

'But then the rest of it . . .'

'Coventry would be a start. You're going to have to come clean one day. What does Mr Stanton say?'

'That we'll know when the time is right to tell them.'

Someone came into the kitchen behind her. Polly. She sat at the table. 'You should teach Sara and me to peel the potatoes and carrots properly, Bridie. We don't know anything useful.' She sounded almost tearful.

Bridie placed an arm around her shoulder. Even now, when the girl was almost a young woman, she felt the familiar delight in touching her. When Polly had been an infant it had seemed impossible that she should be entrusted – expected – to carry the baby, to wash her silken skin and hair, cradle her, sing to her. Polly had been a child that people stopped to admire. From a very young age she'd possessed that old-fashioned quality of glamour. No, something more: charisma. Bridie bent over and kissed her on the cheek, which still felt petal-soft. 'Why did you leave the convent?' Polly asked.

Bridie felt eyes upon them. Sara stood in the doorway leading to the garden, something of a reproach in her eyes. She felt a pang. She seldom kissed Sara, reserving her signs of affection to a half-hug before bed and a peck on the forehead when she left for school in the mornings.

'I'll tell you what I just told Sara.' Bridie drew a breath and let it out fully. 'I don't fully understand all the reasons myself. It was in part because I felt I could serve God just as well as a layperson. I was very young when I entered religious life, lonely, unsure of my place in the world.'

'You'd been in a children's home. Life outside must have seemed . . . alien.'

Sometimes Polly could be very astute.

'I had a job and a bedsit, but nobody around me. Kathleen was still away in Cork. If she'd come over to England earlier, perhaps we could have shared the bedsit.'

She and Kathleen could have lived together as sisters, like Polly and Sara. Instead, Bridie had found sisters of a different kind.

'Why didn't you just go to Ireland instead?' Polly asked. 'To be near Kathleen?'

'There was no work for me there. Kathleen had always said she herself would need to come to England one day.' She just hadn't been able to wait for Kathleen to arrive.

Bridie felt wearier than she had expected the day after her return from convalescence, even though she had done nothing more than vacuum the drawing-room and cook a few meals. After supper she decided to rest her legs and sit down at the kitchen table with her sewing basket and darning pile. So many buttons to sew back onto the girls' clothes – mainly Sara's. And the state of the younger girl's skirt with its worn fabric – did Sara use it as a scouring pad?

'That's a nun's sigh.' Polly said, watching from across the table where she and Sara sat reading. 'I used to think it was an angel's, but it's a nun's.'

Bridie hadn't heard herself make the sound. 'My novice mistress used to sigh when I disappointed her with bad sewing of a seam or a poorly swept floor.' The sigh had usually preceded a verbal expression of disapproval.

'Was she nice?'

'Sister Peter?' Bridie couldn't keep the slightest grit from her voice. 'She did her best to ensure we were trained in all we needed to know.'

'So she was awful,' Polly said.

'I can't imagine you ever sewing badly or sweeping a floor poorly.' Sara lifted her head from her book.

'Even the humblest, smallest task had to be perfect,' Bridie replied. 'Particularly the humblest, smallest task.'

'Why did it matter so much?' Polly screwed up her forehead. 'I mean, things nobody would ever see?'

'God would know,' Sara answered for Bridie.

'God's supposed to be in charge of the whole universe. Why would he bother about a button not being sewn on perfectly? Surely he must have more important things to worry about?'

'We can't know what's in God's mind,' Bridie said quietly.

'Exactly.' Polly folded her arms. 'So you can't tell me that God gives a damn whether my desk is tidy or my shoes are polished. You can't possibly know.'

Sara looked from Polly to Bridie.

'Sorry,' Polly offered. 'I don't mean to be rude, Bridie.' She went up to Bridie and put her arms around her. 'I just need to *know* things.'

'You're a bit like your grandfather.' Bridie stroked Polly's hair, reaching up because Polly had grown so tall this summer.

'Let's go out in the boat, Sara,' Polly said, almost pleading, which was most unlike her. 'Like old times. Just the two of us.'

Sara looked out at the dusk falling, bathing the river in a mink-coloured haze. 'I've already locked up the oars.'

'Just a quick row?' Polly was almost pleading with Sara.

Just do it, Sara, Bridie said to herself.

Bridie watched the girls take the rowlocks out of the shed and fit them in the boat. They worked as a team, quiet and efficient. Once they were in the boat they rowed away quickly and were lost to sight, heading downstream. *One day they will drift away from you for ever. You will just be the nanny their grandfather once employed to look after them. They'll visit you a few times a year, if you're lucky, send Christmas and birthday cards.*

And it will be entirely your own fault. Hadn't Sister Peter always warned her of her innate wickedness? Perhaps she'd been right. Sin and Bridie had certainly recognised one another as sisters when it had come to it.

A TIME OF GIFTS
AND TROUBLES

BRIDIE

25 December 1990

Bridie watched Sara open a small but weighty present to reveal a bottle of Miss Dior Eau de Parfum. Bridie knew how expensive the scent must be. 'Thank you,' Sara said, looking stunned.

Polly gave her sister a smile so open and generous that Bridie felt guilty at her doubts as to how Polly could have afforded the gift. Mr Stanton opened his present and found a Parker fountain pen. Bridie herself found a Jaeger scarf. She could see Sara looking at the presents she'd given the family – paperbacks for her grandfather and Bridie, and pretty gloves for Polly – worrying that they were too humble. Bridie wanted to tell Sara not to worry, that her presents were just right. She hid her unease by folding up the wrapping paper and straightening out the pieces of ribbon so they could be reused next year.

'Why?' she heard Sara whisper to Polly. 'You don't need to. You have your allowance.' Bridie managed not to stare at the girls. *Don't show them you're listening.*

'It gives me a thrill.'

A thrill?

'And you must admit you like having expensive stuff, don't you?' Polly went on.

This Christmas morning had shown Polly's fierce, protective affection for the three of them. It came as no surprise. Bridie had seen her sit with Mr Stanton for hours, finding reference books for him, taking notes, cross-referencing the growing pile of pages that comprised the Great Big Book, as they called it. Bridie never expected the girls to do much around the house. They were young ladies, not like she had been as a girl – poor, bright but incompletely educated – but Polly would stand patiently holding heavy velvet curtains while Bridie stood on a stepladder unthreading the hooks. And again and again Polly would take Sara through the mysteries of algebra and chemistry or test her on irregular verb endings. But then she'd suddenly blank the younger girl, or laugh outside the drawing-room door if she played a scale wrong.

And Sara herself had grown so secretive. Michael. Bridie knew Sara was in touch with that boy of Kathleen's who seemed to combine Kathleen's have-at-it approach with Gerard's forensic intelligence. Once or twice Bridie had seen the child post letters into the box or sneak out to the public telephone down the street. No letters from him seemed to come to Thames End House, but Sara might have asked one of her friends to take them in for her.

Bridie wasn't going to think about her brilliant nephew on Christmas Day. Nor was she going to think about the inexplicably expensive presents Polly had given her family. She and Mr Stanton would talk about it later on, when the feast was over.

But Bridie's fears would not leave her; they brushed up against her like an unwanted but importunate cat as she sat in an armchair. Mr

Stanton was insistent that today of all days was one when she shouldn't rush around, yet distraction would have been welcome. The girls had been sent to lay the Christmas table and prepare the sprouts and potatoes, and he himself pronounced the turkey cooked and carved it for her in his precise, military way.

After they'd eaten their feast, Bridie sat in the glow of the red and gold Christmas tree lights, looking at the label on her Jaeger scarf, frowning. She thought back to what she had overheard Polly and Sara talking about. *A thrill.* But not of saving up to buy presents for her family. Anyway, it would have been impossible for Polly to have put aside so much cash. She didn't have a Saturday job.

'If the colour's not right, I'll change it for you,' Polly offered.

'I love the plum colour,' Bridie said. 'I wouldn't change it for the world.'

'Put the scarf round your neck. And let your hair down,' Sara said. 'We like to see your hair, Bridie.'

Bridie put a hand to her temples. 'My hair?' It was thick, still dark brown – almost black – with little bits of copper in it, but it was seldom released from its bun on the back of Bridie's head.

'You shouldn't hide it.' With a graceful bound, Polly was sitting on the arm of Bridie's chair. Her slim, quick fingers fastened the scarf around Bridie's neck in a loose coil and released the pins from the hair bun, pulling Bridie's hair over her shoulders. 'There.' Polly stood back so that the others could see. 'Doesn't she look different?'

The three of them stared at Bridie. She knew that the plum-red of the scarf must almost clash with her green eyes. Wouldn't that look strange? Perhaps it would somehow make them look even greener. Polly's father, Mark, the artist, would have known how to use colour to take a risk. With this scarf round her neck, the flush from the sherry still warming her cheeks, perhaps she too now looked like someone who'd once taken risks.

'It's a lovely scarf, child. You chose well.' Mr Stanton sounded tired.

'No convent would have you if they saw you now.' Polly was half frowning at her.

'What were Christmases like when our father and Uncle Quentin were boys?' Sara asked, looking at her grandfather. 'Did you have the same traditions as we do? The same food? Having to wait until after church?'

'Indeed. Stockings only until after the turkey.'

'That's cruel,' Sara said. 'Such a long time to wait to open them. I couldn't bear all that waiting.'

Polly sat straighter. 'There comes a point when you just want to know what's inside.' Her eyes were on Bridie. 'You can't just look at the wrapping paper.'

'Everything comes to him who waits,' Bridie told her. Silly proverb, but the conversation was starting to unnerve her.

'I like a bit of mystery,' Sara said.

Polly was still looking at Bridie. 'But after a while you need to see—'

'We should turn on the television,' Mr Stanton said, more firmly than he would usually have spoken the words. 'It's almost time for the Queen's Speech.'

This was Bridie's self-appointed task: facilitating each of his gentle rituals. She should already have switched on the television, ensured that BBC1 was selected, that all the chairs and sofas were turned the right way and that any distracting lights were switched off so that the picture was at its sharpest.

She scraped her hair off her face, snapped back in the hairpins Polly had discarded, and then jumped up to close the curtains, feeling herself contracting back into the carapace she'd built around herself. She felt just as she had at Larkrush, right before everything had changed.

She turned back. 'I think I'll take the food out to Joe now.' It had become a ritual after every family celebration: taking cake and other leftovers to the ferryman and his son. At Mr Stanton's insistence, Bridie had invited the pair to sit round the Christmas table and eat with the family, but Old Joe would have none of it. He and his boy would take the food set aside for them with polite thanks and eat it in the small wooden hut by the jetty where Young Joe took the ferry fares. Did they even have a kitchen at home? Bridie wasn't even sure she knew where they lived.

Man and boy were both in the hut. It was warm enough: a kerosene heater saw to that. Old Joe had strung streamers and tinsel round the windows and put up a small Christmas tree. Young Joe was doing a jigsaw puzzle on his father's desk, and he smiled his angel's smile at Bridie. She handed over a good chunk of Christmas cake, half a dozen mince pies – still warm from the oven – and enough cold turkey and ham to keep them going. Chipolatas wrapped in bacon, too, because she knew all boys liked them.

'Polly,' she said. 'Do you ever see her in the town after school?'

Old Joe finished a mouthful of cake and wiped his fingers. 'That was excellent.' When he spoke, which was seldom, and only to his son, Bridie and a few others, his voice was educated. Mr Stanton said he'd been a schoolteacher before the war. He'd married and had his son later in life. At first Bridie thought Joe wasn't going to answer the question. 'In the shops,' he said. 'But the shops don't do her much good. It's a game, but an angry one. She doesn't want to hurt you so she takes her anger outside the house.'

Bridie couldn't see Joe's face under his hood, which, as always, he wore up.

'Police,' Young Joe said. It was the first time in years Bridie had heard the boy talk.

'They can't catch Polly,' Old Joe said. 'Once, when they chased her down to the river, she jumped into my boat and I rowed her across.' Something like a smile covered the part of his face Bridie could see.

'I'm worried about her,' she said.

Old Joe was silent, too honest to tell her not to worry – all kids Polly's age went a bit wild. 'I watch out for her,' he said at last. 'Nothing in this town will hurt her while I have her in sight.'

'That boy,' Young Joe said.

'Which boy?'

'With the little sister called Fanoola or Noodle or something.'

'Polly sees Michael?' Bridie couldn't remember the last time they'd seen her sister's children down here. Young Joe must be thinking back to the summer when she'd had her operation.

Old Joe looked at her directly for the first time she could remember, and the hood fell back a little. Where his right eye ought to have been was a scaly hollow. He nodded.

'Don't you mean that *Sara* sees Michael?' It was the younger girl who met Bridie's nephew, who had built up a relationship that filled Bridie with dismay. Sara had always assured her that it was a friendship, nothing more. But she'd seen the way the girl looked at Kathleen's boy when he'd left the house with Nuala and Kathleen: lovesick. Well, he was good-looking and had a sharp tongue on him that girls that age found attractive.

'No, Polly and Michael. Whisper, whisper.' Young Joe made talking mouths of the fingers and thumbs on each hand, then helped himself to a mince pie.

FIVE

A SUITCASE AND THE SCENT OF HERBS

BRIDIE

'Whisper, whisper,' Bridie said.

'I'm not saying anything.' Sara turned, looking puzzled. She was packing Bridie's bag for her so they could drive up to Thames End House from wherever it was they were now. The Beeches Home for Children? Larkrush Convent? Somewhere in a big city, where the river was wide, and steel- and cobalt-coloured, and seagulls flew above it.

The school had never alerted Bridie to Polly or Sara playing truant to see Michael, but there were half a dozen ways a teenage girl could play truant for a half-day if she put her mind to it.

'Easy to escape,' Bridie told Sara, who looked worried.

'I've nearly finished. We'll get you out soon.'

This place was surely more comfortable than the children's home or convent. They sometimes held religious services in the lounge, but there didn't seem to be a chapel here and Bridie couldn't be sure the dog-collared man conducting them was a real Catholic. Sara was pulling blouses and skirts out of drawers. Bridie had so many clothes. Reverend Mother must have given Bridie permission to pay a visit. Where? To see Polly. The girl must be back from university, or from wherever she had been with Kathleen's Michael. The two of them, thick as thieves and each as sharp as the other.

Polly was so unhappy about Bridie having once been in religious orders. The revelation had upset the girl terribly, but there'd been some-thing more than just that going on with Polly. Something else had troubled her when she'd been a young girl – vulnerable and on the cusp of adulthood. Bridie sometimes thought she might be able to work out what it was, but then the enlightenment would fade.

Polly's wildness had started even before Bridie had told them about the convent, though wildness was a word Bridie herself would never have used for the girl. She'd been as gentle and considered as always, but more aloof, somehow, seeming to observe the family with a cooler eye. And absent far more often. Eventually she'd gone off with . . . But the name of the boy now escaped Bridie. There'd been something else behind Polly's behaviour other than the revelation about Larkrush. But how could she have found out?

How wonderful it would be to see the older girl, if she really was back home again. Sara claimed Polly was at Thames End House, but Bridie had her doubts. Hadn't she searched the whole town when Polly had run away all those years ago? Hadn't she and Kathleen spent days searching London railway stations, going to pubs in areas of north London where Irish people congregated, asking them if they'd seen the youngsters, after Nuala had rightly pointed out Michael's long-lasting interest in Irish history?

Bridie looked out towards the river again, to where Polly seemed to stand smiling at her, waving. 'Hello, my darling,' Bridie whispered to her.

'What did you find out in Ireland? What did you find out even before you left? Did something happen that summer I left you with my sister while I went into hospital? Kathleen promised my girls would be safe with her.'

Surely Kathleen hadn't blabbed? If you couldn't trust your own sister, who could you trust?

'We'll see Polly within a few hours. Don't worry.' Sara's hands were deft as she folded a nightdress and blouse. 'I'm not taking more than a few days' clothes. We can always wash your things if you need to stay for longer.'

Bridie's clothes were good quality. Sara picked them out for her, paying far more than Bridie thought she ought. When Bridie had packed her case to leave the convent, there had not been much to pack, and before that, when she'd left the children's home, there had been even less. She'd opened her small and battered suitcase as a seventeen-year-old wondering if there'd be something left inside from her infancy that would remind her of her mother. There'd been nothing.

She'd started adult life with a change of underwear, a nightgown and one spare shirt, all made of harsh, faded fabrics, victims of an institutional laundry. The stiff and threadbare textures, the darns on the stockings, the drab colour of her underwear: all this used to make her feel as if she herself had been through a laundry mangle. All she'd deserved, no doubt. There'd been something fundamentally wrong with Bridie, with who she was. *That name they called me in the children's home.* Bridie said it softly to herself so that Sara wouldn't hear.

She'd hated what they'd called her, but there had come an occasion when just saying the words out loud had felt like lancing a deep and festering sore. The awful words had turned to dust in front of her friend's mild, unblinking gaze. They'd been close in a way that the convent did not approve of, enjoying the walks to and from school where they both worked, the occasional coinciding of garden duty, or finding themselves both on the chapel flower rota. Sister Peter had watched them. How could the sharp-eyed old harridan not have noticed the friendship? For the first time in her life Bridie had had a companion who encouraged her to talk, and to read, as far as this was possible.

'She was ill all the time,' she told Sara. 'Mary Margaret had cancer and it wasn't treated properly when they sent her away from Larkrush.'

'I remember you telling me.' Sara broke off from her packing and studied Bridie gently. 'It was so sad for you. And then you left the convent yourself, shortly after she died. I must admit I never understood exactly what had happened. But it was the seventies, everything was changing, especially for women. Perhaps you were just experiencing the spirit of the age.'

Bridie liked it when Sara spoke to her like this. Sometimes she couldn't understand all of what the girl said, or formulate an answer, but expressions like *spirit of the age* seemed to echo around in her mind, a counterpoint to the other, mocking echoes.

There was so much the girls hadn't known about Bridie. She and Mr Stanton had discussed telling them, but there'd always been a reason for delaying the conversation. The past remained locked away in the filing cabinet.

She'd told them about having been a nun, though. Nothing wrong with having been religious, even if she did look back at her time in the convent with a mixture of astonishment, shame and sadness. Astonishment that someone like her could possibly have had a vocation. Shame because she had proved her critics right. Sadness because there'd been times when she'd once believed she could prove them wrong.

Bridie sat down in the armchair by the window while Sara continued her packing, looking out at the plants in the garden between her and the river. There were herbs out there among the flowers and shrubs. The window was ajar to let in the fresh air, and the aroma of the herbs floated into the room, pulling old memories out of the past, making her life as Sister John seem more alive than everything that was happening now.

SIX

BIRDSONG IN A CONVENT GARDEN

SISTER JOHN

Larkrush Convent, East Sussex, April 1972

The herbs in the kitchen garden had nearly dried out in the unseasonably dry April weather. Sister Mary Margaret tutted as she watered them. 'We might have lost all this mint, Sister John.'

Sister John wondered why she worried. The kitchen nuns at Larkrush Convent rarely employed the aromatic plants in their cooking. They'd once had an Italian sister in charge of the cooking who'd known how to use herbs, but she'd long since gone.

'Parsley sauce,' Sister Mary Margaret said. 'Shouldn't admit to such venial appetites, but how I miss it on a slice of juicy ham. Or thyme on a roast chicken.'

'Mint sauce on roast lamb.' Sister John just about remembered the last time she'd eaten that dish. It had been when her sister and stepfather had taken her out for a meal in a London hotel, back in early 1958, just before she'd entered the convent as a probationer. Her stepfather had stared at her solemnly across the table, before pressing a parcel on her. Her mother's lace tablecloth. What on earth was she to do with that frothy piece of linen and lace in a convent? She'd sent it back to Ireland with the two of them, fingers stroking it one last time, imagining her mother ironing and starching it. Hopefully someone somewhere was enjoying feasts on it of the kind she herself could only imagine.

But Sister John shouldn't be thinking about rich meals. What they were served at Larkrush was adequate for their needs. She turned her attention to the weeds threatening a row of cabbages. Cabbage was not a food that would lead you into tempting memories, though her sister had once told her how it was cooked in Ireland, with butter and mashed potato. Another letter from her sister should arrive next month. She might visit, perhaps nearer Christmas, if she had time now she was getting married. *Thank you God for giving me my little sister in the world's sense of the word* sister. *Please let her still have time for me*, she wanted to add, selfishly.

'Poor thing.' Sister Mary Margaret's large fingers were moving with surprising delicacy through the leaves of a sage plant. 'It didn't mind the frost, but that wind back in February was its Golgotha.'

They certainly weren't supposed to use references to Christ's Passion so casually or talk in this easy way at this hour of the day. Or really at any time. Mealtime conversation, when allowed, tended towards the religious. Sister John was out of practice with what the world would call chit-chat.

Sister Mary Margaret was a recent arrival to Larkrush. She'd been in the north, in the Order's house in a city with a large hospital where the sisters nursed. Each year, orders were pinned to the noticeboard and you went where they sent you. For fourteen years Sister Mary Margaret had stayed in the north. This year she'd looked at the board and seen that she was to give up her nursing and go south to Sussex to experience classroom work.

Sister Mary Margaret must have been reflecting on this shift in her work life as they worked in the garden. 'I've no teaching qualification,' she mused. 'Perhaps in the future they'll send me to college and let me become a teacher.' But her face as she contemplated the wasted sage plant told Sister John that she did not expect this to be the case. Why had they stopped her nursing? Word was that Mary Margaret had been an exemplary nurse. Perhaps she had become so good that serving God had taken second place to professional pride. But that wasn't for Sister John to conjecture.

'Be thankful,' Sister Peter had told her when she'd been Sister John's novice mistress, 'that you seem to have no discernible talent for any form of work, sister. We won't have to humble your soul by removing it from you.'

At that stage, Sister John was still accustoming herself to her new identity. She could just about remember what her mother had called her when she'd been a very small child, before the children's home. Now this name: Sister John. She'd let Sister Peter believe that she'd chosen it in honour of St John the Baptist, but it had been for St John whom Jesus had chosen to look after his own mother.

Despite her failure to demonstrate particular talent, they had, however, sent her to college for a year to acquire enough teaching qualifications to teach infants. 'Even you should be able to manage the intellectual needs of five-year-olds,' Sister Peter had told her. Sister Mary Margaret would be coming with her to the same school in the morning.

'What are they like, the children?' Sister Mary Margaret sounded nervous.

How to explain them? 'Most are good.' She'd been going to say more, say that some days the children made her laugh, that some days they taught her things too, but then she remembered herself. 'One or two need close watching or else they'll be slapping their neighbours with rulers.'

Sister Mary Margaret nodded. 'I look forward to meeting them.'

Nuns weren't supposed to look forward to anything in particular. Work was for showing your love for God and obedience to your vows, not for fulfilment.

'I know I'm not a very good example, Sister John,' Mary Margaret said ruefully, perhaps sensing what had flashed through Sister John's mind. 'I've spent too much time working with lay people. Some of their views have rubbed off on me, to use a vulgarism.' She fell quiet, listening to something. A bird. '. . . *thrush / Through the echoing timber does so rinse and wring / The ear, it strikes like lightnings to hear him sing,*' she whispered just loudly enough for Sister John to make out the words. 'Gerard Manley Hopkins. I once thought poems by Catholic poets might be read in a convent.'

Poetry and secular music vibrated through the mind to the senses, luring you away from contemplation of the purely spiritual: this was explained to the postulants when they first arrived. Safer to read the lives of the saints or devotional works. Yet some string, long forgotten and deeply buried inside Sister John, was plucked by Mary Margaret's quotation, emitting a low, pulsing yearning that almost hurt.

'It's time to go inside,' she muttered, turning her back on the light-filled garden with its dangerous scents and sounds of spring. Mary Margaret was looking at something on the path. A snail.

'Part of God's creation,' she said. 'Just like the herbs. Just like the lambs in the field.'

'Snails eat the vegetables. We should stamp on it.'

But Mary Margaret picked the snail up and lobbed it over the convent wall.

For the rest of that day the snail intruded into Sister John's consciousness during all the times when her mind ought to have been given to God. It was as much a part of creation as she herself, and yet they might have trodden on it and killed it and it would have been no sin. Her hands, white-skinned, peeped out of the arms of her habit. They were made of cells, just like the snail.

Sister Mary Margaret walked with her to the primary school in the village. Yet another fine spring morning: the cherry trees were in blossom. A breeze made the tulips in the gardens dance and the last of the daffodils blazed yellow and gold. This part of England had retained its Catholicism: many of the children in the school were locals, descendants of people who'd somehow clung on to the old faith. 'Probably out of sheer bloody-mindedness,' the headmistress, a middle-aged laywoman, had once confided in Sister John.

'I'll see you at twelve,' Sister John said.

Mary Margaret nodded. Her cheeks, usually pink, were pale. 'It becomes harder, changing work, as you grow older, even if you know it's God's will.'

Sister John wanted to tell her that she understood. 'I shall pray,' she said instead, 'that you find your talents readily applied to the challenges.'

Sister Mary Margaret bowed her head slightly.

'It is hard,' Sister John admitted.

'There should be moments of transcendence, too, shouldn't there, sister?'

'These beautiful trees assure me of God's love and my closeness to him.' If this were true, why did Sister John's voice still sound so tight?

At lunchtime they walked the ten minutes back to the convent together. Sister Mary Margaret was quiet, her eyes no longer darting over to the cherry blossom. 'How did you find the children?' Sister John asked, when five minutes had passed without words.

'They are sweet. I think God has given me something I will be able to do.' But she sounded flat.

'And the staff? Were they helpful?'

'Mrs Hughes is a fine Christian woman.' Something seemed to trouble her. They'd reached the gate at the side entrance of the convent. Sister John reached inside her pocket for the key. 'My head is full of new impressions,' Sister Mary Margaret said. 'I must pray for clarity.' She put a hand to her chest. 'There's a trip to the beach tomorrow to plan for. The children are so excited.'

Sister Mary Margaret must have found the morning taxing because she ate little of her lunch. They were not supposed to look at anything other than their own plates during mealtimes, unless they needed to look up to pass a plate or jug. Portions were doled out and you ate what you were given – all of it, mortifying yourself if you did not like a particular food. So Sister John could not help but notice how Sister Mary Margaret managed, without anyone reprimanding her, to hand back her plate through the kitchen hatch with half of her macaroni cheese uneaten.

When they returned in the evening, Sister Peter was waiting at the gate. 'Hurry along, sisters.' If anything they were a few minutes earlier than normal. Sister Peter's eyes scrutinised them.

'Tomorrow you will both take midday meal at school, to spare us having to wait for you.'

'You will need sandwiches,' Sister John reminded her, aware that Mary Margaret might not remember her class was off to the seaside. 'Because of the—'

'Sister Mary Margaret will manage without your counsel, I am sure, Sister John. Now hurry along.'

Hurrying never meant breaking into a brisk walk; you were some-how supposed to convey urgency without speed. Sister Mary Margaret's feet stumbled on the gravel path and she puffed.

'You will need to take a packed lunch for the trip like the children do,' Sister John whispered. 'Ask one of the kitchen sisters to give you something.'

A look of panic came over Mary Margaret. Sister John did not blame her: Sister Maria did not take kindly to requests – even for a humble sandwich – that fell outside the quotidian. She would rage.

As Sister John had anticipated, Mary Margaret walked to school the following morning without any kind of food with her at all. Sister John pulled something out of her own pocket. An orange, given to her by a girl in her class the previous day.

Mary Margaret's broad face was childlike in its wonder at the fruit. 'What a lovely fresh orange.'

'We do only ever seem to have apples and pears. Do you remember the rationing?' Sister John herself had been in The Beeches children's home for the last years of the war and during the even more stringent post-war shortages. Possibly the rationing had made little difference to the quality or quantity of food, though. *Be thankful that you are given anything,* those doling out the thin stew would tell them, with a particularly intense stare for her, as she had been even more of a charity case than the others.

Mary Margaret's face was reflective. 'My father was posted to South Africa for most of the war. We had all kinds of fruit. Yours is one of the few oranges I will have eaten since I became a religious, Sister John.'

'What did your father do?'

'Something in intelligence, making sure the former German territories in southern Africa weren't harbouring spies, I think.'

A patriotic man. A father in whose name you could feel pride. Sister John felt herself retreat even further into the little cave she'd created deep inside herself, a cave whose purpose, she told herself, was to allow her soul recuperation.

'Were your parents kind to you?' Sister John ventured, recalling so little of her own mother, except for her picking up a toy that had fallen onto the dank floor of an air-raid shelter and handing it back to her with a smile.

'They were good and caring. They came to my clothing.' The clothing in the religious habit was the formal reception into the noviciate, the next stage on from being a postulant. 'I could see the love mixed with sadness in their faces. And you, Sister John? Where did you grow up?'

'In the Midlands at first.' That was probably a sin of omission. 'My father died . . . early in the war. Then my mother was killed in an air raid on the East End of London. I went into a children's home.' There was nothing more to say.

'No siblings?'

'A half-sister. But her father took her back to Ireland when we lost our mother.'

'They left you by yourself?'

'Perhaps wartime travel restrictions made it too hard. My sister came to my clothing.'

She'd seen pride and awe in her sister's eyes as she'd walked down the church in her white dress and gauzy veil: a bride about to commit her life to God. She'd seen it again when she had re-entered the church during the ceremony, dressed in black serge and wimple, to receive the white novice's veil from the bishop and kiss the cincture, the long belt that symbolised obedience. But after the ceremony her sister had asked what had happened to the hair they'd cut off before placing the wimple on her head.

'They burn our hair,' Sister John had told her.

A look of dismay had passed over her sister's face. 'Your lovely thick, dark hair.' Their mother had had long, dark hair, too. She could just about remember it. Her sister's hair was a lighter shade, with a wave to it.

Her sister still wrote to her once a month. Sister John wrote back, but all the years of noviciate, during which outbound letters had been read and any expression of personal feelings was not permitted, meant these were dry epistles. Her sister was engaged now, to a good, steady man who was an accountant for a Dublin construction company. She found herself blurting all this out to Mary Margaret.

'Reverend Mother told me she believes further changes to religious life are coming,' Mary Margaret said. 'Perhaps you can visit your sister soon.'

Sister John gazed at her, open-mouthed.

'Look how our habits have changed.' It was true. They no longer wore the long black serge, and their veils fell only to their shoulders now. Sister Peter clung to the old habit, though, as did Reverend Mother.

They'd reached the school gates. Mary Margaret's class were already in the playground, hopping and skipping in excitement at their trip to the seaside. Mary Margaret would need her wits about her to keep them calm while they waited for the coach. Sister John headed for the door. A cry made her turn around. A boy lay on the bitumen, twitching, his classmates gawping at him and nudging one another. She reached them without knowing how her feet had covered the space. Mary Margaret was pushing the children aside. Gone was the look of mild confusion usually present in her face. 'You children move away,' she told them. 'Damian will be fine.'

'What's wrong with him?' Sister John thought the child looked as though Satan himself was pulling at his limbs. The front of his shorts was soaked.

'Epilepsy.' Mary Margaret knelt beside him, a hand on the boy's shoulder. 'You could fetch a blanket or a jumper or something we could put under his head to stop him from hurting it.' She sounded so calm. 'Perhaps two jumpers.'

Sister John grabbed jumpers from two of the boys. 'You'll get wee on my jumper, sister,' one of them objected.

'Take the picnic rug from the basket.' Mary Margaret nodded at the wicker container packed for the class to take with them on the coach.

'And ring his mother. Ask her to bring a change of clothes for the trip.' Her hand did not move from the boy's shoulder.

'He's to go on the trip?'

'Ring her.' Their positions had switched. Mary Margaret was in charge. Sister John almost ran to do what she had been told to do. The boy's mother arrived in the playground just as the boy himself was sitting up – pale, but apparently unharmed.

'I still want to go to the seaside, Mum. Please can I go?'

'I will look after him,' Mary Margaret told the mother. 'Unless you feel another fit today is likely?'

'He never gets a second one on the same day,' the woman told her.

Mary Margaret rose. 'Give me those.' She pointed at the pair of shorts in the mother's hands. 'Come on, Damian.' She peered at the clock on the church tower. 'We've five minutes to get you changed and find you a glass of water and a biscuit.'

'Normally they send him home.' The mother sounded doubtful

'I don't see why he should lose his day at the seaside, do you?' Mary Margaret said, leading the boy away.

'She really likes the children, doesn't she?' Damian's mother watched the pair disappear behind the door. 'Some of your sisters aren't so kind-hearted.' It was true: some of them regarded the children as so dripping with original sin that they needed a daily wringing out. Sister John felt a mixture of awe and foreboding for Mary Margaret.

On the way back to the convent in the evening, Mary Margaret was quiet. 'Did the trip go well?' Sister John ventured. 'Was Damian all right?'

She smiled. 'He loved it: the sea, the sandwiches on the beach. It was a good day for everyone. Reminded me of being a small child myself and my parents taking me to the seaside in South Africa. Except the weather wasn't as warm.'

Sister John was silent.

'Do you have such memories yourself, sister?'

'I only saw the sea for the first time when I was sixteen.' A rare children's-home outing to Brighton. She'd gazed at the sea with wonder, even though it had been hidden under a wet mist.

Mary Margaret said nothing. Sister John liked her for that. There she went again, letting personal feelings about people get the better of her.

'Was it a hard childhood?' The other woman's voice was soft. 'Sometimes I see you looking at those children and their parents with a kind of yearning in your eyes.'

Yearning sounded dangerous. If Mary Margaret had noticed, who else might? Sister Peter. If she picked up signs that Sister John was over-attaching herself to the children, there was no telling where it would lead. Working with the homeless in London or Glasgow, probably.

'I'm not sure anyone apart from me would have noticed, though.' Mary Margaret sighed. 'There I go again, allowing myself vanity at what I foolishly regard as my special ability to read people's emotions.'

'You can indeed read my emotions,' Sister John said. 'I do yearn for what those families have. I still have to work on my gratitude.'

'You said you went into a children's home when your mother died. Were they very strict?'

'They thought I needed careful attention.'

'Why was that?' Mary Margaret's voice was like Father Sullivan's when you went to confession, pulling things out of you.

'Because of my father.'

'The sins of the father were passed on to you? Such an Old Testament view.'

'He had done something terrible. They called me . . .' A deep breath. 'Something . . . I do not feel able to share.' She hadn't understood what they'd meant in the home. At first it had just been something some of the older children whispered at her. God only knew how they'd found out. It was only when she'd been well into her teens, almost old enough to be leaving the home, that she'd sought out one of the kindlier faces in the place, an elderly sister whom she sometimes helped out in the laundry, who hadn't wanted to tell the skinny young girl the truth, who said it didn't matter who her parents were, that she was a child of God.

She had persisted until the elderly sister had laid aside the muslin squares she was folding and told her as much as she knew.

'You do not have to tell me anything more.' Mary Margaret's voice was gentle. Because she did not push for details, Sister John found herself telling her what she knew of her parents.

And Sister Mary Margaret did not look disgusted. Nor did she show any change in her behaviour towards Sister John at all.

A RIPPED VEIL

SISTER JOHN

November 1973

Reverend Mother listened with equanimity to Sister John's confession that she felt her vocation no longer existed. Only the slightest creasing of the lines around her blue eyes expressed concern. She sighed. 'This news saddens but does not entirely surprise me.'

'I am sorry. I have failed.'

'Don't think of it as failure, sister.' Mother Cecilia placed her hands, palms together, on the desk in front of her. Outside, the afternoon was giving up the pretence of daytime and sinking into an early gloom. 'Think of your vocation as having been God's will for you for a particular period of your life.'

'Quite a long period.'

'Fourteen years since you entered as a probationer, I believe, with a year away for teacher training and another year or so in our sister house in the Midlands. But most of it here at Larkrush.'

Somewhere there would exist a file on Sister John, containing beautifully written notes on her progress in Reverend Mother's italic handwriting. Insofar as nuns were allowed or encouraged to like people as fellow human beings rather than souls, Sister John thought that Reverend Mother probably did like her. She knew she liked Reverend Mother, always had done. She opened her mouth to speak, but Reverend Mother was saying something else.

'Who knows what He has in mind for you from now on.' Reverend Mother steepled her fingers and looked down at them. 'You're still very young, sister.'

'Thirty-three this year.' It felt very old. Perhaps it wasn't.

'Like Our Lord himself in his most important year.'

Jesus had died at thirty-three, hadn't he?

Mother Cecilia wrote something on the sheet of paper in front of her. 'I'll have to write some letters to the archdiocese and then I believe they will write to Rome. It may take time. Months, perhaps.' Mother Cecilia surveyed her. 'In the meantime, I'll find you work you can carry on with out of sight.'

Out of sight of the likes of Sister Peter, she meant. Mother Cecilia had always been kind. She had been at the Order's house in France when Sister Mary Margaret had been sent to Wales. For a moment, she toyed with the idea of telling Mother Cecilia about Mary Margaret, about the cruel way that Sister Peter had organised for her to be banished from Larkrush just as she was settling into her new work. Just as her treatment at the local hospital had started to show some benefit.

Sister Peter had watched them so closely, had made it so plain that their *particular friendship* was wrong, was not to be allowed. Had Sister John wished for a cat to dote upon, that might have been allowed, but a relationship with another human being was a threat to her relationship with God. How deftly she had used the opportunity offered by Reverend Mother's absence to employ the temporary powers she had been granted.

'It is the way of the vocation,' Mary Margaret said before she left for the remote valley in west Wales. 'We always know we must be prepared to go and do something different. It's how it has always been. You must not take this to heart, sister.'

'How can I not?'

'Perhaps they are wise to separate us. Our friendship has been strong and true, but possibly it has marked us apart from others. Made us less tolerant of them.' Mary Margaret raised an eyebrow.

'Less tolerant of the foolish.' That was certainly true. 'They're wrong to send you away when you are ill.'

The doctors in the hospital in the town here seemed to have contained the disease that Mary Margaret would never name, the sister saying only that she had been asked to keep the details to herself and thought she should be obedient to the request.

She had died a few months after her removal. Sister John still didn't know what the illness had been. The news had been announced as a joyous event. Sister Mary Margaret would, after some time in purgatory, be nearer to her eternal heavenly home. Sister John had found her lips uttering the familiar words of the prayers for the dead while the synapses in her head relayed shock.

Mother Cecilia must already know all this. And what purpose would it serve to mention it now? Sister Mary Margaret was dead. And with the announcement of her death had come the final unravelling of what Sister John had thought of as her vocation. Had it always been so weak, she had asked herself again and again, that death could sever it? Surely her life as a religious ought not to have ended with Mary Margaret's death? Yet she'd known immediately that her life in a convent was no longer tenable. They could not make her stay and she knew they would not attempt to do so.

Reverend Mother was watching her. She composed her features. 'They changed our habits and liberalised some of the Rule,' the older woman said. 'To make them more appropriate to the modern world.

Of course we should be that. But you can change and change and yet find yourself further and further away from whatever it was you were seeking, sister. Don't let that happen to you. Hold fast.'

'I shall.' They smiled at one another across the beeswaxed expanse of mahogany desk. How she would miss the scent of polished wood, the swishing of robes, the clicking of the beads Reverend Mother still wore around the waist of her long habit, in defiance of the new short version most of the sisters now wore, the smell of cut lilacs before the statute of Our Lady in the chapel. Loss flooded her, filled her with panic.

'I shall pray for you, that you find your true vocation in life and give yourself fully and happily to it. Will you pray for me, too?'

Leaving the older woman's presence, Sister John closed the heavy oak door carefully behind her. That at least she had learnt well: the art of quietness, of not forcing your personality on your surroundings, of letting the atoms in your corporeal body almost merge into the atoms of the materials around them.

She remembered Mary Margaret's hands, red and rather clumsy elsewhere, moving delicately and energetically among shrubs, vegetables and herbs: cutting and pruning and digging almost without sound, almost without seeming to move a single leaf or stem; a daughter of Eve, happy to serve the garden. Though Mary Margaret could talk – oh yes, how she could talk if she felt loquaciousness fall upon her. The conversations they'd had . . .

But now Sister John needed to kneel quietly in the chapel, to pray for the calm she needed to make this transition from one world to another. The chapel would soothe her.

'She told you that the breaking of your vows might be part of God's plan, didn't she?' Sister Peter stepped out from the shadows along the sides of the corridor, her eyes glinting behind her glasses. 'She said not to feel guilt for leaving us?'

She nodded. Sister Peter stood between her and the sanctuary of the chapel. Like Reverend Mother she still wore the old-style habit, long and black.

'Go and hide in there, Sister John. Fall on your knees and pray. It won't change anything.'

Take the fight to the enemy. 'Why do you care?' She stepped towards the older woman.

'I am your sister in this community, in this vocation we share – or rather, *shared*. I helped you when you first came to us.'

'Helped?'

'I taught you patience and resignation.' Sister Peter folded her serge-clad black arms.

'You took pleasure in seeing me fail.'

'You were a novice. You needed reprimanding when you made mistakes.'

'But you so enjoyed it, didn't you? Then again, that was nothing more than what you did to everyone else. But you were responsible for something much worse. And by doing that, you made it impossible for me to continue my vocation here.'

'Your particular attachment, you mean? Sister Mary Margaret? You knew the regulations. No close friendships. And we're always moved on from one job to another. It's part of the life of personal sacrifice to God we have chosen.'

'I wouldn't have minded her leaving if she'd been going somewhere she would be happy. To a school. But somehow you managed to ensure Sister Mary Margaret went to a job she would hate, where she could not be properly treated for her illness.'

'Those decisions are made by the provincial council.'

'But you managed to sway them, somehow, didn't you? While Reverend Mother was away. You fed them gossip about us and made sure she'd die unhappy.'

'Dying is not a sadness at the end of a religious life. It is the doorway to eternal—'

'She was only forty-two.' Sister John was almost shouting. 'She could have lived, she could have carried out her vocation, for years, a decade, longer.'

'How deeply you cared for her, sister. Was that healthy, do you think?'

'She was my friend. Nothing more.'

'Even friendships can distract us from the work we do.'

'I was not distracted. If anything, being friends with her made me more capable of carrying out my vocation,' Sister John said. Seeing the world through Mary Margaret's eyes had felt like seeing the Garden of Eden.

'You see things like the worst kind of adolescent probationer. It's a miracle you lasted this long, sister.'

Again Sister John stepped towards her. 'You hate me. I don't know why, but I know that you do.'

A smile cut its way across Sister Peter's face. 'Dear me, what violent language you use, sister. Can't you wait the few weeks, months at most, until you leave us before you let rip?'

'Why do you dislike me?' She expected the older woman to deny that this was the case.

'I grew up in Coventry, you know, just before the war.'

Sister John felt the blood in her veins turn to sand.

'It wasn't pleasant for those respectable Irish living in the city after your father carried out his devil's work. Oh, there were Irish marches against the violence, letters of support to the local and national newspapers. But the English still spat at respectable women with Irish accents. And their children, well, if a few stones flew at them, who cared?' Sister Peter's voice trembled. 'And if an honest man was thrown out of his rooms with his poorly wife and his children, and if the wife died of her

TB in overcrowded, dirty lodgings shortly afterwards, well, that was just a harsh consequence of your father's bomb going off.'

Sister John tried to push past the other woman, hearing the swish of her robes against Sister Peter's, hearing Sister Peter's gasp of indignation. 'I'll pray for you,' said Sister John. 'For Our Lady to endow you with some of her own mercy and gentleness. And her forgiveness.'

She felt the older woman pull at the short veil she wore in place of the old-fashioned one worn by Reverend Mother and Sister Peter. The fabric was fastened too securely to come off. It ripped.

'You won't shake off your sin, Sister John,' Sister Peter almost shouted after her. 'Guilt will come snapping at your heels. You won't outrun it and it will stay with you until you're on your deathbed, scared about what's coming in the next life, the punishment for your unnatural friendships and your bad blood. You're a viper.'

Kathleen was waiting for her, three months later, when she could finally leave Larkrush, at the end of February, just a few days before Ash Wednesday and the start of Lent. Her little sister stood at the gates wearing a smart belted raincoat, little Michael sitting on her hip, a shiny leather handbag over her shoulder, eyes glinting with the purposefulness of a woman who knew her role in the world. For the first time, Sister John – it was almost impossible to think of herself by any other name – became aware of just how much work it would take to transform herself into someone who could live a similarly purposeful life. She wore the navy corduroy dress that Kathleen had sent her in the post the previous week. The fabric felt of good quality, even if it was too baggy around the chest. The short grey wool jacket that had accompanied it was similarly warm. Kathleen hadn't sent shoes and so she wore her usual black lace-ups. Even she could tell they didn't really go with the dress.

'I forgot about footwear,' Kathleen said. 'Sorry.' She gave her elder sister a peck on the cheek. 'Welcome back.'

It sounded as though she had been away on a very long journey and had reached home again. But where was home? The house in Coventry in which she'd been born had been blitzed, and the rooms in the house in Walthamstow outside which their mother had died had only been theirs for a short period before her death. Then there'd been The Beeches, but that could never be described as home.

No, home had been this convent.

'Don't worry.' Kathleen squeezed her arm. 'You'll be fine with Gerard and me till you're sorted out.' She steered her across the road to a car. The tall, lean man with the worried face in the driver's seat mumbled a greeting as he got out of the car to open the passenger door. She made him nervous, she could tell. There'd once been a young male trainee teacher at the infant school and he had blushed to the roots of his hair every time a nun walked into a room.

'I couldn't sit in the front,' she said. 'The back's fine for me. I could take Michael for you, if he doesn't mind.' She smiled at the boy.

Kathleen looked as though she wanted to dispute the point but then nodded. 'OK. We'll both go in the back.' She opened the door and picked up a carefully wrapped brown paper parcel, flat and soft. 'This is for you.'

'What is it?'

'Mammy's tablecloth. I kept thinking we'd be over to England sooner than we were and I could give it to you then. I didn't really know what to do with it when you went into the convent.'

'You should take it back with you.' She pushed it gently back towards Kathleen. 'You'll have much more use for it than I will.'

'No.' Kathleen walked around to the far side of the car and opened the opposite door to sit beside her. 'It's yours. That's what Mammy would have wanted. Eldest daughter to eldest daughter. She didn't have a long family life herself, with all the First Holy Communions, christenings and weddings where she might have brought it out, but let's give her that wish at least.'

Sister John sat next to her sister and Michael, hugging the table-cloth. She'd never had anything so personal since she was a very small child and had owned a toy rabbit. In the children's home they'd let her keep the rabbit at first because she'd screamed at them when they tried to remove it from her. But when she'd had diphtheria a year later, the rabbit had been taken away and burnt.

Gerard's car smelled unlike anything she had ever encountered before. Plastic and some kind of fabric and fumes: the smell of modernity itself, she thought. 'It's only a week old,' Kathleen said proudly. 'You're one of the first people apart from us who's been in it.'

'It's only done two hundred miles,' Gerard said.

The new car's aroma mingled uneasily with her last convent break-fast of tea with bread and margarine. She hoped she wasn't going to disgrace herself by vomiting in it. To distract herself she looked out of the window. They'd left the village now and were on the open road. A tentative February sun was trying to push through the clouds. She was to spend two or three months helping Kathleen with Michael, and then she'd apply for domestic work. When the new school year started in September she could perhaps return to working in a school.

'Just try and relax, Bridget,' Kathleen told her, squeezing her arm. 'It's a fresh start.' Little Michael turned his head and stared at her as though trying to make her out.

'Bridie,' she said, taking the child's hand and wondering at its softness. 'Bridget's what they baptised me, but Bridie's what Mammy called me until she married your dad.'

SEVEN

MARTYRS
BRIDIE

Oxford, May 1974

Church of England martyrs. Burnt for witnessing sacred truths against the Church of Rome. Protestant martyrs? Bridie read the inscription on the stone memorial in St Giles carefully to be sure. She'd heard of Mary Tudor, known that the Protestants had called her Bloody Mary, but had somehow not thought before about the cleric-burning aspect of her reign. Somehow she'd imagined all saints and martyrs as Catholic. If only Mary Margaret had been here to explain this aspect of English history to her.

Still only nine o'clock. She could probably afford a cup of tea if she could find somewhere quiet. The Jenkinsons didn't need her back until six. Bridie's plan was to buy supplies for a picnic lunch and eat them in Christ Church Meadow or Port Meadow, perhaps with a book borrowed from the central lending library. If the expedition felt too much, she could skip the picnic bit and just hide herself away in the depths of the library. Nobody would stare at a drably dressed woman reading a book there.

But she had promised herself that she would make an effort, not let her fear overcome her. She had thought of Mary Margaret, almost heard her voice telling her to have courage. She'd thought, too, of Reverend Mother, who'd written a letter to her just this week full of encouragement.

One of the department stores had a cafeteria, she remembered – more anonymous somehow than choosing somewhere on the street, but stuffy and windowless and possibly not as cheap as the workmen's cafes in the Covered Market. On she walked, turning left into Broad Street and pausing to admire the outline of the Sheldonian, before she turned right into Turl Street. Another world. Oxford, with its honey-stoned colleges, might have belonged to another century. The convent had been old, too, she reminded herself, but in another sense that she couldn't explain.

Students pushed bicycles and chatted, laughing and greeting one another with arms thrust around shoulders, kisses on cheeks. Boys and girls seemed at ease in each other's company. Bridie tried to remember herself just before she'd entered the convent: a tall, awkward girl of eighteen, already favouring dark clothes; a girl sitting by herself in her room in the boarding house every night, reading the same paragraph of her book again and again. She had not been designed for living alone, that had been the problem.

'Nature intended you to be the eldest daughter in a big Irish family,' the kindly nun in The Beeches had told her shortly before she'd left. 'You should be helping your mammy with the little ones or chatting to her while the two of you do the laundry. Find a nice young Catholic man, Bridget. Marry early. Create that large family for yourself.'

But instead she'd panicked and turned to the convent, too lonely and shy to manage any longer by herself, even though she'd had her job typing up invoices for a furrier and the boarding house.

In a cheap and warm cafe in the Covered Market she sat with a milky cup of tea that reminded her of convent brew. How strange she must look, a woman in her mid-thirties so unsure of herself as to be incapable of ordering a hot drink without stumbling over words and worrying that she would fumble with the coins. The girl at the counter had been patient, but

Bridie could see the puzzlement in her face. They probably thought she'd been in some kind of home for adults with mental problems. Or that she was very slow. Indignation jostled with the old habit of self-deprecation.

Bridie forced herself to contemplate how pleasant it was to sit here and know that her day was entirely her own. The food shopping had been done and the apple pie for tomorrow had already been baked, ready to heat up for Mrs Jenkinson while she was at Mass. Bridie herself would attend the 8 a.m. service so as to be back in time to put on the roast lamb. Nobody knew her at St Gregory and St Augustine's. The Jenkinsons themselves always preferred to walk to the Oratory. Bridie gave herself a mental nudge. Today was supposed to be about exploring life outside, reassuring herself that, with time, with close attention, she could pass herself off as an ordinary woman. Her hair was better since Kathleen had come up to Oxford and taken her to the hairdresser's, and she'd sorted out those eyebrows of hers, though the right hand one was still a little crooked where she'd pulled out too many hairs. Never mind. It would grow. As long as she looked normal, that was enough.

'Stop that,' a woman called to a child. Bridie jumped. And forced herself to relax. Nobody was watching her, nobody cared how she sat, what she drank, whether she chose a bun or a scone to eat with her tea. She pulled her cardigan sleeves down over her knuckles, feeling comfort in its thin wool. Clothes were becoming a problem. Mrs Jenkinson would pay her on Thursday, and a trip to Marks and Spencer would have to be made. That's where they all went, women of her class, if she had one. Spring was here – despite all the dark skies – and lighter colours would be interesting to try on, but she suspected she'd slide back into her default navy and dark green. Possibly even black or grey, if she wasn't very careful. It was probably her memory playing tricks on her, but she thought she remembered her mother once dressing her in a bright red coat. What had happened to that coat when she'd arrived at The Beeches? They'd probably sold it. Good quality children's clothes – at a premium at the end of the war – had been useful sources of income.

A man walking past the cafe halted, grasping at a glass pane, his eyes staring without focus. Bridie saw that he was well dressed, in one of those navy overcoats that men wore if they were going somewhere on business. He slumped onto the straw-covered walkway between the stalls. Drunk? She studied him carefully as pedestrians walked around him. She'd had some experience of drunks, who occasionally showed up at the Larkrush gates. He was shaking. Bridie stood. She knew this, knew what to do. She pulled the door open and knelt beside him, checking the ground for hard objects. Simply a question of pushing him gently onto his side, pulling his lower arm out to steady him. One of his hands was clenched as he shook.

'What's happening here, miss?' The cafe girl had come out, staring at her. 'Should I call the police?'

'No need for that. It's just a fit. He'll be fine in a minute.'

The man's body shook against her.

'He looks possessed,' the girl said. Bridie remembered thinking the same thing when she'd seen that boy at the village school twitching on the playground.

'Shouldn't you put something in his mouth to stop him biting his tongue?' a middle-aged pedestrian asked. 'That's what they do in films.'

'It's not necessary.' Bridie watched the fitting man. The spasms were becoming less vigorous now. His face was blue. 'The main thing is that he doesn't hurt himself.' She rubbed his arm gently. 'You're all right,' she said. 'Come on now.'

Colour was returning to his face. The fingers on the hand he'd been clenching became less rigid. She examined him carefully. Nothing had happened that might cause him embarrassment. If it had, she would have needed to lay her cardigan over his lower body.

Someone tapped Bridie on the shoulder. 'I'm a doctor.'

She stood up obediently to let him look at the man, heard him talking in that confident Oxford way. Probably a medic from the John

Radcliffe, someone who'd really know about epilepsy and would wonder what this woman thought she could do that was of any help. She walked back to the cafe door. 'Your tea got cold,' the girl said. 'I took it away.'

Ah well, it wouldn't have tasted very good cold.

'But I'm pouring you another. On the house.'

'Thank you.' She sat back at the table she'd left and tried not to stare at the man and the doctor. He was standing up now, coming inside. His coat had some straw stuck to the sleeve. He looked down at it and picked it off. Must be feeling better now. The doctor was asking him if this had happened before.

'A few times,' he answered. 'I was supposed to be seeing my own doctor again next week.' His voice was Oxford, too, but deeper than the doctor's. 'Thank you for helping me. It's only a short walk back home.'

The doctor left. The man sat down staring at nothing for a few minutes. She noted his breathing was steady now and his face back the colour it should be. He'd probably be just fine walking home. He frowned at her. 'Didn't you help me, too?'

She nodded. 'But I'm no doctor.'

'Thank you.' He stood up. She watched him carefully for shaky limbs. 'People are usually embarrassed. They step over me, I think.' He gave a sheepish smile. 'Not that I know much of what happens when I'm out of it.'

'When exactly is your doctor's appointment?' He'd find her nosy. She flushed.

'Tuesday. The last fit was pretty bad. I'm not sure how long this one lasted?'

'Five minutes or so.'

He glanced towards the glass display cabinets. 'Look, would you like a bun or something? I feel hungry.'

It would be his blood sugar levels. Mary Margaret had explained epilepsy to her once.

'Don't get anything too rich now,' she warned.

'Toasted teacake all right?'

'Perfect.' He went over to the counter and ordered two teacakes before returning to her table. Was this normal? Did strange men buy women baked goods? 'Are you a nurse?' he asked.

'No. I used to work with someone who knew about fits, though. She taught me what to do.'

He looked puzzled, as though there were more questions he wanted to ask.

'Did you hurt yourself at all?' she asked quickly. 'No bruising?'

'Don't think so.' The teacakes arrived and it was a blessed relief. The girl had plastered the butter on. Bridie started to scrape some of it off, and then wondered with whom she was trying to ingratiate herself. Certainly not God. So she ate the butter-lathered teacake. Oh, it was good. In the convent they'd always had margarine and there was no comparison. He'd ordered more tea for her too, and a glass of water for himself. She looked on approvingly as he sipped at it.

'Do you live in Oxford?' he asked.

One of those casual questions people probably asked one another all the time. At Larkrush such conversations had never been necessary. Bridie could barely remember asking anyone other than pupils at the school any questions. And obviously she had never been interrogated by a man, except for a priest.

'In Summertown,' she said, eyes on the saucer of her cup.

'I live in Jericho. For the moment, anyway.' She knew where the area was: between the Radcliffe Infirmary and Port Meadow.

'Will you be all right to get back there?'

'My brother and sister-in-law will be with me. They've gone off shopping. I'm meeting them at Christ Church at three.' He looked at the smart watch on his wrist. 'Plenty of time for me to get a grip.'

'Have you had epilepsy for long?' She blushed. Too personal a question, perhaps?

'Only since I suffered a head injury a few months ago. The first seizure happened shortly afterwards.' The hand with the watch on tightened. 'There've been two or three fits since then.'

She wanted to ask how he'd hurt his head, but that tense hand made her cautious.

'I was on active service in Northern Ireland,' he said. 'Got myself a bit blown up.'

Bridie rose, pushing at the table in her haste. The teaspoon on her saucer clattered. 'Must go.' She pulled down the sleeves of her cardigan. 'Thank you for the cake and tea.'

'Don't rush off.' He stood too. 'Can't I walk with you?'

'No.' She gulped for oxygen. 'Thank you. I hope the doctor helps you.'

Fool, fool, fool, she told herself. No need to make such a fuss about it. You could leave without all the drama. *Take a deep breath*, she heard that beloved voice from the convent say. She forced herself to push the chair under the table with control, and she felt his eyes on her as she left the cafe.

She wandered around the town for the rest of the day, barely noticing where her feet took her until she stood at the river. It was called Isis here, she remembered Mrs Jenkinson telling her, not Thames. She didn't know much about mythology, but hadn't Isis been something to do with the ancient Egyptians?

Young people strolled hand in hand. A boat rowed past, eight young men straining at the oars, a slight girl steering them, coxing, they called it, Bridie remembered. Swans bobbed at the riverbank. Bridie watched them for a while, before turning back for Christ Church. The sun came out and she sat on one of the benches outside the college, pushing aside a flyer advertising some event. She took in her surroundings, and suddenly spotted the man from the cafe again, now with a man and a woman. The brother and sister-in-law. Bridie blinked. The two men were identical.

She could only tell 'hers' – she blushed at her presumption – because of the clothes he wore. She studied the two men further. The new twin was louder, more expressive, waving his arms as he spoke. Bridie watched them walk up the path through the meadows from the river. She picked up the flyer and pretended to read it, keeping an eye on him. The sister-in-law was fair-haired, with smooth skin and large, expressive eyes. How must it be to look like that? People turned to look at her as she walked past, laughing, linking arms with both men. She was expecting, Bridie noticed, perhaps seven months in. Her posture and general slenderness meant that the bump did not make her ungainly. The brother said something to the porters on the gate at Christ Church and they walked inside.

Bridie stared at the flyer in her hand: 'Art Exhibition for the Works of Mark Stanton'. A photo of one of the twins. The exhibition didn't start until next Monday. Perhaps they were here to supervise the hanging of the paintings, or whatever happened before an exhibition was open to the public. The flyer showed one of the pictures: a seascape, with wild seas and cliffs. Might have been County Cork, which she'd come to know a little by sight, Kathleen having sent so many picture postcards from the coast during their years of separation.

She waited a moment, in case the trio were lingering inside the gate, and then walked back to the river. The day had turned finer and now the water flowed silvery green. Bridie stood, mesmerised by its soft changes of tint.

Mrs Jenkinson could not have been a more ideal employer: kind and although occasionally blunt, not given to asking searching questions.

'I've been clearing out my wardrobe and I left some clothes on your bed,' she told Bridie that evening. 'They're all good quality, hardly worn. Spring's coming and you can't go around looking like a crow.'

Bridie looked down at her black skirt, feeling foolish. She needed to make more effort. In her room she found the clothes Mrs Jenkinson had given her. A bright green mackintosh, far too flashy for her. The skirts were good, though, especially the denim one, slightly flared and coming down just below her knees. Good quality fabric, though she'd never in her life worn denim before. There were shirts – or were they perhaps feminine enough to be called blouses? And a half-dozen lightweight knits to go over them. She drew the curtain and began trying things on. She'd need new underwear at some point; the trip to Marks and Spencer would be made even more intimidating by adding that to her shopping list. Mrs Jenkinson did her best for Bridie, she knew, and she for Mrs Jenkinson, who'd told her that the silver had never shone as brightly as it did now Bridie was in the house. Years of practice had left their mark.

It was a holding place, this job, Bridie knew, not intended to last too long. It had been kind of the Jenkinsons to help her like this. She needed to look into the teaching qualification idea. And soon. Too much of her life had passed already. *Don't be so anxious*, that much-loved voice whispered to her as she refolded the clothes. *We weren't put on God's earth to worry.*

She knew she'd be back to look at the art exhibition on her Wednesday half-day. She'd thought that the little cash she'd saved for the Marks and Spencer outing would cover the ticket, but as it turned out, entry was free. Bridie hadn't seen many paintings like these. She hadn't really seen many pieces of art depicting non-religious themes at all until she'd come to Oxford and the Ashmolean had enlightened her.

Mark Stanton clearly loved the sea. She examined his depictions of the Northumberland coast and the West Highlands, and another of a lighthouse in New England. But the coast used in the painting on the poster was indeed Cork. Bridie wished Kathleen could see it. She reached out and almost touched the surface – such thick brushstrokes, and the oil looked like something that should be stroked. She remembered how one of the sisters, a young novice, had once forgotten herself in front of a statue and had run her hands down the folds of the Virgin Mary's blue gown, enjoying the smooth coolness of the plaster. The novice had been told off for that.

'You can almost taste the salt in the air, can't you?'

Bridie spun round. Him. *Her* twin, the epilepsy man from the weekend. He frowned. 'Hang on, I know you, don't I?' He narrowed his eyes. 'My saviour from last week. You look . . . different.'

'Spring clothes,' she said.

'To match the weather? Good plan. The green goes with your eyes.' He made a face. 'Sorry, that was a bit personal. I often get these things wrong.' He pointed towards a group at the other end of the gallery. 'Come and meet the artist.'

His brother, Mark.

'I can't,' she said. 'I wouldn't know what to say.'

'Tell him you liked his work so much you wanted to stroke it.'

She blushed.

'Seriously, he loves hearing things like that.' He sounded a little wry.

'I couldn't.' She felt foolish. 'But I'm being silly; of course I can.'

He nodded, looking more serious. 'I'm a bit like that myself, not always knowing what to say. I go to the other extreme sometimes and my family tell me I am often inappropriately open with strangers.'

'I don't think you are.' It was more that epilepsy man couldn't know what kind of *viper* he might come across. Sister Peter had thrown that word at her and she'd all but laughed at the older woman, but perhaps she'd been correct.

'The way you looked at that painting of County Cork made me wonder whether you came from Ireland. I can't paint, sadly, but I can tell when people are responding to my twin's work.'

'I was born in Coventry,' she said. 'Grew up in London.' Saying she'd *grown up* made it sound a gentle kind of upbringing. 'But my . . . family knew Cork, though.' She'd been about to refer to her father, and stopped herself just in time.

Mark Stanton had spotted his brother talking to her and was approaching. Bridie looked for the exit, but he was between her and it. 'I need to go,' she gabbled.

'Are you sure? You haven't been here long. Stay and say hello to Mark.'

She couldn't move. Mark approached. 'Hello.' They even had the same smile, the twins, but Mark's was brighter. He put out a hand and introduced himself.

'This is . . .' Epilepsy man looked at her. 'Oh dear Lord, I haven't even introduced myself to you yet, have I?'

'Quent.' His twin managed to convey mirth and reproach in the short name.

'I'm Sis—' She'd been about to give her old name. Who was she now? Sometimes she had to think twice. 'Bridget. Bridie, they call me.'

By *they*, she meant Kathleen and her family and Mrs Jenkinson.

'Quentin Stanton.'

Ah, Quentin, not Quent.

'Bridie, this is my brother, Mark. Mark: Bridie.'

They all shook hands. Very English and very easy.

Mark was looking at her. 'Have you ever sat for anyone, Bridie?'

Her face must have shown her complete lack of comprehension.

'For a painting. I'm trying my hand at some portraits.' He was running his eyes over her face in a purposeful manner that might have felt intrusive had anyone else been doing it. 'You have a quality of stillness that would make you a good subject.'

Stillness. No wonder. Years of being reprimanded for moving as much as a small facial muscle during the hours of services and devotions. Being told, as a small child, that if she fidgeted during Mass she offended Our Lord. As a novice, she'd finally realised that stillness could be her friend. It could allow something she'd once thought of as the Holy Ghost, but could no longer name with certainty, to enter her, allowing her to focus on a single detail – the pattern of bricks on a house, the particular blue of an iris – and find a whole world in it. 'You are stiller than anyone I have ever known,' Kathleen had told her when Bridie had stayed with her and Gerard. 'Sometimes I think you might have died. Do you even breathe when you're like that?'

'Nobody's ever painted me,' she told Mark, pulling herself out of the memories.

'I can be your first, then.' His eyes studied her figure with even more attention. Bridie felt her skin burn. Quentin shuffled.

Mark turned and looked at the door. 'Excuse me, that's my wife coming in.'

'Jenny,' Quentin said. 'She's American. For the last year Mark's dragged her round the coasts of Ireland and Great Britain while he painted. God knows how she put up with him, and the weather.' He took her upper arm gently. 'There's a cafe where we can go for coffee.'

Her legs wanted to take her in the opposite direction, but the habit of obedience was not easily shed. She let him guide her across St Aldate's and into one of the little streets winding west. They passed the open door of a second-hand furniture shop. Bridie caught the scent of beeswax. A pang of homesickness took her by surprise. Not again. She'd made her choice. Complicated arrangements had been set in place for her. Reverend Mother had had much work to do to have Bridie released from her vows. She had no right to feel like this. Feelings could be battled and defeated; the years had taught her that much at least. This, going with a man for coffee, was freedom. It ought not to feel so dizzying. If she didn't sit down shortly she might actually fold up here in the street. She willed herself onwards with him.

'Do you like films, Bridie?' he asked, when they were seated with a coffee in front of him and a cup of tea in front of her. 'Oxford's blessed with cinemas, little ones and big ones. Now I've more time I've been catching up with films.'

'Are you not going back into the army?' she asked, dreading him telling her he'd be going back over to Northern Ireland.

'Not me.' He tapped his head. 'They won't have me any more with this. I'll have to find something else to do with my time.' He didn't sound unduly worried. They were clearly a well-off family; both men wore subtly coloured but clearly good-quality jackets and trousers. Jenny's dress had been a simple shirtwaister, but in a turquoise fabric that hung well over her swollen abdomen and looked expensive. Though what would the erstwhile Sister John know about fashion?

'Are you sad not to go back?' The words came out almost calmly, to her relief.

'I won't miss Belfast. I suppose there was a bit of excitement at first: the danger, the challenge. But it was just sad a lot of the time. All those people hating one another. Hating us. Even though we'd gone out originally to protect them.' He frowned at his coffee. 'It shouldn't have gone the way it did. We could have managed Ireland better in the past, though I'm not a politician and it's so complicated that I don't know what the answer is.' He pulled the sugar bowl towards his cup and saucer. 'Hand the country over to the South? Against the wishes of all those Protestants who want to be British?' He pushed the bowl back towards the milk jug. 'Keep it as part of Britain and continue to alienate the Catholics?' He looked at the bowl as though he couldn't quite remember what he'd been doing with it and returned it to the middle of the table. 'Some kind of compromise, like Andorra, perhaps?'

'It sounds as though you think about it a lot?' This man must regard the IRA as evil in every way. What would he think if he knew he was having coffee with a notorious bomber's daughter?

'Can you speak French?' Quentin asked.

She blinked at the change of topic.

'Though the films do have subtitles.'

'I have no French.' She blew gently at her tea. 'Just a bit of Latin.' Ah, she shouldn't have said that.

'From school? That's where I learned mine.'

'More from religion.'

'You're a Catholic.' He said it seemingly without concern. She nodded. Presumably in Belfast Catholics were potential antagonists, throwers of bottle bombs and missiles and planters of more deadly explosives.

'So you live in Summertown? Do you work?' He rolled his eyes. 'Do you mind me asking so many questions?'

'I'm used to questions.' Probing questions asked either by others or by herself, about the little things she might have done during the day that weren't as good as they should have been: the floors less than perfectly swept, the dishes cleared without complete concentration, the irritation at supper when someone else cleared her throat every thirty seconds, the moments where trying to grow closer to God had been scuppered by distraction. 'I'm a housekeeper.'

'A housekeeper?' He looked surprised. 'Like Mrs Danvers?'

She knew who he meant, which was a miracle; she'd read so little. 'Hopefully less intimidating. And my employer is an honest woman, not like the first Mrs de Winter.' She'd finished *Rebecca* quite recently. Kathleen had told her there were half a dozen novels she had to know about to function in a normal woman's world, and that was one of them. She wasn't ready for some of the other books Kathleen had lent her.

'Have you always done that job?' He sounded curious, rather than judgemental.

'No. Though I am used to domestic work.' The steps she'd swept, the polishing of wood, the starching and ironing of altar cloths and vestments.

'You actually look as though you should be a novelist or a poet.'

She heard her own laugh like a bell through the little cafe. People looked up. Sister Peter would have been appalled.

'Seriously. What kind of work would you see yourself doing if you could do anything in the world?'

She couldn't fully answer that because she didn't really know. How could she possibly understand what was offered by this new world? 'I might like to work in a bookshop or library. The library might be hard, though, as you need qualifications. I do have a teaching certificate, for young children, so I could go back to that.' She looked at him. He didn't seem as pale today. 'What about you? You said you don't paint like your brother, but you must be artistic too?' She hadn't commented as much about anyone for decades. Certainly not to their face, anyway.

'I used to love pottery, sculpture, that kind of thing. But the military life put me out of practice. I've lost the knack.'

'It must be latent, surely?'

'Because of Mark, do you think? That's what they used to say. The two of us are physically identical, but he's always been the brighter and the more creative of the two of us. Perhaps this bang to the head will rewire me and bring me back to art. Or perhaps I could start a specialist art bookshop.' He sat back and looked at her. 'Do you really like your job, Bridie?'

She thought about it. 'Mrs Jenkinson is teaching me to cook properly. Before I could only make very simple dishes. It's quite difficult at times, learning how to make the sauces and the pastries, but it's rewarding when I manage it.' Mrs Jenkinson had praised the shepherd's pies and custards that Kathleen had quickly taught Bridie to cook before she'd taken the job, but she told Bridie she needed her to do more adventurous dishes. Boeuf bourguignon. Crêpes Suzette. It had seemed wanton to use such quantities of beef, eggs and sugar, but satisfying. She supposed she really ought to research how she could return to teaching. It would take more courage than she had just at the moment, though she'd loved it once.

'And the Jenkinsons have a comfortable house. I enjoy Oxford.' To be truthful, it had only been in the last few weeks that she'd dared roam very far. Spring had emboldened her, warmed something up deep inside her: a curiosity about life and people.

'Will you meet me again, Bridie? I really want to go to the cinema to see some of those French films they put on. I haven't had the chance for years. Come with me?'

Go to the cinema, a place she had visited only once, in that in-between period of her life. Seventeen, nearly eighteen: finished with school, but too young for the next bit. *Funny Face*, the film had been.

She'd sat in the auditorium, mouth open, amazed at Fred Astaire, at the easy charm of him, at his conviction that life was easy and charming, too. It had been that or *The Bridge on the River Kwai*. Kathleen was over from Ireland with her father, Bridie's stepfather, and he had said that the latter was too grim for young girls. He hadn't come with them to the 'fill-um', as Kathleen called it, but Kathleen had paid for the tickets and given Bridie half a crown when they came back out onto the street afterwards, telling her it was from Daddy. She'd handed the coin to Bridie with eyes averted, as though giving her one of Judas's silver pieces. No need for that: Kathleen's father had owed her nothing and it had been kind of him to remember her at all. Mention of the cinema brought all this back to her. Quentin Stanton was waiting for her answer.

A church clock struck twelve, the chimes ringing round the cafe as someone opened the door. Bridie's leg muscles responded, and it was all she could do to stop herself from turning to look for a statue with flowers around it, from standing up and starting to recite the old, familiar words. But instead of the Angelus, she heard Mary Margaret's voice again: *Have courage.*

'Yes.' The word sounded very definite when she spoke it to Quentin. 'I'd love to go to the cinema with you. Thank you.' It sounded as though she were saying she'd fly to the moon with him, like in that Frank Sinatra song that Kathleen liked so much, and she wanted to laugh. Nerves. Now would be the time to explain about herself, who she was, who she had been – but that impulse seemed to mingle with the steam from the coffee machine and condense into nothing.

As they left the coffee shop Quentin said he needed to go back to the gallery. They walked together back to Christ Church and shook hands. No attempt at anything more intimate, thank God. She headed back to the Isis, walking along the towpath towards the boathouses, feeling herself and, miraculously, just a little less alienated from the chatting, laughing young people who were walking by the river.

RIVER GODS

BRIDIE

September 1974

Quentin and Bridie stood holding hands by the Isis for so long that she joked they would turn into statues.

'We could be an Egyptian god and goddess,' he said. 'Though I'm never sure whether this river's anything to do with Isis and Osiris.'

'I wouldn't know,' she admitted. 'I don't know much about rivers, and the only thing I know about Egyptian rivers is the story of Moses in the bulrushes.' How clever Moses' mother and sister had been in their plan to have the doomed Israelite child pulled out of the Nile by the Pharaoh's daughter, and to have Moses' mother instated as his wet nurse.

'I don't remember much about the myth,' Quentin was saying, 'but I think Osiris was drowned by his jealous brother in the Nile. Isis, his wife, searched for his body and managed somehow to conceive a son with him. It's all about rebirth. I think some Egyptians still believe that drowning in the Nile is somehow purifying.'

'I can't swim,' she said. He observed her as she watched the river flow.

'But you don't have a jealous brother to throw you in. And if you did, I'd jump in after you.'

'I've only a half-sister. And she wouldn't throw me in, so you're safe.' He looked at her as though he wanted to know more. 'You know a lot about mythology?' she added quickly, before he could ask any questions.

'Not really. My father's the history and myth buff. He's keen on rivers, too, lives right on the Thames about ten miles from here. Can tell you all about Chinese and African river gods who require human sacrifices by means of drowning. He taught us to swim very young and forbade us from going out on the back lawn by ourselves until we were fairly large in case we turned ourselves into unwitting river sacrifices.'

'He sounds like a good father.' She herself wouldn't know what that meant, though.

'He was. Is. How about yours?'

'He died when I was very young.' She felt her hands clench on the bamboo handles of the handbag she'd bought in Oxfam. 'And my mother a few years later. Air raid.'

She could feel his gaze on her face. Of course, he'd be working out that she must have been born at some point early in the war and was obviously some years his senior. Kathleen had told her that life in the convent had simultaneously kept her young and aged her. *Your skin and eyes are lovely and clear, and when you look at people it's like a teen-ager peering out. But you dress like an old biddy and it's those nuns who've shaken all the fun of being a woman out of you.*

I'm not young, she'd told her sister.

Kathleen had told her that the new haircut had taken years off her, and a touch of mascara and lipstick would do wonders. Bridie was wearing some of each today, very cautiously.

'My brother wants us to go out to dinner with the two of them,' Quentin said. 'Sometime this week. Jenny's up for leaving the baby now.' Little Polly was two months old.

A careful note in Quentin's voice alerted her to the fact that this was going to be more of an occasion than the few lunchtime meals they'd shared in quiet country pubs. What would she wear? Jenny was so beautifully turned out, immaculate even as a new mother. You could look at her like you would one of Mark's paintings. Perhaps that was why Mark had married her. What an unworthy thought. But Mark was so observant, in a forensic kind of way. Quentin noticed things about Bridie too, but his manner of noticing and commenting was very gentle. Her lack of pretty clothes hadn't mattered up until now.

She gave absent-minded responses to Quentin's comments as they strolled back towards the town centre, until he laughed. 'Am I that dull?'

'It's just clothes,' she said. 'I never know what to wear. It's . . . daunting.'

He took her hand. 'Isn't it about time we talked about where you were.' His voice was gentle. 'Before you came to Oxford.'

'I . . .' There was something lodged in her throat.

'Because I think it's bothering you. Wherever you were, you know it doesn't matter to me.'

There was a bench outside Christ Church that nobody had claimed. He steered her towards it. 'That's why clothes are complicated for you. I think you must have worn some kind of uniform before.' He tilted his head. 'Women's services? Or were you a woman police officer? Or some kind of servant?'

She laughed. 'In a way you could say I was in service.' This was going to be easier than she had ever dreamed. 'Religious service.'

'You were a nun?'

'A sister. There's a slight but important difference, but, yes, a nun.' She looked down at the ground. 'Do you mind?'

'Should I mind?'

She couldn't think what to reply, and he laughed.

'I think we've agreed that neither of us can think of a reason why I should.'

When he kissed her goodbye on the Jenkinsons' doorstep it was a more lingering kiss than the previous ones had been, as though he wanted to drill down into her. Bridie hoped Mrs Jenkinson wasn't looking out of her bedroom window. She'd already mentioned – a few times – that Bridie had established *quite* the social life. It was perhaps time to think about moving on. The thought was terrifying. If she rented a bedsit and Quentin grew tired of her, what would she do then, all alone? At least there was sporadic companionship with the Jenkinsons. But then Quentin showed no signs of wearying of her.

'Tell me what's in your wardrobe,' he said, letting her go. 'I don't know much about fashion at all, but I know you're fretting about dinner out. Dresses, skirts, blouses, what have you got?'

She listed the garments. It didn't take long.

'The navy dress?' he said. 'Would that do?'

'It's smart. I think it's jersey, good quality. But it's quite plain.' Mrs Jenkinson had worn it to coffee mornings.

'Could you put a bright belt around it? I've seen Jenny do that sometimes with a plain dress and it looks smart.'

'I don't have a belt.' Wasn't she the Moaning Minnie? 'But I could find a silk scarf.' Kathleen had once worn a black dress with a scarf tied round the middle in place of a belt. If she passed Oxfam on the way home she could perhaps look and see if they had anything suitable.

'You'll be classically simple and beautiful.' He stroked her hand. 'You have no idea, do you? No idea what you look like.' There was a choke in his voice. 'Don't you look in the mirror? Didn't anyone ever tell you?'

'It wasn't exactly encouraged.' She tried to remember if there had been any mirrors – *glasses*, they called them – at Larkrush. Not even in the bathrooms. She was remembering something else, though, the line of her mother's cheek, her dark hair falling forward, the smoothness of her skin. 'I don't really remember what my mother looked like, and my father . . . died before I was born.' Had he been handsome? Who could now tell her?

'Those genes came from somewhere.' Quentin's hand pressed hers.

The restaurant, Elizabeth's, was all she had feared: formal service and long menus of foreign-sounding dishes. She ordered asparagus and lamb because they seemed the simplest things on the menu. Mark and Jenny ordered decisively, while Quentin havered between the beef in some kind of sauce and a fish dish.

'Good old Quent,' Mark said. 'Never able to just go for it.' His eyes slipped towards Bridie. Quentin frowned very slightly. This evening the brothers were dressed in a way that suggested mild telepathy at work: different coloured shirts, but both with sports jackets and trousers that were of the same navy brushed cotton.

Mark saw Bridie looking at his shirt. 'Like it?' He had a way of looking at her that made her feel the question he was asking was really another one.

'It's a wonderful blue – like a kingfisher.'

'It's a lovely silky fabric,' Jenny said. 'I bought it for him in New York.'

'Quent could never get away with it.' Mark winked at Bridie. To her annoyance she felt her cheeks burn. She wanted to tell Mark that he was wrong.

'Much too fancy for me.' Quentin took a sip of his red wine and gave an approving nod. Bridie thought she preferred the way Quentin was dressed in his ivory cotton shirt. And silk on a man was perhaps too much of a good thing. Mark himself was perhaps too much of a good thing.

'You might like him in fancier clobber, though?' Mark said, addressing her. 'And he might like you in something that shows you off. Though you wear that navy dress very well, I suspect there's a more sensuous woman in there somewhere.' He topped up her glass. The red wine was nicer than any alcoholic drink Bridie had ever drunk before.

She looked down at the napkin on her lap, almost disliking him now. Did he know what she had been before she came to Oxford?

'Mark.' Quentin said it softly.

'Sorry, sorry.' Mark turned the conversation to an exhibition at the Ashmolean, a museum that Bridie had come to love, spending short periods there every time Mrs Jenkinson needed some shopping from the Covered Market. She started to enjoy herself, debating the merits of Egyptian art with Mark, finding him a more sympathetic person when the conversation was less personal.

'We were talking about Isis and Osiris,' Quentin told Mark. 'The river sacrifice and the concept of rebirth and regeneration.'

'You can see why people might think it would work.' Mark turned to Bridie. 'If you stand on a bridge above a river, don't you sometimes have this crazy impulse to throw yourself into it? Just for the sheer hell of it? Flowing water is so inviting.'

She laughed. 'I'd be worried about the awful cold shock. Perhaps I'm too weak to be good at self-sacrifice by drowning.' She took another sip of wine. Mark topped her glass up again.

'Or perhaps you have nothing to sacrifice yourself for?'

Others would disagree. She thought of Sister Peter. Sister Peter would say that Jesus had sacrificed himself for Bridie. Instead of sacrificing herself in turn, she had repaid his sacrifice by striking him like a serpent: a viper.

She turned to Jenny and chatted to her about Polly.

'I probably shouldn't have come out tonight. I hate leaving her.'

'Nonsense,' her husband said. 'If anything happened we're just minutes away from one of the best hospitals in the country. And the babysitter's highly recommended. Have another glass of burgundy, woman.'

Bridie understood. If Polly had been her child, she would have found it hard to wrench herself away.

Jenny laughed and let him top up her wine. 'You'll have to come round again this week, Bridie. Polly loves you.'

'I love her.' From the moment Quentin had brought her into the hospital to see Jenny and Polly she'd adored the small bundle in the Perspex crib. Jenny had scooped her daughter up and handed her to Bridie. For a second Bridie panicked, unsure where the baby's head should lie, but then some old memory came back and she knew to support Polly's head on her upper left arm. She rocked her gently.

'A natural,' Mark had said. 'You'd think Bridie was the mother of at least five.'

Bridie blushed. She didn't want to let go of Polly.

'Oh yes.' She remembered babies from the nursery at the children's home. The pretty ones hadn't stayed long – someone had always wanted them. The less attractive, less bright or older infants tended to stay longer. She'd played with them often. *You can rely on Bridget to look after the little ones*, they'd said.

During her years as a sister there'd only been occasional contact with babies, and she'd regretted that. Helping Kathleen with Michael before she'd come to Oxford had been a joy, but she'd never seen him when he'd been a tiny newborn. Kathleen was expecting again now: five months, she was. Bridie would be able to help with the little one. The muscles in Bridie's arms and chest seemed to melt at the thought of holding a small infant. All the time in the convent when she had started to miss something, had it been this, this longing for a small body in the crook of an arm? At times she was worried about showing the longing overtly. Jenny might think it strange.

She told Jenny about Kathleen's pregnancy. 'She says she always felt well, both times, just like you.'

Jenny laughed. 'I was sick as a parrot for the first eleven weeks, but after that I just wanted to eat and sleep all the time.'

'Kathleen says she'd love a nap after din—,' she corrected herself, 'lunch, but Michael doesn't agree.' Michael was a little imp, Kathleen said. Worth waiting for, though – Kathleen had been nearly thirty by the time the baby had appeared. That was old to be in your first pregnancy.

Mark had been watching Bridie while she chatted to Jenny. 'Do you ever wear your hair down?' he asked.

She put a hand to the bun at the back of her head. Occasionally she just tied it back into a pony tail but she'd never thought to wear it loose. There'd never been a time when her hair hadn't been required to be off her face. Mark leant forward. She felt herself grow rigid. Was he going to pull the pins out of her hair?

'Perhaps Quent could undo it.'

Not here, not in the restaurant.

'Maybe some other time,' Quentin said mildly.

'Let me tempt you in other ways, then.' Mark had already ordered another bottle of wine, a white one this time, sweet and fruity, to go with the chocolate mousses they had all ordered. Bridie felt her cheeks glow. How much had she drunk tonight?

The three of them dropped her at the Jenkinsons' in Quentin's car. 'Don't you ever stay the night with Bridie?' Mark asked his brother. 'Sneak inside with her?'

'Bridie's domestic arrangements are complicated,' Quentin told him. Nobody seemed to notice Bridie blushing. Quentin got out with her. 'Don't mind my brother,' he said, taking her into his arms at the front door. 'It's all bluster. I know he likes you a lot. He just has to tease people he's fond of. Perhaps you'll be moving out of here soon though?'

'Perhaps.'

'Good.'

He kissed her again, so passionately that she even forgot to worry about Mrs Jenkinson and the two in the car. She moved her hands up and ran her fingers through his hair, touching the slight indentation in his skull caused by the explosive. The skin had healed, but no hair grew over it. He ran his hands inside her coat and over her chest. Instinctively she drew back, then moved closer. The sensation was like nothing she'd ever allowed herself to feel before. 'Do you like it when I do this?' he asked, pulling away for a second, voice sounding husky.

'Yes.' She surprised herself with the firmness of her reply. 'Though I think the wine's making me more . . . free.'

'Mark likes his wine and he likes others drinking along with him.' For a moment Quentin sounded judgemental. 'I'll kill him if he's forced you into an awful hangover. Make sure you drink a large glass of water with an aspirin before you go to bed.'

He pulled her close again, and this time his hands worked their way under the jersey fabric of her dress and under her bra, which was the horrid old one she hadn't yet replaced and now wished she had. 'I'm not sure how much longer I can keep up the restraint.' His voice sounded tense.

This was restraint, was it?

'You're driving me crazy,' Quentin muttered.

Something rustled. They moved apart. Mark.

'Felt a bit stuffy in the car,' he said. 'Thought I'd have a look at the garden. Big house,' he said. 'Is it secure? Do you check the back door is locked before you go to bed? And the windows?' Mark's eyes were scanning the walls.

'Mr Jenkinson locks up at the back.' She was touched that Mark cared enough to ask the question. Perhaps he really did approve of her after all.

'I'd better get Jenny back home. She gets so tired at the moment.'

Quentin murmured a good night and touched her shoulder as he left her.

She tiptoed into the kitchen, managing to pour herself a glass of water without spilling too much of it, hunting down the aspirin in the bathroom cabinet. When she'd washed the aspirin down, she undressed, falling asleep quickly, even after all the wine and coffee, exhausted by the effort of making herself look respectable for the night out and from the outpouring of emotion on the doorstep. Had that really been her, Bridie Brennan, former nun, outside the front door, quivering and sighing like a tipsy teenage girl? Sleep claimed her before she could feel too much guilt.

A small sound, a sigh, woke her. Someone was in the room. She shot up, heart pounding. An arm was around her, a finger moving over her open mouth. Quentin.

'Mark told me there was a window I could climb in through,' he said, his voice seeming to come from far away. So that's what Mark had really been doing: finding an entry point for his brother's nocturnal break-in, rather than checking up on her safety. 'Nobody heard me. We used to get in and out of houses all the time as boys.' Quentin sounded breathless, unusually enthusiastic. 'I can't resist you.' There was almost a choke in his voice. She'd never heard him sound so desperate.

She reached for the light, but his hand took hers. 'Don't break the spell, Bridie.' He spoke in a very low voice; she could barely hear him. 'Close your eyes. In the morning you won't know I've been here, darling. Nobody will. This doesn't count because you're not really awake. It's not a sin. You know how I feel about you.' He was kissing her lips. 'I showed you tonight when we were outside the house together.' The cotton of his shirt felt starchy against her skin.

'But—' She hadn't imagined it like this. She hadn't really imagined getting to this point at all.

'Close your eyes,' he said again. 'Forget about everything else.'

His hands were moving quickly now and she was still trying to explain why this was wrong. But too much talking would risk waking Mrs Jenkinson. This was Quentin: quiet, gentle Quentin who would never harm her. She closed her eyes. She hadn't imagined it could all happen so smoothly, that she would actually want him to continue. At some stage something puzzled her, but even as it did she was distracted by another more insistent sensation, a whispered question in her ear. 'Yes,' she murmured to him. Whatever it was that had confused her faded away.

They lay together for a while when it had finished, then he kissed her gently and stroked her hair. 'I love it when it's loose.' She felt his warm body remove itself from hers with a mixture of regret and relief. He replaced the cotton shirt and the trousers he had worn to the restaurant.

'It didn't happen,' Quentin said. 'Don't worry about it, Bridie. I won't press you again. It was just this one night. We'll pretend it never was.'

She was falling asleep before he'd climbed back out of the window.

November 1974

'Jenny and Mark are going to stay with Dad,' Quentin told her, a couple of months after the dinner at Elizabeth's. It was November now. There'd been no repeat of what had happened on the night of the meal. Quentin's kisses had been gentler again. Perhaps she had disappointed him. 'I'm going to drive the three of them over there on Thursday. Why don't you come too? Dad would love to meet you. Plenty of room in the car.'

'I'd love to, but it's Mrs Jenkinson's dinner party.' Bridie's cooking had come on so much that Mrs Jenkinson had requested her boeuf bourguignon and profiteroles for her guests. Mrs Jenkinson asked so little of her that it would be ungrateful and unreasonable to change her mind now.

'We could pop in and see you on our way over.'

'I'll be in the kitchen,' she warned. 'Getting the food ready.'

'Mrs Jenkinson won't mind, will she?'

'She won't be in. She's having her hair done.'

'You'd like to see Polly, wouldn't you?'

She would indeed. She visited the house at least once a week. On the last two occasions she had even minded Polly for a few hours while Jenny went out to have her hair cut or to shop. 'Jenny won't want to be coming in and out of people's houses with Polly at that time of the evening, will she?' Polly was settling into more of a routine now that she was four months old.

He looked thoughtful. 'Perhaps she will feel a bit tired.' Something of Bridie's disappointment must have shown in her face. He pulled her towards him. 'But I'm sure Jenny won't mind a quick visit.'

Bridie dressed with more care than she would normally have employed to cook dinner. 'My, Bridget,' Mrs Jenkinson said, paying a visit to the kitchen on her way out to the hairdresser to make sure all was in order. 'You look so smart I feel my guests will not live up to your standards.'

Bridie blushed.

'Help yourself to a sherry and let that nice man of yours and his brother and sister-in-law have one too.' Bridie had, of course, requested prior permission for Quentin to come down to the kitchen. Mrs Jenkinson peered out of the window at the thick, grey November night. The sun had barely risen today. 'I hope my guests aren't held up by this dreadful fog.'

Quentin and the others arrived at 5.45; Jenny explained that the baby had demanded a last-minute feed. 'We probably should have left earlier; she'll be all out of her routine now.' As if in confirmation, Polly emitted a cry. Jenny jigged the baby up and down. 'Here, Bridie, you take her for a bit. You're so good with her.'

Bridie washed her hands and walked up and down Mrs Jenkinson's kitchen with Polly in her arms.

'She's looking at the pots and pans,' Jenny said. 'It's taken her mind off her crankiness.'

'I should pour you a drink,' Bridie said. 'Sherry?' Would she ever grow accustomed to offering basic hospitality in a house? Perhaps it felt awkward because this wasn't her own home. She tried to imagine herself back at Larkrush, pouring amontillado for the sisters in the early evening, and the thought made her smile.

Quentin pre-empted them. 'It's a bad night to be out on the roads. I think we should get going.'

Bridie handed the baby back over.

'We'll load her into the carrycot,' Jenny said. 'See you out in the car, Quent.'

'Don't be long,' Mark said. 'It's cold for the baby to be waiting.' Fatherhood seemed to have made Mark more serious. Yet he still watched her in that silent, appraising manner of his. Perhaps he didn't really approve of Bridie as his twin's girlfriend. Girlfriend – what a ridiculous term for a former religious in her mid-thirties. She didn't really approve of herself, either.

When Mark and Jenny had taken Polly out of the kitchen, Quentin pulled her to him, kissing her in the same way he had outside the house after the meal at Elizabeth's. 'I have something to ask you,' he said. 'Not now, not here.' He stroked her hair.

'What do you want to ask me?' Her stomach felt leaden. He'd want to know more about her, about her family. Only last month the IRA had blown up two pubs in Guildford, killing six people and wounding more than sixty others. And just last week an IRA bomber had blown himself up trying to set off yet another bomb in Coventry. Nobody else had died, thank God. Mr Jenkinson had snorted and said it served the bomber right. Coventry, always Coventry.

'Can't you guess?' His look was tender. 'Don't you know how much you mean to me? There's never been anyone like you, Bridie.'

A pan on the stove came to the boil, pushing the lid up. She pulled herself out of his arms and went to turn down the gas.

'You mean . . . ?' This must be a dream. She must have misunderstood.

'I want to talk about our future. I'm very serious about you.'

She clenched the knob on the stove.

'I hope you feel seriously about me, too?' He sounded so solemn, anxious almost.

'Oh yes,' she swallowed hard. 'I feel like that too.'

'There's nothing keeping us apart, is there?'

Her mouth opened. No sound came out.

'You don't regret giving up your vocation, do you?'

'No.' She squeaked the word out.

'Then . . . ?'

She stared at the drying-up cloth hanging over the stove handle.

'I wish we could talk more now but I need to get on to Thames End House.'

Her eyes went to the kitchen clock. Past six. She was falling behind, too. The dauphinoise potatoes were late going into the oven. The beans needed stringing. The table wasn't laid.

'Can you come back? Tonight?' She had to tell him before she went to bed. If she waited even another twenty-four hours, cowardice would overcome her again and she wouldn't be able to explain who she was. What she was.

'Tonight?' Surprise clouded the excitement in his eyes.

'Yes. Tonight.'

He looked as though he was going to say no.

'I know you'll have to drive back specially. I'm sorry. But it's important.'

'You've never asked me for anything before.' He pushed a door key into her hand. 'You won't want me showing up here late. I'll drop the others off and come straight back to Oxford. Meet me at the house.'

The cooking of Mrs Jenkinson's dinner passed in a blur, but the food must have been satisfactory because people smiled and said kind things when she cleared the dishes. The beef was just the thing for such a miserable night, they said.

All the washing up was finished by quarter to eleven. Mrs Jenkinson told her she'd done more than enough. 'You take yourself off to bed, Bridget. You've been an angel.'

Perhaps she really could manage domesticity. Perhaps she wouldn't be such a disaster as a wife and woman. She'd done sex now: she wouldn't be taken aback by it. And cooked a complicated meal. Some people said that was all that men required of their spouses. But there must be something more, mustn't there, than going to bed with them and producing plates of rich food?

She could do this, she really could. She'd tell Quentin about her father and it would be done. Clean sheet: bomber's brat exorcised. Sister John and Bridget Brennan both allowed to die and be reborn as Mrs Quentin Stanton. And the other business could also be admitted and probably wouldn't matter as much now, anyway. Bridie smoothed her skirt over her lower abdomen.

Mrs Jenkinson thought Bridie was going upstairs to her room. It felt wicked to slip out of the front door and make her way down Woodstock Road. Once or twice she nearly missed her step on the fog-greased pavements. Beyond the Radcliffe Infirmary she turned right, weaving her way through the small streets into the one where Quentin's rented house was.

She worried about waking up the neighbours, about them seeing her enter his house, but the key turned easily in the lock. Inside it was all neutral colours and blinds, instead of the flouncy curtains and pelmets Mrs Jenkinson favoured. Bridie found it reassuringly plain – almost like Larkrush, but more comfortable. Interesting oil paintings on the walls – Mark's. She shivered, thinking about him. How could twins have such different personalities?

She curled up on Quentin's sofa. For the first half hour, the memory of his words earlier on were enough to keep her occupied. She ran them through her memory again and again. Then, growing bolder, she managed to switch on the television, an object she had never used before. She even found the BBC and watched the news, sitting up as the headlines sank in. How had she missed it? Bombs in pubs in Birmingham. Many dead, more than a hundred wounded. Bridie felt a low scream build inside her and switched off the television. Had Quentin heard this news? He must have done.

The night passed. His sitting room was warm. She switched off the television and dozed on the sofa, waking to hear the phone ringing. She sat silent on the sofa, not knowing what to do.

When she woke again and looked at her watch it was four in the morning. Panic filled her. She ought not to be here. Understandably, Quentin had changed his mind; he'd phoned her at Mrs Jenkinson's and she'd missed the call. Much as she approved of Quentin, Mrs Jenkinson would not have been impressed at such a late disturbance. Meanwhile, Bridie was stuck here in his house, where she oughtn't to be, where neighbours might observe her. If she left now, darkness would shroud her as she made her way home.

The coldness of the morning air made her lungs hurt. She walked briskly. Nobody stirred as she headed north. She prayed that curtains weren't twitching as she unlocked the door. She crept upstairs and lay on her bed, removing only shoes, coat and skirt, and covered herself with the bedclothes. Two forces fought inside her: one pulling her into slumber, the other warning her to be on her guard. Suppose Mark and Jenny had actually been appalled about Quentin proposing to Bridie? Suppose they'd kept him at their father's house, arguing the point until Quentin had finally capitulated, agreed that it was mad to think of marrying Bridie. *Stay over tonight*, his brother would have told him. *You can go and find her in the morning, tell her you've been thinking things over.* She saw Quentin initially indignant – angry, even – but becoming quieter and sadder as the debate continued, finally agreeing to stay with them. And then he'd have watched that dreadful news from Birmingham.

She couldn't tell him. It would be awful if he decided to stay with her just because of her condition. And yet, if he didn't, she'd be something she had never, ever imagined herself being. An unmarried woman with a baby on the way. A wave of coldness flooded her. What would she do?

Shut your gob, she told herself, using the language of the children's home in an attempt to silence herself. Quentin wouldn't agree to drop her at the behest of his brother. The car had probably refused to start in the damp night air, and he'd spent the night at his father's. She slept again, fitfully.

The telephone went. It was seven, the darkness lifting slightly outside. It would be him. She ran lightly downstairs to the ground floor and grabbed it, praying Mrs Jenkinson wouldn't stir. 'It's Gerard, Bridie. I'm at the hospital. Kathleen's gone into labour.'

'It's too soon.'

'It's happening very quickly. Can you ask Mrs Jenkinson to let you have some time off and come down here to look after Michael?'

She tried to find a way of explaining to him why she needed time – a few hours, even – to sort out the riddle of Quentin's non-appearance last night. She also wanted to ask Gerard if he'd seen the news about Birmingham, but he was already giving her train times from Oxford to Paddington, telling her to take a taxi to Oxford station and then again from Paddington to the Sheehans' house, where a neighbour would be minding Michael until she turned up.

'Is that OK with you, Bridie?' Gerard sounded frazzled. 'Do you have the cash on you? I'm sorry for ringing you so early, but it's not looking good.'

'I'll come right away,' she promised. 'Don't worry about anything.'

INTRUDER

BRIDIE

A week later

No answer came to her knock on Quentin's door. After a moment she took out her key, half expecting it not to fit his lock. Bridie closed the door behind her and leaned against it for a moment. This shouldn't take long. She could have posted the key through the letter box. Letting herself in like this was somehow like being a burglar. She told herself to leave immediately. Another sneakier part of her told her to look around, to see if there was some clue to Quentin's silence. She tried to quash the temptation.

Don't allow yourself to look at anything else, anything that brings Quentin to mind. Or you might be tempted to remove something: a book of his, a record, something to remind yourself of him. But she was no thief. Except she was. She had taken something from him, physical love, that wasn't hers to take in the eyes of God.

She'd taken something of him and was carrying it in her womb. She closed her eyes for a second and drew in a breath. It might all still come to nothing, but she felt . . . different, heavier around the abdomen and chest. At times her mouth felt as though it were stuffed with metal filings.

But women lost babies before they were born: this pregnancy was still young enough to be provisional. Look at Kathleen, who'd just lost the little boy she'd been pregnant with. Stillborn. He'd died before he could be baptised, and his soul would go to limbo, because of the lack of baptism.

If Bridie lost this child, he or she would join his cousin in limbo. Gerard had told Kathleen that it was absolute nonsense to believe that a loving God would consign an innocent to anything other than eternal bliss. Kathleen had listened and nodded. 'Paul may well be in a state of eternal, natural happiness, but I will never, ever be with him again, will I?'

And Bridie had thought of Sister Mary Margaret in the convent garden and wondered what she would have said. Mary Margaret had been clever, knew a lot about doctrine and theology. Knew other things too, about love and how it threaded its way through the souls of the living and the dead, baptised or not. *Help me*, Bridie had whispered to the dead woman at several moments during the last few days.

Concentrate. Leave Quentin's key and a note and get out. She tried not to look at his record collection, at the silver Italian coffee pot still sat on the stove top. Quentin had introduced her to coffee, a beverage she'd rarely drunk during all her years at the convent.

She walked into the little kitchen. There was a shopping list on the table, written in his neat handwriting. *Gin*, he'd written on it. *Eggs. Garibaldis for B.*

He'd been planning on stocking up on her favourite biscuits. Perhaps his declaration in Mrs Jenkinson's kitchen on Thursday had been too much and he'd felt he'd trapped himself. Or else he'd found her insistence that he drive back to see her that night too much. Men didn't like bossy women, did they?

She had forgotten to bring paper for the note she was going to write to him. She turned the list over and found a pencil on the table.

I don't know what happened on Thursday. I hope you're all right? Here is your key. All my love. Bridie.

It didn't seem accusatory. But perhaps she shouldn't have written the love bit. It might look manipulative. But he had wanted to marry her, hadn't he? She needed Kathleen's advice, but she couldn't ask for it just at the moment when her sister was still mourning the lost baby.

The front door to the house creaked. Someone was coming inside. Bridie stood stock still. How humiliating. Quentin would find her in here, like a burglar. Could she hide, let herself out of the back door and scramble over the garden fence?

She couldn't move in time. People were talking in the small front hall.

'I'll leave you to get on. You have my number if you need me?' Mrs Jones, the landlady.

An older male voice was thanking her quietly.

'I haven't seen the young woman this week,' Mrs Jones said.

'And you don't know where she lives? Or even her full name? He only told me that she was Bridie.'

'He never mentioned a surname. Perhaps it wasn't serious.'

Bridie felt her jaw open in silent protest.

Mrs Jones was letting herself out of the door. A man, late middle-aged, still quite upright and fit in appearance, walked into the small sitting room. Bridie could probably move from the kitchen and out of the front door without him seeing her. She picked up her key and note. No need to utterly humiliate herself by letting Quentin's father read it.

She crept forward soundlessly. At the sitting-room door she couldn't resist a peep. The man stood, back to her, his shoulders moving gently and quietly. He was weeping. He turned slightly and she saw that he'd placed a hand over his eyes. Something had happened. Something dreadful, something that explained the silence.

She must have uttered a sound, her senses knowing what had happened before her brain did. 'Quentin's dead, isn't he?'

Her handbag dropped from her hand. The man turned, shock and pain mixed in his face. He had Quentin's eyes, or Quentin had his eyes.

'I'm Bridie,' she said. 'Bridget Brennan.'

A look of recognition on his face.

'How?' she asked. *Why?*

And he was leading her to the sofa, his own grief temporarily laid aside, making her sit, holding her hands, telling her about a car crash on a foggy road, Quentin, Mark and Jenny dead.

'Mark didn't die immediately,' Quentin's father told Bridie. 'The ambulance took him to hospital. Before he lost consciousness he told us that Quentin's car skidded on a bend.' He shook his head. 'Mark said Quentin had something on his mind. The doctors thought Mark would survive, but he must have had some internal bleeding. At least he died knowing Polly was completely unhurt. She was strapped safely into her carrycot, didn't have a single scratch.' He wiped his eyes on the back of his hand. 'I wonder whether Quentin had a fit and that's why he lost control of the car. He was such a steady driver and wouldn't have taken risks with the baby in the car.'

It seemed to happen without Bridie even understanding why or how. She and Quentin's father – his name was Nicholas – left Quentin's house in Jericho together, driving out of Oxford towards the house on the Thames and retracing Quentin's drive of the previous Thursday night.

'It was there.' Mr Stanton slowed on a sharp bend. The road had been swept. Bridie couldn't even see tyre marks. 'I can't believe he was going too fast. Mark must have been wrong.'

If Quentin had been driving too fast, it was because of her, because she'd made him promise to come back to Oxford that night and he wanted to drop off the others quickly and return to the city.

Quentin's father had found an agency nanny to help with Polly. The woman showed her the nappies, tin of formula milk and bottles Mr Stanton had bought.

'Polly hates the bottle,' Mr Stanton said. 'Wouldn't take it at all at first. Just kept turning her head away and crying.' His voice was quiet. 'Perhaps I chose the wrong brand. I've never bought that kind of thing before. Jennifer was feeding her herself.'

'A bottle feels quite different, but she'll take it eventually. If she's hungry, she'll feed.' The memories came back from those years in the children's home when they'd let Bridie help with the babies. They made the mothers feed the babies themselves for the first six weeks, sometimes longer. Then the mothers were sent away.

When Polly had finished her bottle, she lay back in Bridie's arms and sighed, her eyelids closing over her eyes almost immediately. 'Do you think she's wondering where her mother is?' Mr Stanton asked.

'She'll know something's missing, that's for sure.' Some particular scent, the timbre of her mother's voice.

'Poor little soul.' A pause.

The loss of Polly's mother could ruin her life. Bridie held the baby tighter. 'We need to make sure she's all right.' She sounded fierce and bit her lip. What a lot to presume. 'Sorry, I didn't mean . . .'

A look of relief passed over his face. 'You will stay, won't you, Bridie? At least for a while? Quentin would have wanted you to. I can't tell you how much he praised you.' His face almost broke into a smile.

'I can't, Mr Stanton.'

'Call me Nicholas, please.'

She didn't think she could ever do that, but there were more urgent issues to worry about. She needed to stay with Polly, but there was the other problem. 'I need to go away somewhere.'

His face fell. 'Of course. You must have friends. Family. They'll want to take care of you.'

'No, not that.' She looked at the baby in her arms. 'It may come to nothing. But you probably won't want to take the risk. Of disgrace.'

He was frowning now. 'Disgrace? How could there be more disgrace? My son killed his own brother and sister-in-law.'

'But Quentin didn't do it intentionally.' She blinked hard. Her father had purposefully killed civilians in peacetime on a shopping street, one a fifteen-year-old boy. That was disgrace.

'No. Not intentionally.' A long sigh. 'Tell me what else I need to know.'

'Quentin and I . . . There was something he didn't even know. I didn't have time to tell him. I thought it wouldn't matter because we were getting married.'

They stared at one another.

'You do know we wanted to get married? He told you that?'

'Oh yes. We certainly got the impression that he was very serious about you. Mark had already told us he thought Quentin would be proposing.'

She looked out of the kitchen window. Too dark to see much.

Quentin's father followed her gaze. 'We back on to the river. We could have had a reception with strawberries and champagne out on the lawn. It's only a short walk to the Catholic church. He said you were Catholic.'

Strawberries and champagne. For a woman like her. It had never occurred to Bridie that she might have a reception at a house of the kind that had a garden sloping onto the Thames. She'd never been the type to whom these kind of attentions were paid. She imagined Kathleen's face if she'd told her.

She stood up with the sleeping infant in her arms and looked out of the window at the lawn. The Thames was a silvery veil at the end of the garden. Trees waved, boughs lacing the sky. She could hand Polly back to her grandfather, walk away now, make her own way with the baby she herself was expecting, assuming it all came to something. Quentin's father was watching her.

'I'm two months gone.' She blushed. 'You'll think that I was very stupid not to notice before.' Stupid was the very last thing he'd be thinking her. Wicked. Sinful.

'Two months.' A heavily pregnant nanny for Polly, he'd be thinking? Or perhaps he was musing on the wedding that she and Quentin would now never have, how she'd have been all plump in a white gown, like an enormous puff of cotton wool. Perhaps the wedding would have been called off. Perhaps he was thinking that the pregnancy was still at a stage where it might come to nothing. The same thought frequently occurred to her too.

'Please don't leave us, Bridie,' Mr Stanton said. He wasn't the kind of man who would ever have needed to plead. He was the type you'd want to give to, because he was so calm and kind: the way he had bought those things for the baby, not just packed her off to some baby home. He hadn't let Polly go to a place like The Beeches, where Bridie had grown up.

She made a sound to denote that she hadn't made a decision.

'The pregnancy may not . . .' He blushed at his own words. 'Forgive me, I didn't mean . . . But perhaps we are getting ahead of ourselves?' he added gently.

She went upstairs to Mark and Jenny's room with him, while Polly slept in a Silver Cross pram downstairs. 'I bought the pram for them,' he said. 'Jenny'd always longed for one, but they were too expensive. She said she wanted to push Polly by the river.' In Oxford Jenny had used a kind of sling apparatus. 'Mark said they'd fight about whose turn it was to push it.' He smiled to himself. 'Men of my generation weren't encouraged to push perambulators.'

They walked through the rooms to see what Polly had and to work out if anything else was needed. Every room contained light and graceful pieces of furniture in oak or mahogany. The beds were made up with linen sheets or fine, sheeny cotton. There was the carrycot in which Polly slept at night, more nappies, clothes. 'Some of this might be useful for you . . .' Mr Stanton coughed, not meeting her eye. He hadn't referred to her condition again after she'd explained. Perhaps the poor man was still in shock.

'We'll need a proper cot soon,' Bridie said. 'Polly's going to be too big for that carrycot.' He wrote it down in a notebook in very precise writing. Jenny's and Mark's suitcases were in the guest room. 'I'll help you deal with those later,' Bridie said. 'We need to make sure Polly has all she needs first. She's the priority now.'

'What about your job? Won't they mind you spending time here?'

'Mrs Jenkinson always knew it was temporary. She told me not to worry about too much notice if I found something else. I'll ring her and ask if I can go and get my clothes.'

She looked around this room which was to have been slept in by Mark and Jenny. If it hadn't been for her, their clothes would now be laid out on chairs, their shoes paired under the chest of drawers, Jenny's hairbrush and make-up arranged on the dressing table. 'I could help clear out Quentin's house in Jericho, too, if you wanted.'

He looked at her steadily. 'I must admit I was hoping you'd offer. I'm presuming too much, I'm sorry.'

'No, I'd like to help. For as long as I can.'

He swallowed hard. 'Of course. And there'll be the funeral. One for the three of them.' The full loss seemed to stun him all over again. He put a hand to his throat, as though it was choking him. 'Jenny had no family, so we will have to do everything for her.'

'Yes.' They were supposed to be good at death, the Irish, weren't they? Down to earth, respectful, but not afraid to show that it mattered, that it hurt. She should be able to help him a lot, even though she felt so hollow. She couldn't even ask Kathleen to come and support her since Kathleen was still in mourning for her own dead baby.

Mr Stanton drove her back to Oxford, with Polly dozing in the carrycot they'd placed on the back seat. They parked up outside the Jericho house and Mr Stanton carried the cot in so that Polly could slumber on inside. The daily had emptied the fridge and watered Quentin's houseplants. There wasn't much to do in this house. 'Most of his clothes were still at Thames

End House,' Mr Stanton said. 'He just brought some favourite paintings with him. Oxford was just to give him some space while he saw the specialists and decided what to do with his life.' A process she had derailed.

They busied themselves in strangely companionable silence packing things into boxes, taking pictures off walls, until in the wardrobe Bridie found a morning suit, still in its Moss Bros. bag. It looked new, purchased in a sale.

'I might be able to take that back.' Mr Stanton said. 'Unless you'd rather I didn't?' He spoke in that clipped English way, but always asked her for her opinion, in the same way Quentin had.

'We might as well get something for it,' Bridie said. How cold and practical she must sound.

'I'd make sure your baby's all right, you know.' He sat down on the end of Quentin's bed. 'You needn't worry. You'll both be taken care of, it's the least I can do for him.' He rested his face in his hand for a moment. 'It won't make any difference to me: Polly and your child, Quentin's child, will both be my grandchildren. You're my dead son's fiancée, mother of his baby. You belong with us.'

'No.' The word came out like a bullet.

Mr Stanton turned to her, sad. 'I don't understand. What does it matter now if you and Quentin weren't quite married?'

She tried to form the words in her mouth, get them into a shape that could be expressed. 'I can't . . .' Couldn't what? Live with him and Polly? But she owed the child that much at least. Bridie already knew that nobody on earth could cherish Polly as much as she could. But she couldn't inflict her own child on them. She sat down in the chair over which Quentin had draped a jumper, probably planning to re-wear it again within days. She thought she could pick out his scent on it. Bridie clenched her hands together.

'There's something you're not telling me, Bridie.' Quentin's father was looking at her interlaced fingers, knowing something remained unsaid. 'You're not . . . You're not already married, are you?'

Not even to Christ, not any more. Unworthy of being anyone's bride. Unworthy of being normal, which had been all she'd wanted since she'd come to Oxford. Like everyone else, ordinary.

'It's who you are,' she managed at last. 'And who I am. If Quentin had lived, we might have found a way for it not to matter so much. He was clever. He'd have managed it.'

'I don't know what you're talking about.' He sounded resigned.

'There's something about me you don't know. About my father.'

'Your father?'

'He did something terrible.' She was gabbling. 'My mother always said it wasn't him, but the war came and everything changed and then she died.'

'What did they say your father did?'

Her mouth was so dry that she didn't think she'd be able to get the words out. 'They said he set off a bomb. In Coventry.'

'In Coventry?' She saw the puzzlement on his face. 'But that—'

'Not the one this month where the bomber died.' Her face blazed with shame. So many bombs. That other one that had gone off at Birmingham the same night Quentin had died had caused twenty-one deaths, they said: just people enjoying an innocent night out. 'It was just before the war. They said my father and two others killed five people and injured dozens more. One of the dead was just a child. Another was a girl of twenty-one, due to be married.' Now that she'd started to tell Mr Stanton, the words wanted to tumble out. Everything that had happened to her had perhaps been as the result of that stain, that sin on the part of her father, handed on generation to generation. 'He was . . . They hanged the three of them at Birmingham for it.'

His eyes widened.

'They called me the bomber's brat.'

THE BOMBER'S BRAT

BRIDIE

The bomber's brat. A taunt that had echoed round The Beeches home as she grew up. Someone must have found out when she was ten or so. Had a file been opened? Had staff gossiped? Once she was in her teens she'd managed to wrap herself up in a protective layer, which felt curiously like the layer round her now, insulating her from life, from fully feeling things. When she'd left the children's home all the feelings she'd protected herself from had assaulted her.

She'd run into that convent, finding such relief in being somewhere that promised her a home, acceptance and companionship. All were sinners, Reverend Mother had told them once, all were equal before God. Sister Peter had been the only one who'd made her feel more sinful than everyone else. But other than the convent where else could she have gone? Kathleen had only been thirteen, still living in County Cork, when Bridie had left the children's home. There was nobody else to take her in.

All those years had left her ill-prepared for what had happened after she'd left the convent. She was still the bomber's brat, still tarnished.

Quentin's father would be feeling the disgrace, for all that he was obviously a kind and decent man. No doubt even loving and gentle Quentin would have felt it, too, if he'd known the truth. He had suffered that head injury and had probably had friends killed or wounded by the IRA in Northern Ireland.

Quentin's father looked at her with those sharp eyes of his, and she felt her face turning pink. She found she was praying, silently, unaware of what she was praying for. Still he said nothing.

'I'll go away now,' she blurted. 'You won't have to see me again. I never wanted to cause any problems to Quentin's family.'

'Did Quentin know about your father?'

The shameful part. 'I was going to tell him. Before we were married. I was frightened.'

'Why?'

'Because there are probably still people out there who knew my father. Or knew of him. Who think he's either an innocent victim or a martyr and that his daughter ought not . . . be with a former British officer.'

'You were scared for Quentin.'

She nodded. 'But then . . .'

'You found yourself pregnant.'

'I was going to tell him.'

'And that's why you think you can't stay with us. What do you plan to do about the baby?'

'I don't know.' She thought again of the children's home: the obvious way of dealing with a situation like this: give birth in one of those homes. Stay there with the baby for the first weeks. Then hand the baby over to a new family and walk away. Thousands of women had done it before Bridie.

'You don't have to go. You can have the baby. I told you I'd look after you both. What you've just told me doesn't change anything.'

How easy it would be to give in.

'I don't deserve my child.' Everything she'd done since she'd left the convent had been wrong, wrong, wrong, and now an innocent would pay the price.

'There must be a way.' Mr Stanton was frowning at her, probably still stunned that something like this could have occurred in his smart, respectable family.

Yet some instinct pulled at Bridie, insisting she stay here. The Stantons' house on the river with its sunny lawn, its flowerbeds, the books on the shelves: this was where Quentin's child should be brought up.

Mr Stanton took one of the cushions off the bed and seemed to be looking for an answer in its quilted surface.

She waited. Sister Peter seemed to laugh. *Doesn't take much to tempt you, sister.*

He smoothed the satin cushion cover. 'The simplest way is that we say – imply – that you were actually married to Quentin before he died. A quiet, private service in a Catholic church in London, perhaps.'

'No.' Funny – the thought of that lie seemed worse than the alternative. 'That would be very wrong. Quentin and I weren't married. Not yet.' It would make things too easy and she didn't deserve them to be easy. 'And that still won't get over the problem of who I am.'

'Why do you want to punish yourself, Bridie? Hasn't the loss been great enough?' He said it almost reprovingly, as though she wasn't feeling Quentin's death enough.

'I don't know.'

'You can't help who your father was.'

'Perhaps I feel it was my fault.'

'The accident?'

'Quentin was in a hurry to drop the others off and get back to me. I'd begged him to return that night.' He would have done anything she had asked. She hadn't been used to being the centre of attention.

'If he felt enthusiasm for someone or something he had to act on it.'

She knew what Mr Stanton meant. That sudden rush to buy a bunch of freesias or a packet of freshly ground coffee because they smelled so good.

'I used to think the army would teach him to be calmer. Perhaps it did, most of the time.' He looked at Bridie. 'And being with you probably put him on a more even keel.' Quentin had said so himself. Told her he felt calm and quiet when he was with her. Said she was his point of stillness.

She looked at her watch. 'We should get going. Polly needs a feed.' Something inside her warmed as she thought of the infant waiting for her. Later she'd take her for a walk out in her pram. Forget her own plight. Polly was all that mattered. Kathleen would have her and Polly to stay. The Sheehans had a spare room and Bridie could help with Michael. Gerard wouldn't mind – he was spending time away from home, working on projects up north, so Kathleen was often alone. Would she mind seeing Polly, who was just a few months older than her own stillborn child would have been? Bridie's mind whirred.

Mr Stanton was thinking, too. 'We have a holiday home,' he said. 'A cottage, down on the Sussex coast. You and Polly could go down there for a while. I'll come down too, at weekends. I'll ring the woman who keeps an eye on it for me and ask her to give the place a good airing. If you stay away from Thames End House until . . .'

Until she could go back to being the person she'd been when she'd stepped out of Larkrush and into Gerard's car, before she'd seen a man having an epileptic fit in the Covered Market.

'It will give us some time. But I tell you this again, Bridie: you and your child must be part of our lives.'

She picked up the carrycot and looked round Quentin's little sitting room for the last time. With his paintings removed from the walls and his books packed into cardboard boxes, the room no longer seemed to have anything to do with him.

They drove back in silence, broken only by an occasional murmur from Polly, who seemed to be deciding that she was hungry. 'Back home soon, darling,' Bridie told her, finding it the most natural thing in the world to talk to the baby.

The Sussex idea sounded appealing. Perhaps she could ask whether her sister could spend time with her down there, too. Michael would love the seaside and it might help Kathleen recover full health.

She heard someone laugh, a woman, spiteful, and she almost turned to see if Sister Peter was actually in the car. Of course she wasn't, but something of her presence was there. *Tempted to do what that poor bereaved father has suggested in his moment of grief? Want to foist your love child, your bastard, onto a respectable family, do you?*

'Are you all right?' Mr Stanton asked.

'You needn't worry,' she said, very clearly so that there could be no going back. 'I'm not going to do anything to harm your family. Polly: she matters most. She's the one we need to protect.'

No stain must besmirch Polly.

And for the months immediately following Quentin's death, it seemed that the plan might work.

There had come the moment, of course, when she had to tell Kathleen. Kathleen stared at her. 'Mother of God, I could see you'd rounded out a bit. I thought it was just good food. Well, I've been distracted with what happened to me, I suppose.' Normally, her younger sister would have been asking her sharp questions for weeks now.

'What are you going to do?'

Bridie told her of the plan she and Mr Stanton had put together. Kathleen's eyes widened and then narrowed as she listened.

'So after you've given birth, you bring both children back to his house and you are both . . . vague about the exact date of the car crash, making it seem as though it happened months and months later and there was a small baby brother or sister in the car as well as Polly?' Kathleen looked as near to flabbergasted as Kathleen could look. 'And what does Mr Stanton do in the meantime? Pretend his sons are still alive? What happened at the funerals, anyway? You said it was a joint service, in Oxford?'

'It was very quiet.' Only a few of Mr Stanton's closest friends had been present, he'd told her. He said he trusted them to be discreet in the future. Perhaps he'd told them the truth.

Kathleen looked stern. Her Irish view of what a good funeral should be must have been sorely offended. You needed a good crowd to support the bereaved.

'He's going straight off to France afterwards.' Outside the crematorium Bridie had watched the taxi drive him to the station, his face pale and set.

'That poor man. And him just having lost both his children.'

'I think the friends in France he's staying with are ones he can talk to.'

'Well, let's pray they can support him. When's he back?'

'Not until after I've had this baby.'

'And then you become the nanny to both children? Including your own?'

Bridie stared at the carpet.

'Gerard took me to a play once, at the theatre. *East Lynne*, it was called, based on a Victorian novel. The fallen woman who'd run off with another man and then lost her looks came home in disguise to become her own children's governess.'

Bridie looked up. 'How did it end?'

'Oh, the mother died, I think.'

Bridie took a breath. 'I have to ask you something.'

'What?' Kathleen looked at her hard. She was still recovering from the stillbirth, still not quite her usual self.

'It's not to lie or anything. I wouldn't do that.' She was deceiving most of the world, but she wouldn't lie to her sister. 'When I go off to have the baby, would you look after Polly for me?' She glanced at the sleeping infant.

'You love that little girl, don't you?' Kathleen's voice was softer.

'I sometimes wonder if I could ever love any other child as much.'

Michael toddled in from the next room and examined Polly in her pram with interest. 'Baby talk?' he asked his mother.

'She's too wee for that, but I'm sure she'll have plenty to say when she's bigger,' Kathleen picked up her boy and turned to Bridie. 'Of course I'll look after Polly for you. Don't mind my tone. It's just . . . not what I expected of you.'

'It wasn't what I expected of myself.' Lies, evasions, deceit. And all so that a granddaughter could live with her grandfather. And, to be strictly honest, so that she could stay with her own child without additional shame. What would Mother Cecilia have said about Bridie's long fall from grace? 'To this day, I'm not quite sure . . . how it happened.'

'I'll draw you a diagram if you want,' her sister said drily. 'Oh, there I go again. I'm sorry. Was there drink involved?'

Bridie nodded.

'Explains a lot,' Kathleen said. 'And you a complete innocent. At least you won't be going into one of those homes for fallen women where they make them wash other people's dirty sheets in penance while the fellas waltz off.' Kathleen must have remembered that Bridie's *fella* was dead. Her voice softened. 'But this plan of yours and Mr Stanton's has got so many holes in it you could use it for lace.'

Bridie couldn't dispute it. 'He wants to make it work,' she said.

'If these friends in France know the truth, don't you think it'll come out eventually? Isn't there a risk someone happens upon the car crash dates in an old newspaper?'

'Mr Stanton says we'll tell the children when they're old enough to understand.' She felt her cheeks glow at the thought of confessing. 'And, of course, there's always a chance that I might . . . that it might not . . .' She broke off, not wanting to say more in front of her sister.

'You might lose the baby, you think?' Kathleen considered her. 'Like me? Well, I suppose it's a possibility. It would get you out of a mess, but I wouldn't wish it on my worst enemy.'

'Certificates,' Kathleen said, after a pause. 'Birth and death. You'll need to keep them out of the way of the children.' Bridie could see her sister's mind whirring. 'And surely Mark and Jenny must have friends who'd know there was just the one little girl?'

'They'd been in America for some years,' Bridie said. 'And then touring round Britain and Ireland so Mark could build up his portfolio. Mr Stanton says they'd not seen many people they knew.'

Even so.

'Eventually we *will* tell the child, the children,' Bridie repeated. 'There'll be an end to the deception.'

'I pray to God you know what you're doing.'

From France Mr Stanton organised a car to drive Bridie and Polly down to the cottage on the West Sussex coast. Bridie had feared being back in the same county as Larkrush, but reminded herself that Mr Stanton's cottage was not in East Sussex.

Kathleen joined them in April, driven down by Gerard. She was set to burst back into her usual energetic self, Bridie could tell. She brought Michael with her, now a real handful, Kathleen admitted.

The spring weather sometimes relented and granted them a little sunshine, and they'd push Polly out along the promenade in her pram, with Michael sometimes in his pushchair and sometimes trotting along beside them, his attention always ready to be snatched by an interesting dog or screeching seagull. Kathleen's funny leg, as she called it, made long walks hard, but she was happy to get her share of fresh air, looking less pale every day they spent on the coast. It felt companionable – sisterly – in a way Bridie hadn't expected. This was how it could be, having a child, raising it, spending time with other women who had small children and talking to them about feeding and sleeping, comparing notes on development.

They travelled by bus to Arundel Cathedral one Sunday morning for Kathleen and Bridie to attend Mass, leaving the pram and pushchair behind. 'We Catholics don't get the most beautiful churches so we might as well enjoy something smart while we can,' Kathleen said. 'Even if we have to manage these two on the bus.'

The cathedral was certainly striking. Gothic Revival, Bridie had read in a guidebook in Mr Stanton's cottage. The Larkrush chapel had been built in the Gothic style too, at a similar period in the nineteenth century. It still felt strange attending Mass as a layperson. Stranger still as a layperson with a baby inside her. She hadn't been to confession after that night with Quentin back in September, a lifetime ago. Easter Sunday had been and gone, and confession would need to be made by the end of the season of Easter if Bridie wanted to continue to go up to Communion. Kathleen pointed to a notice inside the entrance listing confessional times. 'There's one today. Just after Mass. We could both go, take it in turn to look after the little ones.'

What exactly would Bridie tell the priest? What would he tell her to do in penance? She imagined she knew. Give up the child, for sure. She crossed her hands over her abdomen. 'Polly gets awfully restless late morning. I'd rather wait for another time.'

Kathleen gave her a sharp look, but said nothing. Probably knew that Bridie would have to face the priest in the confessional at some stage. 'We'll leave it for now, then.'

Polly dozed in her arms during Mass, yet Bridie found it hard to concentrate on the service. Uncertain as the weather was outside, it was a relief when it ended. Boards had been set up by the entrance with photographs and leaflets pinned to them. An order of nuns had started a new medical centre in a central African country, alongside a new convent.

They were raising funds for children who would be cared for and educated at the new site. How different might it have been if Bridie herself had been part of such a venture, sent to Africa to care for sick boys and girls and teach them? Perhaps her vocation might not have withered away.

She pushed two of Mr Stanton's pound notes for household costs into the collection tin. She wouldn't let Polly lack for a thing, but would cut back her already meagre expenditure on herself.

'Very generous,' a voice said behind her. She turned.

Sister Peter. In a short habit now, with a veil exposing a small band of surprisingly fair hair.

'Larkrush Convent has formed a new association with the sisters carrying out this work,' Sister Peter told her. 'I'm in charge of ensuring that the same standards apply in our house in Africa as in England. It may be the other side of the world, but you'll recall how important it is that things be done properly.' Sister Peter's eyes swept over Polly. 'You have done well for yourself.'

Where was Kathleen? Bridie looked for her sister, but she must have taken Michael on so that he could run around away from the crowd emerging from the service.

'Quite a sweet little girl. And so quickly acquired.'

Bridie flushed.

'Don't look so startled. Of course I realise she can't be yours, sister— Oh, excuse me, old habits die hard, if you'll forgive the pun. Not unless you had already committed some terrible breaking of your vows while you were still at Larkrush?' Her eyes slowly travelled the length of Bridie's body. Even the shapeless coat she wore would not be able to hide her condition. Thank God she'd already pulled on her leather gloves and Sister Peter wouldn't be able to look at her fingers.

'I'm looking after her.' Bridie clutched Polly more tightly. 'I work for her family.'

'And that other young woman I saw you with, the one with the small boy, must be your sister, who came to collect you from Larkrush?'

Sister Peter must have been watching them during Mass. Bridie nodded.

'Dear me, there's a strong likeness between the two of you. And don't you both look happy and carefree with these two dear children. Not a worry on your faces despite all your old family . . . troubles.'

Bridie could have told her that Kathleen didn't share the family troubles, but why should this woman have to be told anything?

'It's heartening to see that your life has moved on.' But her thin lips didn't really form a smile, not a proper one, and her eyes were cold. 'Children truly are a gift from God, aren't they?' Sister Peter made another slow study of Bridie's abdomen.

Bridie muttered an excuse and walked away, feeling the older woman's eyes on her back. Suppose when the child was born Sister Peter sought Bridie out and taunted them both? The bomber's brat and the bomber's illegitimate grandchild.

Whatever desire Bridie had had to enact Mr Stanton's plan and bring this own child of hers into his household, it was now too dangerous. Polly, who was growing so attached to Bridie, innocent and deprived of her own parents: what would happen to her if there was a scandal and Bridie had to leave Mr Stanton's household? The child had already suffered such a big loss.

Kathleen was waiting for them on a bench, Michael on her lap. 'You're as white as a sheet. What's up?'

Bridie nodded at the bench. 'I need to talk. I've got this all wrong.'

EIGHT

WASHING OUT A STAIN

BRIDIE

2002

For all the 28 years she had known him, Mr Stanton had retained his upright bearing, his attention to spotless, smart – but never flashy – dress, and moderation in all his habits. He liked a lightly boiled breakfast egg, a post-lunch brisk walk along the riverside, and a single glass of claret – two at weekends – at supper. And for all those 28 years, she had evaded his attempts to persuade her to call him Nicholas.

Polly's disappearance ten years earlier had shaken him so greatly that Bridie feared his heart might give up on him back then. But he'd rallied, throwing himself into looking for her in Ireland and farther afield. When the search had proved fruitless, he'd remained positive, telling her that Polly would be back.

Even 9/11 hadn't dealt an immediate blow, despite the fact that it rendered completely unpublishable, in his view, the book on the nature of conflict in the late twentieth century it had just taken him over a decade to write, showing what he called his utter lack of understanding of what had been brewing in the Middle East.

'You didn't hold yourself up as a prophet,' she told him. 'You were putting forward a thesis, your view. You're not responsible for the doings of evil men.'

'I'm an anachronism,' he'd said. 'What I and my family stood for is irrelevant now.'

Bridie wasn't a blood relative of Mr Stanton's but sometimes she felt she knew him better than anyone else she'd ever known, Kathleen, Quentin and Sister Mary Margaret included. She knew exactly how many inches to open the window of his study, how to dust his desk so that the papers were returned to exactly the same position, how long to roast his beef. He knew her too: buying her a new coat every winter, in colours that were always muted, as she preferred, but cut from cloth that spoke of quality. He took her to the theatre or opera in London once a month. Every time he visited the city he returned with a bag of books from Hatchards for her.

'Those years in the convent, I never thought I'd read novels like this,' she'd told him, removing *Madame Bovary* from the bag with wonder.

'The nuns might have objected to Emma Bovary,' he said, watching her stroke the cover, raise the book to smell the clean paper scent. 'You are a true bibliophile indeed.'

Mr Stanton no longer wrote himself. Perhaps he still read, made notes, but there were no more pages for her to proof. The manuscript she'd been preparing to post on 11 September 2001 remained on his desk. The publisher had given up telephoning him about it, and the advance had been quietly but firmly repaid. Sometimes she'd see him watching the dreadful unfolding television news with a look of something that was almost shame on his face.

When Kathleen had died, he'd been such a support to her, standing quietly with her by the grave, speaking softly to Nuala as though she were his own daughter.

One morning, they admired a blackbird standing out on the frosted back lawn like a comma on a sheet of paper. He continued with his egg and toast at the breakfast table. Bridie went down to the basement with a load for the washing machine and fiddled around in the utility room, cleaning out the machine's soap dispenser and sweeping stray washing powder from the floor: silly tasks that could have waited another hour, another day.

When she returned to the kitchen with a pile of folded dishcloths it took her a moment to work out that he really was dead, not merely quiet because he was listening to something particularly interesting on Radio 4.

'You're gone.' She put her fingers on his neck. No pulse, the skin only slightly cool. It seemed so peaceful, no sign of a struggle, of panic. A very polite, very English, way of leaving the world. He'd told her only the week before that he wouldn't want to be revived if he was terribly sick. He'd been fortunate, he said, to have enjoyed such good health into his eighties. She rang 999, all the same.

The old rites and habits had swept Bridie into praying for him while she waited for the ambulance, a last act of contrition even though he wasn't a Catholic and probably didn't believe prayers made any difference as to whether you got into heaven, perhaps didn't even believe in an afterlife: you couldn't tell with Anglicans.

Sara flew back from university in America to stand with Bridie at the graveside. The church had been full during the funeral service. Bridie recognised academics and newspaper editors, archivists and friends from Mr Stanton's army days. Most of those attending had gone ahead to the house, to be greeted by Fionnuala with sandwiches, fruit cake and the bottles of whisky, sherry and brandy that Mr Stanton's will indicated should be opened for the occasion. Bridie looked for Polly between the still winter-shorn trees. Surely she would come today? But there was no tall, elegant figure with long blonde hair. A cold tongue of anger rippled through Bridie, gone almost as quickly as it had appeared. There'd be a reason Polly wasn't here. Her letter, with a Jordanian postmark, had been so brief, but there had been real emotion in the words: *I always knew Grandad would cherish and love me whatever happened. There will never be another man like him in my life.* Sara had looked scornful, but later on Bridie had seen her rereading the letter with a softer look on her face.

Bridie and Sara threw their handfuls of earth onto the wooden coffin and Sara thanked the vicar, who couldn't join them for refreshments because he had another funeral about to start. A busy time for death, the first weeks of spring, apparently.

The unspoken question of Polly hung between her and Sara as they ate breakfast the following morning. Sara had packed her bag, was almost ready for the taxi to Heathrow, and from there she would fly back to America.

Bridie had spoken briefly to the family solicitor, and anxiety nagged at her, competing with the other feelings. An amount of Mr Stanton's estate would have to go towards paying the inheritance tax, and the house couldn't be sold to raise the money if they couldn't find Polly. Was Jordan a big place? Perhaps Bridie could fly out there and look for her.

'Don't worry about the tax,' Sara told her when Bridie expressed her anxiety. 'I've had a quick look at the accounts and I think there's enough money in Grandad's savings to pay the tax. Nuala's helping me with it.' Nuala was training to become an accountant. 'Let Polly stay away if that's what she wants.' There had been such resignation in Sara's last words.

'I was thinking of perhaps taking in a few bed and breakfast guests, if you didn't mind. I might only make fifty pounds a week or so, in the summer, but it would be something I could give back to you.'

Sara took Bridie's arm. 'You don't need to give anything back to me. I have a good job. Grandad left me some money. And Polly, too, wherever she is.'

'I like the idea of doing something with the house, though,' Bridie said. 'It's big enough and wouldn't need much sprucing up for paying guests.'

She was good at breakfasts too: English, Irish, continental, Ulster Fries.

'I think it's a great idea.'

Bridie pictured herself serving perfectly fried eggs and crisp toast and chatting to her guests about riverside walks and the opening times of the local art galleries and museums, and something that wasn't quite contentment, but might have been a degree of serenity filled her. She might still do something useful with her life: serve the girls, make something of their family house for them. Or for Sara, at least.

'You could have family rooms,' Sara said. 'The bedrooms are big enough. You'd like having children around the house again. I like the idea too. Thames End House was made for families.'

'I'd have to warn their parents about the water,' Bridie said. 'And keep the back door locked so the little ones couldn't fall into the river.'

'It'll be fine. You never lost Polly or me to the Thames.'

No, she'd never sacrificed a child to the river gods. Bridie shivered, remembering Mark and Quentin talking about human sacrifices years ago.

Sara was looking at her with a particularly intense expression on her face. 'Your back was never turned, Bridie. And you always . . .'

Bridie looked at Sara, at her daughter, and what she saw sent a big, cold wave of fear over her. 'I always what?'

'Nobody could have been a better mother than you were,' Sara said very slowly and deliberately.

'I was the nanny.' Her words sounded strangulated. 'Your grandfather employed me to look after the two of you, he—'

'Polly found my birth certificate, Bridie: the full version, not just the short one that gives only my name and birth date. She found the death certificates, too, for Mark, Quentin and Jenny. She told me about it the last time I saw her in this house in 1992. She came across them when you were in hospital and the Sheehans stayed here with us in the summer holidays.'

Bridie held on to the cupboard handles. The world spun around her. Sara couldn't know. She did know. Her daughter was waiting for her to say something. What could she say? So many years of deception. 'Why?' she murmured. 'Why didn't you . . . ?'

'Say something before?' Sara asked. 'I went to Grandad, just before I went off to university, when we'd given up the initial search for Polly. I didn't want— Well, he'd had too much to deal with.'

Sara had waited, keeping her pain to herself, because she thought that her grandfather had suffered enough from the loss of Polly.

'I told him what Polly had told me and what I'd found in the filing cabinet. He confirmed that you were my mother. He asked me to give you time, to let you tell me all the . . . other details yourself. Or to wait until I was getting married or having a child. He was worried that telling you I knew would harm you. You were still in shock after Polly had gone.'

'You didn't have to worry about harming me.' Didn't she deserve to be harmed?

Sara had made no move towards Bridie: empty space still lay between them. It was too late.

'I wanted to protect you,' Bridie said. 'I wanted you to grow up free of it all.'

'All of what?' Sara's eyes narrowed. 'Grandad wouldn't say much, just that you'd had a harsh childhood and wanted me to have everything you hadn't had: security, a good home, love.'

'He was right,' Bridie said. 'I didn't have those things, not after I was four.' She should be saying, doing more. She should be moving towards her daughter, the child she'd hardly dared touch when she was young in case something yearning in a caress had given her away. Her response to Sara was inadequate, dreadful. Emotions were blasting her mind, but she knew her face would look calm, nun-like and unruffled, as though she didn't really care. *Say something to her, go to her.* She felt her right leg shake. Pins and needles. She needed to sit down at the table for a moment. 'I'm sorry,' she almost gasped. 'Just give me a moment.'

'Can you at least tell me who my father is?' Sara asked. 'I think I know but—'

Bridie was going to fall. She managed to slow her descent to the ground by grabbing at the edge of the table, hanging by her arms for a moment before she could haul herself back into the chair.

'Bridie!' Sara was helping her up. No harm done, just a bruise on the thigh and a sore shoulder joint where she'd tried to stop herself. At least she hadn't banged her head. A bad head injury could cause all kinds of trouble. She thought of dearest Quentin, with his epilepsy caused by the wound to his head, which her fingers had made out each time she'd run her fingers through that lovely fair hair of his. Something about this memory stirred a question in her mind, a question she had occasionally felt nip at her heels, but one which had been easy enough to drive away.

'Your father . . .' she muttered. Her head was pounding now, after all. She put a hand to it.

'What's wrong?' Sara's voice was coming from a long way away.

'Nothing. Your questions—' The room shook. 'I'm sorry for everything, I know I've handled it all wrong. Your grandfather always warned me . . .' *We will do what you want, Bridie,* he'd promised, *but think very carefully about what's best for Sara, about telling her before she finds out. Because she will find out one day or another.*

'Does your head hurt?' Sara was asking. 'Let me get you paracetamol.'

Without meaning to, Bridie was preventing the poor girl from asking the questions she needed to ask. After Sara had discovered who her mother was, had she looked at the photographs of Mark and Quentin as children and wondered whether one of the identical boys was her father? Of course she had: there was enough of a family resemblance between Sara, Polly and her grandfather for it to be an obvious conclusion. 'I'll tell you,' she said. 'Just let me take a breath.'

The kitchen seemed to lack oxygen. She needed to open a window.

A car hooted outside the front door. The taxi. 'I'll wait,' Sara said. 'To make sure you're all right.'

'My head's fine. It was just the surprise.' She forced the muscles in her face to smile and she managed to stand.

'I'll take you down to the GP and catch the next plane.'

'No. Don't you worry about me.' She nodded towards the door. 'Have you got the money to pay the taxi driver? Your passport and ticket?' How easy it was to take refuge in the everyday worries. Wasn't that what she had always done: relied on cleaning, polishing, cooking and cajoling the girls into good habits? Shame washed over her. How badly she had let down her daughter. How cold she had been with her.

'We'll talk,' she told her the girl, when Sara was getting into the taxi. 'I can't tell you in a rush, just as you're leaving. There's too much to explain. I'll write to you.' It would be easier to express herself in writing.

Sara's face expressed distress. To keep her waiting for days would just be cruel.

'No, I'll email. So you get it when you arrive. Then you can ring me and we'll talk about it.'

The taxi hooted again.

'You'd do that?' Sara looked amazed. Had her daughter anticipated so much evasion from her?

'You need to know.' She took the girl into her arms. Thank God she felt a little more substantial these days, no longer the skin and bones she'd been when she was younger.

'At least now you know that I know I'm your daughter.' Sara had looked younger as she'd said the words.

Bridie felt herself look behind her, expecting to see Sister Peter standing just there, waiting to taunt her. *Still think you can get away with it, do you? She doesn't know the whole truth, does she?*

Bridie waved Sara off. She needed to think her email through before she started typing it out. She packed up Mr Stanton's clothes for the charity shop, framing her explanation in her mind as she worked. The clothes were all good quality, made of fine material. As she folded his cashmere overcoat she felt the smooth evenness of his breath on her cheek. Had she loved Mr Stanton? He and she had perhaps shared the kind of purely companionable relationship she had not enjoyed since Sister Mary Margaret had left Larkrush.

She took the bags down to the shop and walked back quickly to sit at Mr Stanton's desktop computer. Composing the email was hard work. An hour passed and she had already deleted three drafts. She noticed that her right leg felt as though it no longer belonged to her body. She gave it a good rub. It didn't hurt but it felt very stiff, heavier than the left one.

She would leave her attempt to write the email for now. Sara would still be in the air. There was shopping to be done. Mr Stanton had always claimed that a walk was the best way in which to get a piece of writing moving again. Anyway, the best of the fruit at the market would be gone if she didn't get there soon.

Bridie stood, with effort, and removed her net bag from the peg behind the door. Really she'd feel happier with her trolley. The girls had always laughed at the trolley, but it was something to hold on to. Though really for a few bits and pieces it was ridiculous to wheel it out of the pantry.

When the market trader handed Bridie her loaded net bag, it felt heavier than usual, even though it was just a few apples and grapes and an onion or two. She was growing older and more feeble, though she didn't usually feel like this. She walked back towards the river. The bag pressed her down into the pavement. She broadened her gait, feeling like an old sailor. This wouldn't do – she needed to get back home to finish her email to Sara. But her thoughts were no clearer; if anything, they felt even more jumbled up.

Bridie sat on a bench beside a mother and toddler. She tried to exchange a word with the young woman about the sun coming out, but the words sounded like gibberish. Fear was replacing confusion. She had the mobile telephone Sara had given her. She should perhaps call someone: the doctor's surgery might be an idea. She could take a taxi there and ask the GP or one of the nurses to check her over. Sara had put the telephone number for both taxi firm and GP practice into the phone. She just needed to press a few buttons . . . She wanted to fall asleep, but something told her not to let this happen.

'Are you all right?' the young mother asked, bundling her child into her, eyes full of suspicion. Probably thought Bridie was drunk.

Bridie handed her the mobile. 'Doctor, please,' she said, or at least she thought it was what she said. The woman took the phone, saying something Bridie couldn't understand and there were other people around her now. Young Joe was beside her – he must have been buying his lunchtime sandwich – holding her hand in his large palm. A vehicle was pulling up that was not a taxi, but larger and whiter.

'Don't fall asleep,' someone said as they laid her on a stretcher and lifted her inside the white vehicle.

She found herself in a hospital bed, with the net bag of fruit and vegetables sitting embarrassingly on the table beside her, and Sara, looking anxious, sitting on the other side. 'Oh Bridie.' Sara took her hand. 'Thank goodness. You look more yourself. Can you talk?'

Talk! Of course she could talk. They were a family of talkers, weren't they? She and Kathleen and the girls had always been chatty. Surely her mother and father must have talked a lot, too; they were Irish, after all. Perhaps that was another reason why convent life hadn't suited her. So much silence. Gerard had apparently complained that Kathleen talked too much, but that was just Gerard, he'd been such a quiet man, God bless his soul, and Michael, just like him.

'Tea,' she heard herself say.

'You'd like a cup of tea?' Sara stood up. 'I'll ask the nurse if you can have one.'

But she'd been trying to ask Sara if she'd be staying on for tea, as they had called the meal the girls had eaten when they'd come in from school and were too hungry to wait until Mr Stanton had supper at half past seven. Would Sara walk her back to Thames End House and have a meal with her? Polly would have known what Bridie meant. Polly was not her flesh and blood, but had always known her so well.

But Polly could not have helped her with the question she needed to ask herself now. Something about the feel of someone's hair through her fingers . . . No, not the hair itself, about where it would not grow. About a man's hair growing on a part of his scalp where no hair should grow. That night with Quentin, so long ago . . .

They wouldn't let her out of hospital, but perhaps that was no bad thing.

The torment of the gruelling exercises – people moving the affected arm and leg, talking about flexion and extension, making her push against them, making her walk when she'd been able to get out of bed – all this was blessed distraction. But they weren't on at her all the time. Sometimes she sat alone in the day room. Released at last from decades of suppression, the memory gained strength and vividness every time she let it flood through her.

Don't think about it, she heard Kathleen's voice tell her. *You can't be sure. You're getting your head in a muddle because of the stroke.* Had she ever talked to Kathleen about the memory? Her little sister would have been very shocked. Perhaps she'd kept it buried so far down inside her that she herself really had forgotten. She could hear the spiteful voice of Sister Peter telling her that sinners were well able to deceive themselves.

'No car.' She hadn't meant to say it aloud.

'I came down from the airport by bus and train,' Sara said, sounding weary. Bridie had forgotten she was visiting. 'Nuala managed to reach me when I arrived in the States and I took the first flight back to Heathrow. I'm going to take you back to Thames End House in a taxi.'

Scar, she had meant. There hadn't been a scar. The horror of the realisation was such a strong sensation that she slumped in the chair.

'Do you want another pillow?' Sara asked. 'You don't look very comfortable.'

Holy Mother of God, how could she ever be comfortable again?

Sara took her home in the cab. Bridie sat at the table in the kitchen looking at the watery light playing over the walls, while Sara busied herself with the kettle and the teapot. Bridie hoped she'd use the brown earthenware pot; it made the best tea. She tried to find the words to explain what she meant. 'Brrr,' she managed. *Brown.*

Sara took out the white china pot that poured badly. 'Are you cold?' Sara asked. 'I'll close the window.'

Bridie shook her head and waved her unaffected hand in dismissal. Oh well. It was only a teapot, not a disaster. Bridie could almost hear Kathleen saying the words, except Kathleen too was dead now. November 2001, it had been. She'd forgotten about that until just now. Heart trouble. Neither of the sisters had had the most reliable circulatory systems, it seemed. At least Kathleen had gone before this stroke had happened or else her sister would have felt obliged to come over here and look after Bridie. The two of them hadn't produced the large brood of children who'd help stand in at such times. They hadn't fulfilled that old Irish Catholic cliché, and look at them now: one dead and one helpless.

Kathleen dead. The guardian of so many secrets. Buried next to her husband in a cemetery in west London. Heart attack. Impossible to think of anything being strong enough to strike down that doughty heart. Bridie felt a craving to stand at her sister's grave with a bunch of flowers. Perhaps even say a prayer or two for her sister's soul, which was probably, if Church orthodoxy was to be believed, still doing time in purgatory, even though it was hard to think how Kathleen could have better lived her life as sister, wife and mother.

Bridie pictured Kathleen's soul circling heaven like a plane in a queue trying to land at an airport: *stacking*, Sara had once told her this was called. Was Kathleen caught in stacking? And their mother? And Quentin, too, though he wasn't Catholic? And Gerard and Mr Stanton? And possibly Michael too, if their darkest fears were correct?

If Bridie wrote down about visiting Kathleen's grave, Sara would drive her there, she knew. But writing the request would make the trip look urgent. Sara would worry. Some things were better spoken, not written. And the girl needed to get back to the university in America. Sara poured the tea, and the pot dribbled onto the saucer. Bridie stared at the spilled liquid as Sara told her how she'd be having more speech therapy, as an outpatient. Sara had to return to America, and carers would come in twice a day to look after Bridie. She wanted to protest that this was the wrong way round – it had always been she who had done the caring. An ambulance would drive her to the hospital, Sara told her. Nobody could tell her whether the words would return in full to her lips. Kathleen had died with some of the secrets so nobody else would ever know them.

'You've regained almost total mobility,' Sara said. 'They just don't know exactly how much the bleed into the brain will affect you in . . . other ways.'

By *other ways* they meant her mind, she realised.

And they'd been right to express doubt. Little by little, the familiar outside world had become a less understandable place. And the interior world had become puzzling to Bridie as well. Not her soul, that part of her that didn't belong to her body: she could still care for that tattered rag and say prayers for its salvation. Occasionally the priest – she couldn't remember his name – came to the house, and she prayed with him and the words came out right. What she really wanted to ask the youngish African man with his bright expression was how to confess her guilt to those who had been harmed. But she couldn't get the words out. The priest would make the sign of the cross over her and give her his kind smile.

She was the only one left who knew the truth. And now she couldn't express it.

NINE

A FRAGILE THREAD

BRIDIE

15 July 2005

'That's the truth of it,' Bridie told Sara, who seemed to have finished packing her clothes and was fiddling with a mobile phone. These girls couldn't keep their hands still: they'd have never have made it to noviciate. 'I found myself walking out of Larkrush and getting into that car with Kathleen and Gerard, not knowing where I was going or what I was going to do with myself. *Desperately telling myself I was making a fuss about nothing. I'd chosen this path, after all.*'

Bridie realised that she hadn't said the last bit, even though she was sure she'd heard herself speak the words. *Oh yes, I chose my path and it was strewn with boulders and the farther I went the more it twisted,* she continued, in silence.

Sara was still listening, still wanting more. Bridie should have told her all of it years ago. Perhaps she could attempt to write it down, but even writing a postcard was probably beyond her now. She still knew how to form the letters – she wasn't stupid! – and which words they should make up, but somehow they didn't transmit themselves down her hand and through the pen onto the page. No, writing it all down would be too difficult. What was she to do?

To give herself time to think, Bridie went to the basin and folded her face flannel very precisely, as she'd been taught as a child, and placed it on top of the suitcase. A glance in the mirror reassured her that her face reflected no tumult.

She noticed that the straps on the top of the suitcase were unevenly buckled and so she tightened the one on the left to make them symmetrical. Another suitcase, another journey. Her mind was not in Putney now, or even at Thames End House. It was in Oxford. She was back with Quentin, dear, darling Quentin. She'd go through all the memories one more time: from the first encounter with Quentin in the Covered Market up until the night of his death. Then perhaps she could explain what had happened to Sara.

A telephone rang. Sara jumped to answer it. Bridie hoped it wasn't Reverend Mother's telephone, which none of the sisters could use without express permission.

'The car's here,' Sara told Bridie. Then she and Sara were in the smart rental car, driving home from the convent in London that wasn't a convent. But Sara had never been in the convent; it had been Sister Mary Margaret who'd been there with Bridie, and she was dead. And there had never been cars at Larkrush, although Father Sullivan who came to say Mass had occasionally offered them lifts in his old red Morris. The two of them were definitely going to Thames End House, though. That part was right. There was a girl . . . Which one? Polly and Sara. And Bridie herself and Kathleen, from whom she'd been separated so early in life. The one clear memory she had of the infant Kathleen was of the night in the cellar during the air raid, but often she felt as though she was observing the events through the eyes of her own mother.

'I'm turning into Annie,' she told Sara. 'Feeling like her.' Sad, trying to hold everything together. Trying to hold on to Polly, though she was slipping away now. Feeling the melancholy sweep over her, except she wasn't sure for which of them she was grieving.

'Annie?' Sara sounded genuinely interested, distracted away from whatever it was that caused her to frown from time to time. 'Polly was talking about an Anna, but I think I misheard her.' Sara's whole frame seemed to open up with interest, distracting her away from her anxiety. 'You never talked about her before. Who was she?'

'I was only a small child when she died.' They'd been living somewhere in or just outside London. What was the place's name? Walton? Witham-something? Her father had died by then. Her parents had been living somewhere in the Midlands. Kathleen had once told her Annie had worked in a laundry. She and Kathleen had pieced together what had happened the day the bomb went off in Coventry.

Annie would have been in her overalls. It must have been hot in that laundry at the end of summer. 'My mother was just expecting me,' Bridie told Sara. 'Pregnant in all that heat. Then the shock of the bomb going off and what happened afterwards.'

TEN

STEAM AND BLOOD
ANNIE

Coventry, early on the morning of 25 August 1939

Tell him her suspicions or not? He'd looked at Annie in a funny way at breakfast, but hadn't said a word about her dash for the lavatory in the outhouse. Or about her lack of interest in her food. He'd pulled her into his arms and kissed her goodbye, taking his time about it, stroking her shoulders and back. Annie could feel him hard against her, but it was time to leave for work. She laughed. 'You'll make us late.'

'So I will.' He'd given her another lingering kiss before sighing and releasing her. 'Need anything from the shops, sweetheart?'

'And what would you be doing in the shops?'

'Dentist, remember? Foreman's given me permission to work through dinner and go for a half-two appointment.' He tweaked her hair. 'Fancy a nice new hat from Owen Owen?' He screwed up his eyes. 'Or perhaps some beautiful silk undies, like the ones that pass through that laundry of yours?'

'The ladies don't send their scanties in to us.' She picked up her handbag. 'They have maids to do personal garments. At least we could afford for you to have your tooth seen to.' Dentists were very expensive.

He winced as he took his cap off the peg.

'Is that your tooth? Or your stomach again?'

'It's my gut. Jesus, I hate the bread over here. What I wouldn't give for a farl with some bacon.'

He still missed his mother's potato bread. She'd make farls for him at the weekend.

'Don't work too hard today, missus.' For a second his expression was serious as he took his cap off the peg and waved goodbye.

'I won't. Off you go.' Her hours were almost as long as his. The laundry was hot as hell, but at least she had work and it was convenient, just across the road from this house. She was looking for office work, but nothing had come of the search so far. Perhaps they didn't like Irishwomen in offices, though there were plenty of her fellow country-men and women in Coventry, mainly in factories.

Another bout of nausea made her stop and take a deep breath. If this was a baby coming, it would change everything. They'd hoped for a few more months of saving money, finding a house that was more suitable for a respectable young married couple. Annie eyed the kitchen linoleum with distaste. She'd scrub it again tonight. None of the other lodgers seemed to care about basic cleanliness. She couldn't have a baby here.

As she walked across the street, she reflected on how much a child would change life for the two of them, even if he or she was a blessing. Jesus, she felt sick. What a pair the Brennans were with their delicate stomachs.

And the heat of the laundry didn't help. As the morning passed she felt herself droop. Basket after basket, parcel after parcel of tablecloths, sheets, pillowcases, shirts, vests, blouses. She knew better than to watch the clock, so kept her eyes on the task in front of her, whether it was winding sheets through the presses or starching shirts.

Nearly twelve. Annie tied a bow in the string around a brown paper parcel and wiped her brow on her sleeve. Not long until the midday break. She'd have 45 minutes' rest. Time to get home, make a pot of tea, put her feet up. If the other lodgers were still at work, the cups she'd washed at breakfast would be clean and the table wiped. She could sit in the cool by herself.

The clock showed twelve. Annie removed her overalls with relief. Thank God she'd only put on a short-sleeved frock and petticoat underneath. Could she get away without her petticoat this afternoon? But then her perspiration would soak the frock and it would need washing. She'd only worn it twice since it had last been laundered.

Annie left by the delivery entrance, exchanging a few words with the delivery men who were leaning against the wall and smoking while they waited for the completed laundry. Most of them were nice enough. She felt almost too drowsy to walk across the road for her meal. But there was some of the despised bread at home, and milk. Back in the house, she sprinkled brown sugar on the bread and poured on milk. Her husband was right: the bread really wasn't that good. But she felt human again.

Someone had left a *Midland Daily Telegraph* on the table. Too depressing to read more about the inevitable war, so she flicked through to Situations Vacant. Factory work in abundance for the men today, but little for women. A few office jobs, but mainly requiring years of experience. The only other jobs for the female sex were parlour maid, receptionist or hairdresser. She fancied receptionist, but with a Cork brogue? Perhaps she could try to flatten her accent into a more local one.

She couldn't resist the advertisements for household goods in the Owen Owen sale. Mahogany dining-room tables and chairs. Oak dressing tables. Linen sheets. Perhaps one day a child of hers would sleep in linen sheets. Or at least in undarned bedding. At least she had her lace tablecloth, given to her by her mother on her wedding day. It was as fine a piece of linen as anything that passed through the laundry. Not that she'd used the tablecloth since coming to Coventry. This house wasn't good enough for it.

Annie yawned. This kitchen was peaceful, if nothing else. They were doing well enough, the two of them. Some people said the glow came off the marriage after a while. Well, it was nine months now and there still seemed to be a sparkle to the relationship. The day before their wedding they'd walked along the beach at home and he'd found a washed-up bottle, cork half in, half out of the neck. He'd asked her if she'd a pencil and paper. Scrabbling around, she'd found an old receipt and he'd discovered a stub in his trouser pocket. He'd scribbled some words on the scrap and folded it, then removed the cork from the bottle and carefully inserted the paper. She'd asked him what he'd written, and he'd told her that it was words along the lines of him always being with her. She'd pictured the brown glass bottle gently drifting across the Atlantic. Perhaps it would never be washed up on the shore, but would float eternally around the seven seas.

She nodded off, waking with a start. The watch he'd given her last Christmas showed her that she had five minutes to make it back to the laundry. She rinsed her plate and cup and walked briskly across the street.

Annie didn't mind work that afternoon. She lost herself in folding sheets and moving from presses to steam cleaners and from there to folding tablecloths and checking laundry marks so that the garments could be placed in the correct parcel. She wrapped paper around piles of shirts and handkerchiefs and stacked them in wicker baskets for the delivery vans. And not a minute of feeling sick this afternoon. She might even be able to manage a piece of fish that evening. They both loved a slice of fried fish with potato chips, so they did.

She was out in the yard, handing over a batch of tablecloths to a driver for delivery to one of the hotels, when she heard the rumble. The driver straightened, frowning.

'You hear that, Annie?'

'An exhaust backfiring?'

'Civil defence,' he said confidently. 'Probably a pretend air raid or soldiers firing blanks from mortars.'

Grim to know the real thing was just around the corner. Her baby might be a war child. They could go back to Ireland; there was always that option, if there was any work for them. The thought of Ireland was like a cool cloth on her hot brow. *We could just go home, or to Dublin if nowhere else.* If all went well, perhaps she'd have a little one in her arms, named after his father if he was a boy. If the baby was a girl, they'd name her after Annie's own mother, Bridget.

The brown-paper-wrapped laundry piled up at the delivery gate. Where was that driver? He was taking his time, sure he was, and here they all were tripping over the wicker baskets.

The driver returned at just gone three. 'They closed the town centre.' He looked pale. 'That was a real bomb we heard, on Broadgate.'

'Who on earth would do a thing like that?' She placed the last parcel in a wicker basket and straightened, catching sight of his face. His eyes, normally genial, were flinty.

'One of yours, they're saying.'

For a moment she didn't understand. Then she twigged: the IRA. Did they not know how terribly wrong this bombing campaign of theirs was? It was strange that she could feel so cold with all the steamy air coming out of the laundry hitting her, but she saw goose pimples standing up on her skin.

She pushed the basket at him. 'It's a wicked thing they've done, then.'

He scribbled a number on the basket label without saying a word.

'Placing bombs in town centres and hurting innocent people is a sin, so it is.' She raised her voice, aware that others were listening, very clear that they should hear her say this.

'If you say so.' He picked up the basket without making eye contact.

'Thing is,' a woman chipped in from behind, 'you never can tell. I mean, you *are* Irish.'

'We've heard you say yourself that Ulster should be part of the Free State, Annie,' the driver added.

'That's a whole different thing from hurting people to do it.' They both had family in the North as well as in the Free State. Not surprising they might dream of a united Ireland. But never like this.

Annie wanted her husband. She wanted him to tell her this had nothing to do with them. She wanted to tell him about the baby. 'Were people . . . ?' She could taste the bile in her mouth.

'Killed?' the delivery man asked. 'Oh yes. Dozens injured, too.'

Annie crossed herself. Mother of God, help us all. She went back to the press, watching the white sheets flying round and round the rollers until they took on a red hue, to calm herself. Nausea made her rush for the lavatory out in the yard.

She still hadn't started. It must be a baby coming, no other explanation. She'd always been so regular. Annie sat in the lavatory, where the whiff of Vim mixed with urine made her midday bread and milk bubble in her stomach, and tried to pray.

FRESH STARTS
AND ASHES
ANNIE

Walthamstow, East London, 18 April 1944

The baby wriggles on Annie's lap and her face crumples into that familiar expression, demanding a feed. Please don't let Annie have to pull up her blouse with those disapproving eyes on her. At least Bridie is a such a good girl now, nearly four, though you might think her older. She's distracting her little sister by jiggling the rattle in front of her. For now, the entertainment is doing the trick.

The basement tiles start to vibrate. Oh God, oh God, was she right to stay in the house tonight? There's no Anderson in the back garden because the feckless landlady seemingly couldn't be bothered to take advantage of the free installation for those on low incomes. There's a rumour of measles in the nearest public shelter, and Annie daren't risk such a young baby being exposed. Anyway, the raids haven't been as bad this side of London this year. Just a few more weeks now until Daniel's finished at the munitions factory and they can move somewhere safer, perhaps even back to Ireland . . .

But the baby likes the droning rumble of the planes with its irregular rhythm and even forgets her desire for a feed. Her eyelids flicker over her navy-blue eyes and she sleeps, her head a warm weight against Annie's shoulder. If the raid grows livelier she may not be so content.

Hush yourself. Might just be a raid farther west. Even Knightsbridge and Chelsea haven't been spared this spring. Bridget sits on the floor at Annie's feet and cradles her toy rabbit in her arms, mirroring her mammy. Even Daniel can't resist a smile at the child when he sees her being the wee mother. And Mrs Jennings, their fellow tenant, who has told them several times that she dislikes both the Irish and small children, is now looking at Bridget and her rabbit with something approaching softness.

The rumble is now more of a pulsing roar. Annie can hear the two-tone throb of the engines. Jesus, where are those bombers going? Daniel's working nights this week at the factory; will they be sure to send them down to the shelters in good time? If only he'd left that damn job before now, but £10 a week, before overtime . . .

A quiet rhythmic murmuring comes from Dana. She'll be saying her rosary. Annie should say hers, too. A hand pulls at her skirt. Bridget is pale. The pounding has got to her. She's such a sensible girl that it's easy to forget that she's only wee, too.

'I wish I'd gone to the shelter,' Mrs Jennings says. 'Don't like the sound of this. They're too close.' She sounds less snooty now, more like any other woman of a certain age who's scared she'll wet her drawers at the Luftwaffe.

'If it's a direct hit it doesn't matter if you're in the fanciest shelter,' Dana tells her. Dana's only sixteen, daughter of another woman in this house who works nights, but she's got a good head on her. 'We're grand here.' She recommences her Hail Mary.

Grand as they could be. Something crumps close by. Oh Jesus, it's going to be here tonight, the feckin' planes aren't moving on, they're dropping bombs and coming back, or so it feels. Mother of God, it's just houses down here, why would the Luftwaffe bother? But Daniel's told her how the Allies pound German cities and kill their civilians, so why should Goering hold back? Please God, let Daniel be safe in the factory shelter. It can't happen again, not after all she and Bridget have come through.

Annie watches a chunk of plaster detach itself from the wall. Dust trickles onto the tiled floor. Another crump. The house shakes. Darkness. Bridget cries out. 'Just the electricity going out, darling. Here.' She moves Kathleen onto her left side and scoops her elder daughter, her big girl, onto her right knee, kissing the top of her head. 'Where's your bunny, Bridget?'

The child points to the floor.

'Here.' Dana, bless her, picks it up. Annie can only see the girl in the gloom because of the brooch she's wearing on her coat. Her boyfriend gave it to her last week. He's joined up, another young Irishman gone to fight for the British. It had stuck in Annie's craw, but she'd said nothing. The Nazis deserved a beating, but the thought of an Irishman in British uniform took some adjusting to. Funny, because she'd really liked the English people she'd met in the laundry. They'd turned quickly enough, though. Some of the things they'd said to her when Jack was arrested . . . And she'd lost her lodgings, too, within days of Jack's arrest, had to sleep, pregnant, on friends' floors until she could find work in Birmingham.

Mr Richard O'Sullivan KC, the traitor Irishman, as Annie thought of him, had built up his case of lies, ignoring every attempt to show him how wrong, wrong, wrong it was. *M'lud, the accused had family connections with an uncle in Belfast who belonged to the IRA . . . He'd visited a house where two other suspects lodged.*

Jack had been searching for rooms advertised in the newspaper and had knocked on the door to ask for directions.

That's even before we read the witness's report of seeing the accused wheel the bicycle into position.

The witness? Some little English girl, Dorothy somebody-or-other, who'd got the wrong end of the stick, sworn she'd seen Jack wheel that bike onto Broadgate. Or lied because she was like the rest of them: bigoted.

The character witnesses, the English factory foreman and Father Matthews, their parish priest, had counted for nothing. *A good and conscientious worker: the other workers, English included, admired him . . . Ran the Boys' Brigade football club . . . decent Christian man.*

Annie can feel her rage bubbling up again and hugs the baby closer to remind herself of what she still has: two healthy girls and a good husband. He's not like Jack, not so handsome, so bright. *Will you shut your gob – he's a decent man and you've more than most women.*

In a few more weeks they'll be somewhere where the name of Bridget's father is not treated with contempt. Annie is Mrs Daniel O'Doherty now. Daniel wants to adopt Bridget formally. The nosy and vengeful should be thrown off the family's scent.

Move on, move on, she tells the Dorniers silently, ashamed at wanting them to go somewhere else, some other borough. Back in 1940, when she'd been living a shadowy life with Bridget in Birmingham, finding scraps of work where she could, she'd felt a savage joy at the destruction in Coventry. *Serve them all right. Let that little English girl Dorothy tremble in her bed.* The priest at the church where she went to Mass had seen the sinful gloating in her eyes, had taken her aside, talked to her gently. She'd told him of her shame at feeling glad at the news of the many Coventrians who had died in those big raids.

The house shakes. Dana screams. Bridget is thrown from Annie's lap. Annie's arms feel numb. Kathleen gives a high-pitched shriek. Where is she? It's all right. Mrs Jennings's fallen against Annie, but

Kathleen is still safely cradled, squashed and bawling but very much alive.

'Sorry,' the elderly lady tries to stand up. She manages to push herself off Annie and slumps on the bench beside her.

'Where's Bridget?' Annie peers through the smoke.

She hears a faint moan from the corner of the cellar. 'Take the baby.' Annie hands Kathleen to Mrs Jennings and stands, reaching for her torch, which must have fallen to the ground. Can't find it. Mother of God. Her eyes adjust and she picks out Bridget's outline, pushed against the far corner, between the chair that Mrs Jennings was sitting in and the covered bucket they brought down. Annie doesn't even see her daughter move, but feels her in her arms. She lets her stay there for a second and then runs her hands over the child's limbs. She's wet. Must have knocked the bucket or had an accident in the fright. Never mind. Annie has a towel and change of clothes.

'Where's your bunny, sweetheart?' she asks her. 'Will we find him now?'

'He's dead,' the child tells her.

'Sure he's not. We'll look for him.' She raises her voice against the roaring and crashing overhead. 'Everyone all right?' How is it that she, the *bomber's wife*, spat at in the streets of Coventry, is taking charge here?

'I'm fine.' Dana is sitting up straight. A beam of light shines; she must have picked up the fallen torch. The beam shows Annie that Mrs Jennings is still cradling Kathleen. Praise be to God. The baby actually seems to be dropping off to sleep again in the old bat's arms. Is one of her legs hanging in a strange way? Annie squints at the child.

The bombers are still droning away overhead, but the crumps of the bombs are farther away now. Are they going on towards Daniel's factory?

Dana is sniffing. 'Something's burning.' Panic in the girl's voice.

They are supposed to wait for the all-clear, or for the warden to tell them to move.

'Stay here,' Annie tells her. 'Give me the torch. I'll have a quick look. Take care of Bridget for me.' She gives the child a little push towards Dana.

As she heads for the stairs, Mrs Jennings mutters something that sounds like a plea to be careful. Jesus, who'd have thought the old trout would warm up like this?

The kitchen is full of dust. Annie sniffs. No smell of gas. The torch beam leads her through to the scullery and out of the back door into the garden. When she steps outside, the night air reeks of aviation fuel and smoke. She peers at the neighbouring house, just the other side of the low fence. The glare of a searchlight illuminates its brick back wall, cracked, a large section crumbled away into the garden. Not a direct hit, but damage from one fallen close by, she estimates. Flames crackle inside on the first floor, bright behind the blackout. Incendiaries as well as explosives tonight. She runs as quickly as she can to the street. There'll be a fire engine, a warden. The blaze makes her blink: fires burn in houses across the road. Two engines tear past her, not hearing her scream at them to stop.

Who is next door? It's such a transient time; people come and go as houses are lost, work appears and disappears. Annie tries to remember. An elderly couple. They usually go to the shelter. Had she heard them leave this evening? She runs up the front path and peers through the letter box. 'Anyone there?'

She thinks she hears a shout from inside, and she returns through the passageway to the back garden, pausing at the rear door. She should wait for the warden. The blackout on the kitchen window moves: the old woman is there, mouthing something at her, blood on her cheek. Annie opens the back door. 'You need to come out,' she shouts through the opening.

'My husband's stuck, the table's fallen on him.' What's left of the back wall shudders. Annie takes a step back.

'I'll go for help.'

'The ceiling's going to fall,' the woman shrieks. Annie grabs her, pulling her out of the door. The woman's so light she almost falls into her arms. The woman shakes herself free. 'I've got to help him.' She scuttles back through the kitchen door.

'Come back.' Annie follows her into the kitchen, shining her torch around until she spots the old man, pinned under a rubble-covered large table that's lost all but one of its legs.

'Help me.' The woman is pulling at one end of the table fruitlessly.

Annie places her torch in the belt of her coat and picks her way over the rubble to hoist up the other end of the table. She's strong – all the women in her family are – and the weight is nothing to her.

'I'm clear,' the man cries. 'Pull me to the door, before the roof comes down.'

His legs are crushed, useless. Annie grabs him under one shoulder and his wife the other.

A whistle blows, and someone grabs her by the shoulder. 'We'll take over, get under cover.' Ambulance crew brush past her. 'Into the shelter with you.'

She tries to explain about needing to go to her children, but a warden appears and grabs her arm. 'Go into the Anderson in number ten's garden. There's room for one more.'

Again she starts to tell him about Bridget and the baby and the others in the cellar next door as he drags her out onto the street. 'Stupid Irish bitch, want to get yourself killed?'

'Leave off, Watkins,' another voice yells from the path behind. 'The bombers are coming back. Hurry up, missus.'

A roar overhead that seems to consume the houses and the air. The road shakes. Roofs tremble and cave in. A tree shoots upwards, roots and all. For a second everything seems to stop dead. Then the world turns black. Annie falls backwards, hitting her head on something hard. Time passes: seconds, minutes, a lifetime? She opens her eyes, sees the warden slumped against the back of the house, clutching his chest, a long shard of glass stuck in it. There's Dana too, clutching the baby, Bridget clinging to her skirt. The girls need to get back into the cellar. She tries to tell them, but it's hard to keep their figures in sight: it's all darkening.

In Ireland, as a very small child just starting infant school, she'd once accidentally run into a nun, finding herself caught up in layers of fusty black habit, the voice of the sister a harsh and confusing percussion as she tried to pull herself free. How can it be that she is four years old again, and that suffocating and blinding black serge is all around her?

Then she's free of the stifling dark robe. And he's standing over her. She always worried that the rope would sear into his neck before it broke it, that it would choke him before he died, that there would be pain and fear. But he looks perfect. Now she understands. Quick. She needs to ask God for forgiveness, make an act of contrition before it's too late.

'Try and keep still,' a woman's voice tells her. 'We're getting a stretcher for you.'

But Annie knows it's too late, that the darkness is falling over her again and it won't lift this time. She's not scared, just distracted because of Bridget and the baby and . . . Oh my God, I am heartily sorry for . . .

ELEVEN

FRAGMENTS PASTED TOGETHER

SARA

15 July 2005

Bridie murmured an act of contrition under her breath and crossed herself. 'My mother was lying there on the ground, dying, and she could see the mark around his neck where the rope had been,' she told me. 'I know because a girl who was with us told my stepfather. He told Kathleen when she'd grown up and Kathleen told me.' Bridie reflected for a moment. 'I was left with a mark, too.'

'You were injured in the air raid when your mother died?' I turned for a second to stare at her. 'You never told us that.'

'Not that kind of mark. That was Kathleen. One of her legs was damaged. That's why she walks crookedly.'

I remembered Kathleen's uneven footsteps. *I walk a jig*, she'd told us once.

'My mark was washed away in the lamb's blood,' Bridie murmured to herself.

This was the language of the religion that had guided those long years of hers in the convent. If only I had asked her more questions about Larkrush and could understand how it still informed the way she thought. Somewhere inside Bridie's head, I was convinced, a line of narrative still ran like a bright ribbon, but the highways of her brain she relied on to communicate it to the rest of us were choked up.

Even so, she'd told me enough for me to start to piece fragments together. The IRA bomb in 1939. My grandmother, Annie. My grandfather – hanged? All this kept a secret from me for so long. Had she ever intended to tell me, or was this only emerging because of Polly's return? Polly herself had told me that Bridie was *part of this*.

'Jack Brennan was my father and I was the bomber's brat,' Bridie told me. 'The viper.'

'No,' I told her. 'You could never have been a viper.' My eyes were pricking at the thought of it. 'And whatever your father did, you were innocent.'

'The sins of the father,' she muttered.

But there was no time to say more now. We were approaching Thames End House, slowing down at the entrance to the narrow road in which I would have to try to find a parking space.

The front door was already opening as I manoeuvred into the one remaining place. Nuala came out the house, tears in her eyes, as I was helping Bridie out of the car. 'Polly's gone, Sara. Just a few minutes ago. I'm so sorry. I'd just popped out to the corner shop to buy milk.'

'Polly's dead?' The words sounded impossible.

'Not dead. Vanished. From her bed. God knows how she had the strength to drag herself out. I've called the police.'

'Polly's gone,' Bridie echoed, walking inside. I followed her helplessly into the kitchen, where she placed her handbag in its old place on the wooden oak table and stood at the window. 'Goodbye, my sweet.'

I made Bridie promise to stay inside the house while Nuala and I searched the road, the garden, the gardens of neighbours. We ran into local shops, some of them ones my sister had stolen from as a teenager, and churches: including the Catholic one Bridie and I had attended and the Church of England one Polly had sometimes gone to with Grandad. Nobody had seen Polly; everyone shared our anxiety. The priest persuaded a church finance group meeting to give up their number-crunching in favour of searching the small park adjacent to the church.

I knew it was fruitless. I knew where she was. Nuala did too, because a police boat ploughed up and down outside the house, its wake splashing against our jetty.

I watched them for a few minutes before removing my shoes and cardigan and plunging into the river, gasping at the water, which even the fine summer days had not warmed. I dived down to where the water was clear, weeds swaying in the current, small silvery fish gliding past.

Would Polly have been strong enough to swim more than a few strokes? Surely not. The current was strong today – had it washed my sister's body downstream? The policemen in the launch shouted at me to get out of the water. I was in the way and they'd run me over.

Nuala stood on the bank, with a towel for me. 'Oh, Sara,' she said as she wrapped it round me. 'Where is she?' She rubbed the back of her hand over her eyes. 'I had no idea she'd do this.'

'Nor did I,' I said. 'Nobody could have guessed she'd even have the strength.' I held the towel round myself with one hand and put the opposite arm around Nuala's small, neat figure. She felt as warm as she had when she'd been a small girl and had curled up next to me so we could look at a book together.

'I think she was worried about Bridie seeing her,' Nuala said. 'She was so excited at first. But when you'd been gone about an hour she went very quiet. Said she didn't want to upset Bridie, that Bridie would be shocked by how she had deteriorated. I thought I'd reassured her.'

Polly was Bridie's golden girl, the source of so much pride in her glowing health and beauty. Perhaps my sister had been right to fear what a shock her appearance now would be for Bridie.

'Polly's Polly,' I told Nuala, echoing her own words back to her. 'Once she makes her mind up about something, that's it.' I felt myself shiver.

'You need to change, Sara.' Nuala led me gently back to the house. When I had put on dry clothes from the wardrobe in my room, we stood on the lawn, watching the launches go up and down. Grandad's boat was still moored to the jetty. If I could find the keys to the shed and retrieve the rowlocks, I could help with the search. *Polly, it wasn't supposed to end like this for you. Did your cells harbour the cancer for years before something triggered its growth? All those years when you were such a golden girl, was your fate already written into your body?*

I looked up. Across the river Young Joe was rowing the ferry towards the town, looking over at me. 'I wonder . . .'

I ran through and out of the house, along the street, and up to the bridge where Young Joe was just about to turn the ferry for the return leg. 'Joe! Don't go, wait.' He paused, about to untie the rope from the mooring. 'Have you seen Polly?'

'Polly's very ill.'

'Did she come out to the ferry, Joe?'

'She wanted to be by the water. Said she felt hot.'

'Where did you take her?' I knew not to rush him, not to raise my voice or I'd scare him and the words would dissolve before he could speak them.

'She rang me.' He pointed to the rectangular bulge of the mobile in his shirt pocket. 'I rowed to your house.'

Of course. Polly would have been far too weak to walk all the way to the ferry jetty.

'I took her there.' He pointed to the far bank. I looked at the bridge, teeming with pedestrians.

'Would you row me over too, please, Joe?' Miraculously I found a silver coin in my pocket. Even now, even in this crisis, it would have paralysed Joe had I asked him to take me over without payment. I knew my sister would have had a coin for him too.

'She said she was coming back here.' He blinked. 'I thought it would be like it was before, when she was a girl.'

So Polly had rung Joe ahead of her return here. She must have made her plans in advance.

When we reached the opposite bank I jumped out. 'Which way, Joe?'

He blinked at me, silent.

'Polly needs to be in bed. She needs her medicine to keep the pain away. I've brought Bridie back to look after her.'

'Bridie.' His face brightened at the mention of her name. He'd be remembering all the cakes and pies Bridie had made for him up until she'd had her stroke. Young Joe pointed upstream. Now I knew where Polly had gone: to the water meadow alongside which we had rowed as girls. I suspected what was on her mind and I knew she wouldn't have wanted to do it in the proximity of the house.

Polly hadn't gone far. I found my sister, for this she would always be, tangled up in a tree's roots fifty metres upstream of the ferry. She could only have swum for a short time before exhaustion overcame her. It would have been the way Polly would have liked to go: welcoming the water as it rose over her head, knowing it was better than anything else on offer. I jumped into the water to untangle her, but the water had made her clothes heavy and I couldn't move her. The kind female constable that Nuala had sent after me in the police launch tried to persuade me to leave before they brought her to shore, but I wouldn't move. Water trickled off my sister's head as they lifted her out, glistening gold in the light so that for a second it looked as though she had regrown her lustrous blonde hair. Her eyes were open. She didn't look afraid. A swan on the opposite bank raised its wings into a silver arc. An empty beer bottle floated past on its way downstream to London and the sea. Things Polly would have noted herself so many times in the past.

I had to tell Nuala and Bridie what had happened to Polly. The police launch took me the short distance back downstream to Thames End House. How much the young Polly and I would have enjoyed such a dramatic arrival by water. I got off at the jetty and walked up the garden path and into the kitchen, as I had a thousand times as a child. The two of them were sat at the table. On hearing the news, Nuala put a hand over her mouth fleetingly and crumpled where she sat. I could make no sense of Bridie's response. Her eyes opened and closed. Her hand touched mine fleetingly over the oak surface, but she said nothing, and nor did she utter a single word for the rest of the night.

Nuala and I prepared a simple meal of soup and sandwiches, and the three of us sat in the kitchen watching dusk settle over the garden. I could almost imagine that Nuala was Polly and the three of us were back together in the kitchen again, waiting for Grandad to come home from a meeting with his publisher in London, a bagful of books for us in his hand.

The shadows had joined one into the other and the darkness was almost complete when I stood up.

'Where are you going?' Nuala asked.

'Polly must have left a note or a message of some kind.' She wouldn't have re-entered our lives just to leave us with so many questions unanswered.

'I thought so too,' she said. 'I looked everywhere in her room and down here in the kitchen. There was nothing. Have you checked your email?'

I logged on to the laptop Nuala had brought with her. Nothing. I wasn't even sure Polly knew my email address. Polly had been enigmatic during her lifetime, but even she surely wouldn't leave me without a word, having promised an end to the story, would she? Or had the cancer cells metastasised into brain, altering her judgement?

The following afternoon we walked through the town to the same undertakers that we had used for Grandad's funeral. When we went to look at Polly, she was wearing a wig that Nuala had given the funeral director: very realistic, and almost exactly the honey shade of Polly's own hair. Her face was still but serene. Perhaps drowning is a kind death, as they say it is. Or perhaps undertakers are just very skilled in their work.

I knew my sister would have preferred to have the waters close in over her head than to die a drug-muffled death by cancer. *It was just the shock*, I told her. *I know you did it because you thought it was best for us. I'm not cross with you, not really.* When we'd been little and Polly had done something that had hurt me, she'd come into my room and ask me if I was still cross with her. I'd always had to say that I wasn't before she'd go to her own room. Sometimes she sat on my bed for hours until I did. *I can't sleep if you're not my friend*, she'd say. *It's not enough just being my sister.*

Bridie pushed an invisible hair from Polly's cheek and straightened the neckline of the delphinium-blue silk shirt that Polly had told Nuala she wanted to be buried in. 'Nice and tidy, darling,' she told Polly. I wondered whether she thought that Polly was about to go off to school at the beginning of a new term. Bridie rattled something in her hand and I saw it was a rosary. She placed it in Polly's hand. 'Do you think your grandfather will mind as she's not Catholic?'

'He'll be pleased,' I told her. No point in reminding her that Grandad had been dead for three years.

'Polly has such a long journey and I don't want her to be alone.'

I knew she was imagining Polly progressing through some kind of purgatory in order to reach eternal rest. I could have reminded her that the nominally Protestant Polly would never have believed in purgatory, but how could I be sure of anything to do with Polly?

'Perhaps her journey won't be as long as we think.'

'She was always a good girl.' Bridie took my hand and pressed it. 'Sometimes she got herself into trouble, but she was a kind person, Sara, thoughtful.'

'I think my brother was a good person, too,' Nuala said quietly, as we walked back to the house.

I felt a pang. At least I had some sense of an ending to the mystery of Polly's disappearance. Nuala's brother was still missing. Yet she had cared for Polly, helped look for her when she'd left the house for the last time, supported Bridie and me when Polly's body had been found. We exchanged a long glance in which I tried to express the sense of the debt I owed Nuala and my recognition of the long loss she'd suffered.

'She said she was trying to find out something about your father, Bridie.' We'd reached the front door. 'Was it something to do with what you were telling me about . . . how he came to die?' I asked, as I pulled the house key out of my bag.

'My father?' Bridie looked interested, but not distressed, as I had feared she might. 'He died at the beginning of the war.'

'Would you tell us about him?' We were walking into the kitchen. I hoped that being in this room, the heart of the house, would perhaps relax her so that she would feel able to look into the past and make sense of it for me.

She stared out of the window. 'Mammy had to move to London with Daniel O'Doherty and Kathleen and me. Kathleen was just a little baby when the bomb fell on Mammy. And then I went into the children's home. And Kathleen and Daniel went back to Ireland.' Her eyes blazed for a moment. 'Daniel O'Doherty took my lace tablecloth with him when he left. It should have come to me when Mammy died, because I was the elder daughter. Perhaps he thought those nuns would steal it from me. Kathleen gave it back to me when I came to work in Oxford, years later.'

This I already knew. The lace tablecloth would be carefully unfolded onto the dining-room table at home because Polly's funeral would be one of the solemn events that merited its use. I had seen it deployed on only a few occasions: Grandad's funeral tea, my First Holy Communion celebration and the publication days of Grandad's books. The prospect of Bridie taking it out of the sideboard and shaking out the creases filled my heart with liquid concrete. And it wasn't just because of the sorrow of the funeral to come. The ivory linen cloth, with its delicate hand embroidery, was like a cloud manifesting in fabric. But for me it represented unresolved and heavy secrets, secrets which I feared Bridie could now never reveal to me, even as my fears grew and massed, inter-cut with the sharp pain of losing Polly.

'Do you know what Polly was going to tell me, Bridie?' I asked when the three of us were in the kitchen, drinking the inevitable tea from the brown earthenware pot.

'They must have found out,' she said. 'It explains it all.'

'Found out what? Something about your father?'

'I'm guilty,' she said matter-of-factly, folding her arms. 'By delight and by consent.'

'You weren't responsible for your something your father did or didn't do.'

'Through my fault, through my fault, through my most grievous fault.'

I vaguely recognised the words of some old piece of Catholic liturgy that I might once myself have uttered. 'I wish . . .'

She stopped her murmuring. 'What do you wish, darling?'

My heart leapt at the endearment. Could this be the moment that she would truly admit who she was? That she was my mother?

'I already know I am your daughter, Bridie.' I couldn't quite bring myself to call her Mum or Mummy or Mother or whatever else normal women of my age called their elderly parent. 'Remember? We talked about it after Grandad died. About three years ago, it must have been, just before you were taken ill.'

I could hardly bear to remember the time I'd confronted her with my knowledge, airline ticket in hand, the taxi about to whisk me away to Heathrow.

'I just need to know about my father.' I went on, when I could steady my voice. 'Are you able to talk about him?'

'You can't be my daughter,' she told me. 'I had to pay the price.'

'The price?'

'I gave my baby away. I was no good for her.'

'No, I'm here. You kept me.' I tried hard to keep my voice steady.

'I gave you away to The Beeches home. They always said I'd be coming back. Girls like me usually did.'

She started to tell me a story about a woman who'd just given birth, describing events with great precision, but as though she herself were not the recently delivered mother in the bed, as though she were observing another woman altogether.

TWELVE

TWELVE

NO RING
BRIDIE

'I've seen you before, haven't I?' The elderly nun had eyes like shards of flint. 'I'm good with faces.'

The woman in the hospital bed pulled the sheet further up her chest, saying nothing.

The nun placed the folded pile of terry nappies next to the woman and examined the card on the end of the bed, raising a thin eyebrow.

'At least you haven't lied and called yourself Mrs. Or put a ring on your own finger. How old were you when you left the children's home here?'

'Nearly eighteen,' Bridget said.

A door opened. Whoever it was walked up the corridor in the opposite direction.

'Women like you, you're like dogs with bones, you can't keep away.' But the nun said it gently.

The precise tapping of a pair of traditional men's shoes on linoleum made them both turn towards the door. 'Visiting time isn't for another two hours,' the nun told the man.

'I won't be long.' The voice was firm, mature.

The nun opened and closed her mouth.

'I need to speak to this lady.'

The flinty eyes glinted at the last word. She picked up the nappies and glided away, speculation oozing out of her pores. The man standing at the foot of the bed certainly wasn't as youthful as you'd expect to see visiting a recently delivered woman, but he was upright, active-looking, with piercing eyes. Not the type who'd be put off; persuasive, for sure. Bridget felt herself sitting up on the pillows, bracing herself.

'How are you?' he asked. 'Are they looking after you?' His voice shook a little and momentarily he didn't look quite so sure of himself. 'I was worried.'

'I'm well.' For an elderly primigravida of nearly thirty-five, Bridget hadn't done badly, the midwife had told her. The baby's head was a little bruised where the forceps had grabbed it, but the swelling would go down. That was why the infant had cried so much in the first few days: it probably had a headache. They'd wanted her to feed the newborn, which she hadn't been expecting, and the midwife had unbuttoned her nightgown and shown her how to position the baby on her chest. For six weeks she'd be doing this, they said, until the child was taken away by its new family. The Beeches was a kinder place these days, they claimed: the mother and baby ward was run on modern lines. She still wasn't sure why she'd come back here, like an animal crawling back to deliver its young in the familiar cage it had previously escaped. 'They're kind enough.' Most of them.

'Where is the baby?'

'In the nursery. They bring them to us for feeding.' She blushed at the thought of the feeding and was relieved to see that the clock showed another hour before this would happen again. Would the infant know that it was not supposed to feel hunger for another sixty minutes? How did a baby experience hunger, anyway? Perhaps it felt painful.

'The birth went well? Your message was . . . brief.'

She'd just told him the sex and that they were both fine. 'Eight hours in labour. Seven pounds and one ounce.'

He looked pleased.

'They said the baby was healthy,' she went on. Easier not to call it *my* baby.

The man was watching her. 'I'd like to meet the child. Did you have any ideas for a name?'

'No.' There hadn't seemed much point, as presumably the adoptive family would want to choose their own name.

He sat on the chair beside her bed. 'Don't do this, don't sign those papers.'

Her mind was on the other child she'd had to leave to come into The Beeches. 'How's . . . ?'

'Fine. Don't worry. Think about the new baby.'

'You need to watch that cough of hers. It could turn to bronchiolitis. If you're both distracted with . . . me and . . .'

'The child's fine. Misses you and wants you to come home. Both of you.'

'No.' How could it be possible? It would bring disgrace on them all. Divine retribution on the newborn, perhaps, too. She needed to protect those she loved. Her mind went back to an old Bible story, to the Israelites in Egypt painting lamb's blood on their doors to let the Lord pass by without striking down the firstborn child. You had to sacrifice a lamb.

'You said you wanted the baby. We were working towards that end, sorting out the house for you.'

'I thought some more about it. How could I possibly have a baby? We have to set our priorities.' She looked over his head, towards the door through which the midwife took the baby after each feed.

'You were supposed to go into a maternity unit either in Sussex or Oxford, not down to London to give your child away.' His voice was so quiet that she could barely hear him. 'If you're worried about the original plan, I suppose I can change the story again.' There was a weariness to him. He was a man who wouldn't like rewriting the harsh truth to fit convention.

'We were never married.' Just saying this made her cheeks burn.

'Who needs to know that?'

It's a cheat's way out.

'You cannot want your own child taken from you. You love children. There must be a way we can make my plan work.'

She looked down at her hands, clenching the white sheet. 'It's a lie. I'm not married. I don't deserve to keep the baby.'

'I urge you not to do this. Don't let this child be lost to us.' His voice shook.

'Everything that happened was my fault. No child should have a mother like me.'

'That baby has a good home waiting. And you. Me.'

It was true. Apart from the bit about herself. Poor man, such a time they'd both had of it. A ring on her finger, and it would all have been different. She'd blown it through her own sin. What to do for the best? She tried to question the voice inside her, but could only hear the distant crying of a baby – not hers; she already knew the infant's cry – and the old nun scolding another mother in the next room.

You'll pay, she'd been warned once. *There's no dodging the price.* Perhaps there really was no such thing as free will. You were destined to make a mistake, to sin, and it didn't matter what you did to try to avoid the transgression. It would seek you out.

'I . . .'

The nun was on her way back.

'Think about it,' he said fiercely. 'Don't sign anything.'

'We really must ask you to leave now, Mr . . . ?' The nun stood at the bedside, eyes bright with speculation.

He rose. 'I'm going.' He leaned over and kissed her on the cheek. The nun's delight was almost palpable. 'But I'll be back.'

The burst of adrenaline after the delivery had long since left her. She could have slept for a hundred years.

'My, aren't you the lucky one?' the nun told her, watching the visitor open the door. 'I've seen the girls walk out with such deadness in their eyes when they have to leave their babies here. And that gentleman of yours is so respectable and well-to-do. Do you think he might do the right thing by you, dear?'

Perhaps the nun wasn't being entirely malicious. Perhaps she really had just seen it all a hundred times before: the mother with no wedding ring and the baby and the forms to fill in. Perhaps she liked what she thought was a happy ending: the woman taking her child home to the man: the Virgin Mary finding St Joseph to be a kind and generous husband and stepfather to her Christ child.

Except that Bridget wasn't Mary the Mother of God. And there was no wedding ring in the world that could provide her and her baby with a happy ending.

'Nearly feeding time.' The nun was looking at the clock on the wall. 'One of the midwives will help you.'

She wanted to ask if the child could not be fed with a bottle. By someone else. So she didn't have to risk seeing it. But it wasn't the policy of the mother and baby unit to allow bottles to women who were perfectly well able to feed their babies themselves, giving them a healthy start in life even if they couldn't provide homes.

'Drink your water. You need to keep your fluids up for the feeding.' She steeled herself to meet the baby again.

I cannot be this child's mother.

THIRTEEN

NEW PASSAGES
SARA

'You went back to the same children's home you'd been placed in yourself at the end of the war?' I asked. 'To give me to them?'

My mother had taken me to a place where she herself had received little affection. Would she actually have gone through the process of adoption – signing the forms and leaving me there to be taken home by someone else – and returned to Polly? Polly, who could be denied nothing because Bridie held herself responsible for the loss of her parents? Bridie had decided to sacrifice me for Polly.

Polly again. Always the more worshipped. I couldn't completely quash the jealous little voice inside me, even though Polly's pale and cold face filled my heart. Nuala, beside me, gave my arm a little squeeze. Had she known about this? Had Kathleen ever told her?

'Your grandfather made me get you back,' Bridie said. 'He told them nobody was taking his granddaughter from him. He told me not to be afraid of *her.*'

My grandfather had never told me that he loved me: men of his generation and background didn't. But he had taught me how to row, had often stood beside me looking at the river, a hand on my shoulder. He had read me stories and been a quiet presence in my life until he had died.

'Not to be afraid of who, Bridie?' Nuala asked. 'Who were you scared of?'

She looked at us blankly, the name clearly gone from her memory. 'Your grandfather made them get you out of the nursery, Sara. Wrote them a cheque that was big enough for them to stop all their screeching. He told me to get up and get dressed because we were both coming home.'

Were you *glad Grandad made you keep me?* I didn't say it because it would have been cruel. Not that Bridie would have answered. I could see her mind drifting away somewhere.

'Couldn't give myself to the river,' she said. 'But there has to be a price paid somewhere.'

I wanted to ask her what she meant, but I could tell her attention had already switched. 'Eat some toast, Polly,' she told Nuala. 'You looked very pale back there at the viewing. Perhaps you're short on iron. We'll go to the chemist and get you a tonic.'

Polly. Dead or alive, we still came back to her. She wasn't my sister, really. I'd known that for years, and she no longer existed on a plane where I could talk to her, ask her questions. And yet I felt myself reclaiming her, understanding her better than I ever had since we'd been teenagers growing up.

For three years, Polly had kept the secret of my parentage from me. What a strain it must have been on a teenage girl: knowing that the girl she'd thought of as a sister might be a half-sister or even a cousin. Or, possibly, no relative at all, for all Polly knew. She'd kept the discovery from me because she didn't want us not to be sisters.

Tiny fragments of our past now made sense, such as why Bridie had rushed to arrange my passport for me when I was fifteen, about to go on a school exchange trip. She hadn't wanted me to see my birth certificate with its absence of a father's name and her name where my mother's should have been.

'Quentin,' I said softly. 'Quentin was my father. I just need you to say it.'

Bridie's eyes softened at the name.

A SLOW TIME
FOR DEATH
BRIDIE

Sara named Quentin as her father, and hearing the girl say his name was like a rush of warmth. But now Bridie was weary, confused, trying to explain all of it: the near-adoption of Sara. And before that, Mark, Quentin. The night in her room in Mrs Jenkinson's house.

Nuala was taking her by the arm, leading her upstairs to her old bedroom to rest because she needed to build up her strength for Polly's funeral the next day. The girls had done well to organise it so quickly. Perhaps July was a slow time for death, unless you had been on those trains in London in which the young men had blown themselves up. Bridie had seen the pictures on the news, but hadn't told Sara because she didn't want to scare the girl, who had to travel by public transport for her work. But was it Sara who'd been at risk from the bombers? Surely it was people in Coventry, and that was in August: the end of the holidays, a time of innocence, the last innocence before the war.

Another funeral; another death. There would be time enough to try to tell Sara the rest of the truth when Polly was buried. *In a minute there is time*, Sister Mary Margaret had liked to quote. *For decisions and revisions which a minute will reverse.*

When Bridie went back to that convent by the river that wasn't a real convent but wasn't Thames End House, she would have all the time in the world. But time to yourself wasn't precious when each minute of it hung empty and silent. Growing up, Bridie had never been alone or silent. Impossible, with all those other children around you all the time.

She would beg her daughter's forgiveness. Too late to beg Polly's. It had all come out wrongly, the truth. Polly had found out half of the secret years ago, even though she had never said anything.

And then she'd grown so silent – cold, at times – alternating between aloofness and presenting her family with beautiful gifts, like she had on Christmas Day when the girls had been about sixteen and seventeen.

Sara had found out that Bridie was her mother much later on – too late. She and Mr Stanton had lacked courage, had delayed the revelation that should have come while Sara and Polly were still children. And when she had found out, Sara had waited years patiently before trying to talk to Bridie about it. Too late. Her memory had started to play its tricks on her.

Nuala brought her down to the kitchen for a cup of tea. Polly should have been here too, but didn't seem to be in the house. Perhaps she was off with Michael again. Young Joe said they'd been seen together. Bridie remembered now: Michael was Nuala's brother. They were both Kathleen's children. Kathleen was her own sister. It was good to have siblings. Quentin had had his twin brother, had grown up with a companion.

But Quentin's twin had seen the wickedness in Bridie and responded to it. He'd looked just like Quentin, but they had been different sides of the same coin. What had his name been? Matthew? Martin? Marcus?

'Mark,' she said.

Sara looked at the table and then at the tiles above the sink and lastly at her own outfit. 'Where?'

Not that kind of Mark.

'Mark. Shirt.' The shirt had fooled her, one night, years ago, in Mrs Jenkinson's house. Identical twins. A dark bedroom. And Mark had somehow swapped his bohemian silk shirt for Quentin's plainer cotton one. She couldn't have known – not at first. But then when he'd got into the bed with her and things had moved on so quickly, she'd run her fingers through his hair. There hadn't been a scar on his scalp. Quentin had a scar because he'd been injured in Northern Ireland: the bad head wound which had started his epilepsy.

And there'd come a moment when she'd known it wasn't Quentin. There'd still been time to tell him to stop. Mark would have stopped. He was bad, but not bad enough to take a woman by force. Had he known that Bridie had seen through the deception, that the dullness that the wine had thrown over her senses had lifted? And that she hadn't wanted him to stop because it felt so good. She'd moved her hands from his head and closed her eyes and let him do it. Perhaps that had made it even more exciting for him: knowing that his twin's girlfriend found him so irresistible. Had the brothers always been so competitive?

It had all come down to a shirt being swapped for another and her not noticing in time. 'Shirt,' she said again, not realising until she heard the word that she'd spoken it aloud.

'Polly's blue shirt is just right,' Nuala said, sounding sorrowful. 'No marks on it. It's beautiful and it's what she wanted to be buried in.'

Bridie made one more attempt. 'The shirt was what did for me. And all the wine.'

They looked at her blankly. But Quentin was outside in the garden now. He waved at her. *Don't worry, darling*, she heard him say. *Mark and I were identical twins, so what does it matter? I wanted to be Sara's father, anyway.*

A SILENT MUSICAL BOX

SARA

20 July 2005

'Musical box,' Bridie said.

The funeral tea was laid out on the linen tablecloth which Nuala had discreetly ironed to avoid the potentially dangerous combination of Bridie and a dangling electrical lead.

'Polly's box? Do you think we should bring it down here?' We'd already displayed photos of Polly as a girl and the few we had of her as a young woman: very few, because she'd disappeared for so long.

The idea of displaying the musical box with the photographs pleased me. Polly had kept that box by her bedside until the day she'd walked out of Thames End House. It had been a much loved part of her childhood. She'd left it in the house when she'd run away, and perhaps I had taken that as a sign – a promise – that she would one day return.

But Bridie was shaking her head. 'Not down here.'

'Would you like to take it back to Putney with you?' I could have kicked myself. Why remind Bridie that she wasn't living at Thames End House any more?

'Go and look,' Bridie said.

I glanced at the flowers in the vase I was arranging.

'Now,' she said, sounding as she had when I'd been in need of a stern nudge to do my piano practice. Was she anxious that the musical box wasn't there? I tried to remember if I'd seen it when I'd gone up to Polly's room just this morning to open the curtains. I hadn't been able to go into the room for a few days because yesterday would have been Polly's birthday. Thank God we'd arranged the funeral for the day after.

The box was indeed on the bedside table. But something about it didn't look right. The lid wasn't properly closed. The reason the lid wouldn't shut and the ballerina didn't twirl in her endless pirouette when I opened the box was clear. Inside sat a square white envelope with my name written on it in Polly's handwriting, still very much her elegant italic script.

I sat on the bed and opened the envelope. I found a CD and a single sheet of writing paper.

> *Dearest Sara, I wanted to tell you myself what I've put down here, but there's no time. I know the end is very close now. Please listen to my recording, which I'm making in short bursts while you are in Putney. My laptop should still be in my room. All my love, Polly.*

I found Polly's laptop on the floor beside the bed, noticing what I hadn't observed before: that she had fitted a small microphone to it. I slotted the CD into the computer.

> *Sara, I know you were on that tube train, so close to one of the trains that was blown up by a suicide bomber. I might have lost you before I'd even found you again. That bomber's death*

was a horrible, murderous sacrifice. I want to make my dying something gentle. I can't face Bridie seeing me like this – it will destroy her. And, to be honest, I can't face the last days.

I know I'm being a fool, but perhaps if I go into the Thames and let it wash over me there will be an end to the bombs and the pain, for our family at least. Death's just the other side of the river, but it looks kind and welcoming.

Polly broke off for a moment.

. . . I need to do it now, while you are away, before the drugs make me even weaker. When I've finished here, I'll ring Young Joe on my mobile – did you know he has a website now? – and I'll ask him to row over to the garden.

Her voice became more businesslike. I heard the rustling of paper.

Until that summer in 1989 when Michael and I opened Grandad's file, I'd always felt you were the one person I still had left who belonged to me. Our parents – my parents – were gone. Then I found out that you weren't actually my little sister at all. That you and Bridie had this shared blood. That Nuala had as strong a blood link to you as I did.

I told you how messed up I was when I went away: resentful that Bridie and Grandad wouldn't tell me the truth. Jealous of Bridie's relationship with you. Jealous, too, that Michael had this closeness with you. Half platonic but half something more – the fascination, perhaps, of knowing you to be his secret cousin, so like his family and yet at the same time so different. I remember watching the three of you play Monopoly and thinking how alike you all were. I think Michael's feelings for you became ever more charged as the years passed.

So I was jealous. And angry. I stole things from shops, half hoping the shopkeepers would say something to Bridie and I'd explain what I'd discovered and how it made me feel. It didn't work. I stopped shoplifting and stole Michael from you instead.

It was just after my eighteenth. I told him how fed up I was that this big family secret was seemingly never going to be discussed. Growing older has taught me that Grandad and Bridie were probably waiting for a time they thought was best to tell us both. Or that they might have felt out of their depth, unwilling to risk a huge family upheaval. But I was too young and angry to see that at the time.

Meanwhile, as I said before, Michael was desperate to talk to the old IRA men, to find out the truth about the Coventry bombing, as I'll go on to explain. We both wanted to be somewhere else, do the same thing: clear Jack Brennan's name. He wanted to solve an old injustice, and I longed to come back and tell Grandad and Bridie that I'd sorted it all out for them, to show them how foolish they'd been to keep this family secret hidden from us.

My excuse is that I was only eighteen. I thought it was all that simple.

But somehow I found myself . . . crossing a line with Michael that I hadn't meant to cross. It was hurtful and wrong. I'm sorry, Sara. You didn't deserve that.

A break.

I'm going to switch to less personal matters now because I'm feeling weaker by the minute. As you'll have perhaps worked out by now, Sara, Bridie's father, your grandfather, Jack Brennan, was wrongly hanged for wheeling that bicycle with the bomb onto Broadgate. The real bomber somehow escaped to Ireland, leaving three men to be arrested and charged. The cuttings which were in Grandad's file along with your birth certificate concerned the bomb and named Jack as having been found guilty. But perhaps even if you'd unfolded them and read them, it would all have been a bit oblique. I needed Michael to point out that Bridie's surname was Brennan, like Jack's. We never really used her surname when we were growing up. She was just Bridie to us.

And as you'll have concluded, Michael and I foolishly thought we could ease into the bars along the border and whisper a few names and get introductions to the old men who remembered what had happened back in the late thirties. Or whose fathers had told them of the mainland bombing campaign running right up to the early years of the Second World War. We thought they'd give us answers because it was all such a long time ago and an innocent man had died.

As you know, Special Branch were on to us almost immediately. They were harsh: talking of prison and disgrace. They knew who Grandad was, and they quoted some of his words condemning terrorism at me. I didn't want anything to do with bloodshed. I didn't really want to be in Ireland; I wanted to be back by the Thames with you and Bridie and Grandad. But I'd said I'd help Michael find out the truth about Jack, and I meant to keep my word. I begged the men who came to see us not to tell Grandad where I was. They didn't like it, but eventually they agreed.

By now I'd got completely caught up in Jack Brennan's story. The other hanged men had had some involvement with what had happened on Broadgate in 1939, even though they hadn't actually planted the bomb, but Jack's involvement was purely circumstantial. Nobody could find a motive, not even the prosecuting counsel. The presiding judge cautioned the jury to consider the evidence very carefully, but perhaps he should also have warned them that even apparently rock-solid evidence without motive means nothing. So many people spoke up for Jack, but all for nothing. I picture him becoming steadily more crushed by the knowledge that he was going to be unjustly convicted, and more panicked about Annie, about the baby she was expecting, Bridie. And he was so ill, too, I'd discovered even before I left Thames End House, with the coeliac disease probably nobody would have diagnosed back then, and which he passed on to you. His last weeks must have been horrific.

The Special Branch officer we spent most time with was actually quite sympathetic when we told him more about Jack. He agreed that your grandfather was almost certainly innocent, and pointed us towards some articles in Irish and British newspapers which we hadn't read.

In return, as I told you, Michael was asked to carry on building up a relationship with some paramilitaries he'd met, and was fed good material to pass on to them. Michael had been born and schooled in Ealing, didn't sound Irish and had never lived in the country. His parents had no interest in politics. But when he told the IRA men where to find vehicles on the mainland to transport explosives, or remote barns in the north of England to store them, or safe houses in Manchester or Crewe for men on the run, the hard men were impressed. I should add that Michael never told them anything that caused a single person's death. As the IRA started to trust Michael, they began to include him in 'operations'. I told you before about the dud bomb. We also evaded some of the other 'tests' by claiming Michael had shingles once to avoid involvement in a punishment shooting, and sabotaging our own Ford Fiesta so we couldn't leave the cottage on a second occasion when he was going to be involved in forcing some poor soul to drive a bomb-laden truck into a Belfast checkpoint. We knew they wouldn't tolerate a third excuse, and our British contact made plans to get us out. But Michael vanished before then. Was he taken by the IRA? There were no other Disappearances during the nineties, so it seems anomalous.

I sometimes wonder whether he vanished of his own volition, so I could go home safely. Or perhaps he died in some other way, by accident, overseas.

The Special Branch officer I liked must have had contacts with overseas intelligence personnel. A job offer came through, teaching English as a foreign language in Jordan, where I also learned Arabic and occasionally did bits and pieces for the intelligence people. I was really quite an Establishment person by the end – Grandad might have been proud of me after all.

But I hadn't forgotten about our original mission of proving Jack innocent. I felt I owed it to Bridie, and to you, to continue researching the case. And to Michael, too. I kept reading and ordering documents from British and Irish archives once these were digitised. Some Irish journalists gave me more names of men suspected as having been involved in Coventry. But most of those named were dead. A couple of British journalists expressed interest when I spoke to them, but they couldn't find anything concrete either. After the Good Friday Agreement in 1998, a lot of people wanted to put a lid on the Troubles.

Whoever the bomber is, villain, idiot or someone who lost his nerve at the last minute, the full story may never be known. There are still government and police files that can't be opened for years yet. Perhaps the truth will be found in one of them.

I am so bone-tired now . . .

There was another pause.

I told you how I worried that the violence might follow me back to you, Bridie and Grandad. Even more terrifying was the fear that perhaps you – justifiably – wouldn't want to see me after such a long time. But I've seen you now, Sara, and I know you're still my little sister: that hasn't changed. I couldn't love you more. You'll be fine, you and Bridie. And you have Nuala, too. She's the best of all of us, Stanton or Sheehan.

I'm leaving you my share of the house and enough money to cover inheritance tax. Perhaps you and Ben could live in the house, maybe even get live-in help for Bridie to stay here too. I know you and Nuala will do what's best for her.

The most important thing I can leave Bridie is to tell her that I know her father was innocent. Perhaps some day this will all be made official, just as it was for those wrongly convicted of the Guildford and Birmingham bombings.

I'm going to slip downstairs quietly now, while Nuala's at the corner shop. Joe will meet me with the ferry. I have the coins for my last crossing of the river. I'll slide into the water by the willows and let the Thames carry me away.

I'll leave this recording in the musical box, where I know one of you will think to look.

I can't tell you how much love I'm sending you.

The three of us stood at the graveside. The church had only been half full during the funeral service. I'd been surprised that Polly had wanted a conventional burial, but she had specified all the details of the service, requesting sandwiches and Bridie's tea loaves for the refreshments back at the house, and plenty of gluten-free alternatives for me. I'd been surprised again when Bridie had put on her apron and baked the tea loaves from memory. She hadn't turned the oven on before she put the tins of batter in, but Nuala spotted the omission and switched it on when she wasn't looking.

We threw our handfuls of earth onto the wooden coffin as we had when Grandad and Kathleen had died. I thanked the vicar, who had another funeral about to start.

'Come on,' I took Bridie's arm. She was looking out for someone. I wondered whether it was Polly herself, or my grandfather, or her sister, or my father, Quentin. Or perhaps Michael, the brilliant child, the boy who'd won all the school prizes so effortlessly, who'd eaten up books and never sated his appetite for knowledge. A tall figure moved in the shadows under the yews. Young Joe. I knew he wouldn't come back to the house for the refreshments, but Bridie would pack him up some of the sandwiches and cake and walk the food down to the ferry, with Nuala and me along to keep an eye on her.

Back at Thames End House, Bridie's attention was taken up with boiling the kettle, making pots of tea and finding the best glasses for the Madeira, sherry, and whisky that was on offer alongside the sandwiches and cake. Watching her, you wouldn't have known that she was not the old Bridie of before the stroke. But she preferred not to attempt conversation with the guests, mainly men and women of retirement age. People who'd known us for decades; people who'd known Grandad, too.

An elderly woman wrapped in a grey pashmina approached me. I'd noticed her at the graveyard, standing slightly back with her companion, a woman of a similar age holding a white stick. 'My name is Anstey Clement,' she told me. 'My friend is Dorothy Jenkins.'

I stared at her.

'Don't worry.' She smiled. 'No reason why you should know us.'

'Dorothy . . .' I tried to remember. 'The witness at the Broadgate bombing?'

'Exactly. We met Polly and Michael some years ago, when they came to visit us.'

'Visit you?'

'The summer of 1992, it must have been.'

'Just before Polly left.'

Anstey sighed. 'They were so determined. I wished we could have stopped them.'

So did I.

'Dorothy and Polly occasionally wrote to one another. She knew Polly was very ill and was coming back here. We saw her funeral notice in *The Times*.'

I had the sense of the very beginning of a chain somehow looping itself back to the end and completing a circle.

'Dorothy would love to talk to you.'

'Now?' I looked around the room. The guests were thinning out. A few women of roughly our age whom I recognised as Polly's classmates were already making their excuses. Polly had been so popular, but even golden girls faded from their contemporaries' lives and minds.

Nuala and Bridie would be able to manage for a short period. 'I'll be back soon,' I told Nuala. I introduced myself to Dorothy and led the pair into Granddad's study, guiding Dorothy into his comfortable desk chair. Anstey and I sat on the upright chairs Polly and I used to sit in when we'd been invited in to have cocoa with our grandfather.

'They wrote to me first,' Dorothy said, without preamble. 'They'd done some sharp research to find our address in Leamington Spa.' She sounded admiring. 'I used to do ceramics—I turned to that from painting after I lost my sight. Polly managed to find someone who'd once managed a gallery where I'd exhibited some of my pieces.'

'Polly was a historian's granddaughter,' Anstey said, glancing at the books on the shelf. 'And I gather you've followed in the family line too, Sara?'

'In a very niche way.' I told her briefly about the book on Victorian female education I was researching. Or had been, before the suicide bombers had blown themselves up.

'Did you mind Polly and Michael tracking you down?' I asked.

'I was suspicious at first, I'll admit,' Dorothy said. 'Probably because I still felt some residual guilt about my part in Jack Brennan's prosecution. But Polly wrote to me a week or so after the Baltic Exchange bomb in London.' She sounded weary now. 'Three dead, including a girl of fifteen. It seemed the violence would ever end. Polly's letter came at the right time and it was eloquent.'

It would have been.

'I was receptive. I had to put them off for a few months because I was having an operation on my knee, but I wanted to see Polly and Michael.' She nodded to herself. 'You'll need to get back to your guests,' Dorothy said after a moment. 'So I'll just tell you quickly what happened when Michael and Polly came to visit us.'

FOURTEEN

GUESTS FOR TEA

DOROTHY

Anstey has put out their best Clarice Cliff mugs for the visitors. She's had to dust them first because it's been so long since they've been used.

Dorothy picks one up. She can see the pattern through her fingers just as she can feel the art deco angles of the handle. Will the young guests even notice the special china? Perhaps they just drink without looking or feeling, or prefer mugs that can go straight into a dishwasher. When she'd been a girl in Coventry, before the war, she'd always appreciated lovely things. But life is different now.

'Don't be so nervous, Dot,' Anstey says. 'They're coming to see you because they're interested, that's all.'

'They will be so angry with me.'

Anstey's hand is warm on the top of Dorothy's head. 'They just want to know what you tried to do.'

'None of it was of any use. Jack Brennan hanged.'

'Time, or rather timing, was against you, Dot. Polly and Michael know that.'

Trying to insist that a miscarriage of justice be remedied at a time when the country was fighting for its very survival. Trying to make the point that the very reason they were fighting the war was because justice and a fair legal system mattered. All useless.

Dorothy's ears pick out the sound of footsteps and Anstey walking over to the window.

'The girl has long blonde hair,' Anstey says. 'She's tall and slim. The young man has dark reddish-brown hair. Can't see their faces yet. She has more money than he does: her clothes are better cut, even though they're casual. She's trying to look ordinary, but she's not. He's not ordinary either. He could be a heartbreaker in that very Celtic way. Actually, they could both be actors.' Anstey is good at almost instantly making these little verbal sketches of anyone they meet.

'Are they a couple?' Dorothy asks.

Silence for a few seconds. 'Not sure,' Anstey says. 'If they are, it's recent. They haven't quite mastered how to walk side-by-side on the pavement without jostling into one another.'

The doorbell rings. Dorothy tells her muscles to unclench themselves. Anstey walks to the door and lets them in. Introductions. The girl sounds nervous, but interested. The boy says nothing. Perhaps they aren't as confident as she thought they might be. It makes Dorothy feel a little better.

'Here they are.' Anstey never falls into the trap of sounding unnaturally bright when she introduces people.

'Hello,' says the girl. RP accent, hesitant.

The boy greets her too, his accent a London one, but educated.

She lets out a breath. 'Sit down, please.'

'I'll get the tea.' Anstey pads out.

'I'm glad someone else cares about Jack Brennan,' she says, the words coming out in a rush. She hadn't expected to start like this.

'We do care about him,' young Michael says. 'We both know he was innocent.'

'How do you know this?' Dorothy asks, leaning forward.

'Motive.' The boy sounds so certain. 'There was nothing in his background or previous history to suggest he had any interest in the IRA. His involvement was purely circumstantial. He just picked up a bicycle, that's all.'

Anstey is bringing in the tea tray, the teaspoons rattling against the mugs. She has been to see the actual bicycle in a museum in Coventry and described it to Dorothy. It made Dorothy feel nauseous to think of that black twisted metal structure living on without its blasted-out handlebars and basket.

'Jack had been to the house in Clara Street where the wife and mother-in-law of the other accused men lived,' Michael says. 'He'd been seen there.'

'Jack was looking for new lodgings,' Dorothy says. 'He said in his evidence that he'd knocked on plenty of doors in Clara Street because he'd been given a wrong house number.'

'The other problem is that a clerk in the Coventry post office also remembered him buying a postal order and it was traced to an uncle who had been an IRA member,' Michael adds. 'Which was taken as proof of his true political colours. In his evidence Jack explained that his uncle was now elderly and sick, picking turnips for a living, but the jury obviously wasn't convinced.'

This all sounds less positive. But even if, in the very worst case, Jack Brennan *had* had IRA sympathies, had even handled the bomb, it didn't mean he had intended it to go off in a town centre and kill civilians. He might have intended placing it at the telephone exchange or in a left luggage office, less costly targets in terms of casualties, as other IRA bombers had done throughout 1939. Perhaps he'd panicked, left the bike and run for it. But that wasn't how she remembered it. His face had been so open, so unworried. Not the face of a man who knew he was wheeling explosives. No, she couldn't believe he'd been involved.

'Annie Brennan refused to let her husband be disinterred and reburied in Ireland and commemorated,' Polly said. 'I found an old Irish newspaper that covered the reburial of the other two hanged men and it mentioned that Jack Brennan's remains were staying in England.'

Pressure is building in Dorothy's head. She puts her fingers to her brow and is aware of Anstey's worried glance. She promised not to let herself become upset.

'Jack kept saying he was innocent,' Michael says. 'Bishops and politicians from Ireland telegrammed to beg for clemency. The government simply ignored them. Did you know Jack was actually quite ill while he was in prison? Crippling headaches. Stomach problems. The hospital doctor was concerned, but put it down to the strain of the trial.'

'Stress, they'd call it today,' Dorothy says. 'It would have made everything worse.' She remembered how she hadn't wanted to leave the house after the IRA bomb in 1939. After the Coventry Blitz, she'd been in hospital for some months, at first in Leamington Spa and then in a home for the blind, where they tried to teach her and some RAF men who'd been burnt in their planes how to function again without sight. And all the time she'd been begging for the police to come and see her, for them to listen to what she had to say, for a lawyer to take another statement, for someone to find Jack Brennan's widow. Dorothy feels the girl's gaze on her face.

'It was the Coventry Blitz, wasn't it, where you were blinded?' Polly asks.

She's done her research thoroughly.

Dorothy is back there, back on Broadgate with the German planes above her, searchlights scoring the sky above, wrenching the steering wheel of the ambulance to avoid the craters in the road, springing out of the ambulance to open the back doors, tasting the hot oil and smoke and raspy hot metal in the air, despite the globules of Vicks she'd stuffed up her nostrils before they left the station.

'How did it happen?' Michael asks. The girl must have frowned at him because he apologises. 'Didn't mean to be nosy.'

'We were collecting casualties. My attendant had gone ahead to see what was happening. I was waiting with the ambulance. He tripped over something, a bicycle, and propped it up again.'

She could see him rubbing his ankle, then kicking at the metal structure on the cracked and shrapnel-pocked tarmac behind him, before propping it against what was left of the shop front, out of the way.

'Something pulled at my memory, something about being back on Broadgate, watching a man pick up a fallen bike and prop it up so that people wouldn't trip. The thought was still churning around in my mind when . . .'

When the burning timber from a shop front had struck her. Dorothy's still on the cratered street, feeling the oxygen whoosh away. 'I was on the ground when I regained consciousness. My head hurt. It was like the last time, when the IRA bomb had gone off, but this time I couldn't see. I'd been wearing a helmet, though, and that probably saved my life. Everything was dark, yet images were flickering through my mind as I lay there on the cobbles.'

The fire-heated cobbles had felt warm beneath her back, she remembered now.

'It was as though someone was showing me the early scenes in a film that I'd missed before. I could see Jack Brennan. I could see the bike. He hadn't been wheeling it along Broadgate at all. He'd only picked it up where it had fallen.'

The insight had been like a piece of burnt paper crumpling into ash as she tightened her hand on it. The sound had switched on again: someone shouting and the roaring of bombers' engines and flames and the water hissing on the burning buildings. The recollection had dissolved into pain. Her face. Her eyes. Burning. Everything dark.

'Have some tea,' Anstey says firmly. Teaspoons clink as Anstey unloads her tray. As usual she places Dorothy's tea on the little side table to her right. There is a pause while the youngsters juggle mugs and plates and express obviously genuine delight at being offered slices of Anstey's chocolate cake.

Dorothy herself had been about Polly's age when the Broadgate bomb had gone off. 'I wasn't expecting it to be like this,' she says. 'I thought you'd be angry with me.'

She'd felt defensive before the youngsters arrived, but relating how she'd been blinded had somehow cleared her mind. Perhaps sharing the old pain, seldom talked about now, even with Anstey, had helped.

'We knew you'd tried to tell the authorities there'd been a mistake,' Polly says.

'I even employed a private detective,' she tells them. 'I hoped he might unearth something new. He found no evidence that Jack Brennan was an IRA member or supporter. Jack had simply voiced his opinion on Northern Ireland on a few occasions, saying that the province shouldn't be part of Britain – but he had no interest in violence. When IRA members bombed electricity stations and railways in the Midlands he was not impressed. He sent money to his uncle because he was an old and impoverished man.'

She wipes a tear from her eye and hopes the youngsters know it's the product of anger rather than sadness. Dorothy remembers the Irish in Coventry organising protest marches against the IRA bombers, expressing their dismay at the bombing in letters to the newspapers and in the pulpits at Mass. She recalls the comments of the vehement minority who thought every Irishman in Coventry should be expelled from the city. A community about to enter world war, fighting amongst itself. The evil done by the real bomber had spilled out to touch the innocent: those out shopping on the street, the girl due to be married, Jack Brennan's unborn daughter.

'There was another IRA bomb in Coventry years later, wasn't there?' Polly asks. 'I'd have been a baby at the time.'

'1974, outside a telephone exchange this time.' Dorothy gives an ironic half-smile. 'It blew the IRA volunteer up.' She feels her features harden. 'So many bombs that year. The M62 coach bomb. The Guildford and Birmingham pub bombings.' How Anstey had gasped at the television images of the wrecked pub interiors, the survivors with the blood running off them. Dorothy had made her describe the horror. 'But they convicted the wrong people for Guildford and Birmingham. And they had to let them go eventually.' But if you put a noose around a man's neck there was no chance to put things right for him. All you could do was clear his name, put history right, make things better for any family or descendants. She turns towards Michael. 'What are you going to do about all this?' She hears a harshness in her tone.

'The home secretary won't budge on re-examining the evidence against Jack Brennan, so I'm going to try and track down the real bomber.'

'You're going to do what?'

'It can't be impossible. Ireland's not a big place.'

'After all this time?' And Michael Sheehan's just a boy of, what, twenty or twenty-one. 'Surely the man will be dead?'

'Probably. But someone in Ireland, north or south, must know who he was. I think he managed to get himself into the Republic in autumn 1939, hiding away until the trial was safely over and the three men were hanged in 1940.'

'Turning private eye and investigating old gunmen sounds dangerous, Michael,' Anstey says. 'How will you get them to talk to you? The IRA don't strike me as the most trusting and reasonable bunch.'

Dorothy shudders.

'There're people on my mother's side who live in the North, near the border. They know which bars to go to.'

Dorothy hears Polly shift slightly on her seat – obviously not entirely keen on Michael going to Northern Ireland and to persuade people to open up to him about an old crime. Sensible girl.

'But why are you so interested?' she asks. 'I know you're of Irish descent, Michael. And you mentioned something about a family connection to Jack Brennan, Polly?'

'He wasn't a blood relation,' the girl says. 'But he's my . . . cousin's, whatever you want to call her, grandfather. Sara doesn't know anything about this.'

'Why not?'

Dorothy hears the girl sigh. 'It's complicated. Sara's mother, Bridie, is my grandfather's housekeeper.'

'And the housekeeper is Jack Brennan's daughter?' Clever Anstey has worked it out.

'My mother and Bridie are half-sisters,' Michael says.

'It's complicated. There've been so many secrets in our family.' Melancholy of an almost too mature kind drips from Polly's words. And there's something else, too. Dorothy thinks the girl sounds guilty. But about what?

'My aunt Bridie has never acknowledged Sara as her daughter. We think it's to spare her from knowing her grandfather was hanged for terrorism,' Michael says.

'There are probably other reasons too, for Bridie keeping it a secret.' Polly still sounds leaden. 'She wasn't married to Sara's father. She has a very black-and-white view of morality. But proving Jack Brennan's innocence would lift a weight from her.'

'So you two have researched all this about Jack Brennan, but you haven't shared it with anyone else?' Dorothy can detect the amazement in her own voice.

'Even though you don't approve of all the secret-keeping?' Anstey sounds the closest Anstey ever could to tart.

'We weren't supposed to find out,' Polly says. 'We came across newspaper cuttings relating to Coventry when we were snooping a few years ago. We wanted to know why my grandfather had kept the cuttings with Sara's birth certificate and . . . other things.'

Michael takes over. 'We read as many accounts of the trial as we could find. The case against Jack seemed very thin.'

'You must care a lot for Bridie,' Dorothy says to Polly.

'I do.' Polly says it very quietly. 'It hasn't been easy knowing that she has this closer relationship with Sara. It's changed things between the three of us.'

The girl must feel less loved at some level. Perhaps unjustly, but emotions run very deep when you are Polly's age.

'I haven't behaved well. This is my chance to show them all – Bridie, Grandad and Sara – that I'm sorry. I just want—' the girl takes a breath. 'I just want things to be like they used to be.'

The yearning in Polly's voice makes Dorothy almost approve of this mad scheme.

'So much of Bridie's life has been constrained by other people,' Polly goes on. 'She was a nun for some years from her late teens. Then she met . . . Well, I assume it was my uncle Quentin. The birth certificate didn't say. Quentin died in the crash that killed my parents too, before he could marry Bridie. She turned herself into our family's housekeeper and nanny.' Polly's voice is solemn. 'I can't stand it when everyone apart from us thinks she's just a servant.'

People have looked down on Dorothy and Anstey because of their eccentric, as they term it, relationship. It has been more painful for Dorothy to know that Anstey has been mocked than it has to know it of herself.

Dorothy feels tired, as though she's buried up to the neck in decades of emotion: hers and other people's. 'What do you want me to do?' She feels Anstey's concern as a heightened vibration in the room, hears her pick up her mug and pour herself more tea.

'We wanted to ask if you'd kept copies of the statements you gave the police and ask you if you'd seen anyone else that lunchtime. We can't find the statements anywhere in the public records,' explains Polly.

'The files may still be closed to the public,' Michael says.

'My father made me go home and write out what I could remember telling the police. He kept my account locked up in his desk. But my parents' house was badly damaged by incendiaries late in the war. His study was burnt out. By the time the fire hoses had sprayed everything with water, there was nothing worth keeping.'

'Can you remember anything that might be important that the police didn't ask you about?' Michael leans towards her. She can almost feel his young man's breath on her, slightly animal-like in a fresh, not unpleasant way. She lets herself be seventeen again, impatient to get on with life before the war starts and it's all too late.

She's standing on the pavement outside Burton Menswear. Who's there? Two road sweepers. A girl with a smile on her face. That will be Elsie Ansell, aged 21, looking forward to getting married in two weeks' time, probably shopping for a few more things she needs for her trousseau or new married life. A woman with a perambulator. Two middle-aged ladies talking about the Owen Owen summer sale. The man who moves the bicycle, Jack Brennan, also with a look of anticipation in his eyes. His wife's expecting their first child: Bridie, this must be, mother of Sara. Does Jack yet know about the pregnancy?

Who else? Is there someone in the shadows, looking on furtively? Or perhaps sweating with anxiety, heart thumping, wanting to do something, to shout a warning, because that bicycle with its deadly load isn't supposed to be parked here in the town centre, ready to blow the lives of scores of people into chaos?

Who is there?

Dorothy tries to see. So many bombs in her youth. *Focus on this one, on Broadgate, that last summer of peace when the only thing on her mind had been frocks and her new status as an adult.*

Is there someone there who shouldn't be present?

Nobody. Just shoppers: chatting, laughing, bustling. 'I'm sorry,' she says, as much to the absent Bridie as to anyone else.

'It's all right.' Michael sounds resigned but not surprised. 'We still have our plan B.'

'Plan B being to go over to Ireland and use your family connections to track down old IRA men?'

The youngsters are silent.

'Probably best not to say more,' Polly says sadly. 'You'll only try and stop us.'

Dorothy is filled with a sense of doom, almost as though she is once again out on the streets of Coventry during the Blitz.

'We've discussed it.' Michael's voice is resolute. He might make a good teacher or even a leader of some kind. A politician, perhaps. 'There's no other way.'

'It's dangerous.' Doesn't the boy watch the news? Sometimes Dorothy is glad she can't see the pictures that make Anstey gasp with horror. 'You've read the press articles, you say? Didn't some of the Irish newspapers in the sixties name someone?' Dorothy tries to recall the details. 'Wouldn't it be better just to try and get the Irish authorities involved?'

'People are named, but there's nothing more than names,' Michael says. 'We need evidence.'

'I should ring your families and tell them what you're planning,' she tells Polly and Michael.

'We're both over eighteen now,' Michael says. 'They can't stop us.'

'You can't want to take Polly into such danger,' Anstey almost shouts. 'What about Bridie and Sara? What about her grandfather? He's elderly, isn't he?'

'I'll come back and see them all soon,' Polly says. Dorothy can hear a gentle zipping noise coming from her direction. The girl must be pulling a jewel or metallic ornament up and down a chain worn round her neck, making a slight rasping sound. Polly isn't as sure of herself as she would like them to believe.

'Don't do this,' Dorothy says.

'It's too late.' The zipping sound stops. Dorothy hears a gentle clink as Polly replaces her mug on the tray. 'I have to.' The slight creak of the loose floorboard under the Persian rug indicates that she's standing up. 'Thank you for the tea.'

FIFTEEN

COVENTRY: AN ENDING

SARA

1 August 2005

It's a straightforward train journey from Oxford to Coventry. Bridie hasn't been on a train for some years, and her face brightens at the sight of a young mother with a baby and toddler in the row next to us. The mother has to take the toddler to the toilet and entrusts the baby to us. Bridie holds him carefully and he smiles at her. Nuala and I expect a fuss when they get off at Leamington, but Bridie hands the boy back to his mother cheerfully.

I myself am feeling more cheerful than I could have expected to feel so soon after Polly's funeral, as this morning I have finally received the email I have been longing for: *Only just got your messages, on way to airport, back within 24 hours, Ben xxx.* I showed it to Nuala, whose beaming smile indicated just how worried she has been about me and how relieved she must be that Ben is finally on his way home. This time tomorrow he will be in Thames End House filling the rooms with his laugh, his photographs of Peruvian creatures, his maleness: a welcome corrective to our all-female house of mourning. I am not worrying as much about Bridie because I think that the money Polly has left will be enough to pay for a live-in carer for her at Thames End House, with me perhaps coming down more often, possibly even moving in myself, if Ben is happy to come with me.

'Sara heard from her young man before we left this morning,' Nuala tells Bridie. 'Has she told you about Ben?'

Many times. But she denies it.

'What does he do?' Her eyes are shrewd and interested and she smiles at the mention of the monkeys, but she loses concentration when I start explaining more about his work.

Nuala winks at me. 'Just start planning the wedding and she'll be getting out the lace tablecloth again.' I kick her under the table and Bridie frowns at us.

'I will not tolerate poor behaviour in public places. You two will not let your grandfather down.' I try not to meet Nuala's eye.

The unmodernised railway station does not appeal to Bridie. I feel her about to comment and usher her quickly into a taxi. I know she will think this is extravagant, but Nuala and I want to save her energy for the city centre.

'The town centre doesn't look anything like it would have done when your mother and father lived here,' I warn Bridie. 'The Luftwaffe and the city planners more or less destroyed the medieval parts, but it's beautiful around the cathedral.'

A shame. In my internet search for old photos of Coventry, I've pulled up images of a fascinating skyline of old Tudor merchant houses. If Bridie is up to it, I'd like to go to the museum and look at more of the old pictures I saw when I made a reconnaissance visit to the city last week. I'd like to see more of the city my grandparents courted in, the places they'd have known in the early months of their marriage.

I have a photo with me of Broadgate just before the August 1939 IRA bomb. When we stop at the place that I estimate must have been where the bomber left the bicycle and where Jack picked it up, we find ourselves in a shopping precinct. To the left of us is a long empty space which must once have been the centre of the road, down which the trams ran. I spot the statue of Lady Godiva and point it out to Nuala. I wonder if Bridie's seen the statue too. I brace myself for a comment. She's sharp on historical meaning even if she can't remember what the day is, so she might forgive Lady Godiva her otherwise unnecessary nudity.

I want to close my eyes and try to picture myself back in time, back in 1939, but I dare not take my eyes off Bridie, who can still amaze us with a sudden dart towards some attraction she's spotted: a balloon-seller, a dog, a toddler.

'Here,' Bridie says, looking around the expanse of concrete at a clothing shop in one direction and a coffee chain in the other. Pedestrians peer at us with suspicion. 'He did it here.'

'Hard to tell.' Nuala screws up her brow in concentration and looks just like her mother used to when calculating how many potatoes to peel for us children. 'Looks about right, though, from the old map of the city.'

Bridie's father – my grandfather – was on his way to carry out some lunchtime errand. He couldn't have known about the pregnancy yet – his wife, my grandmother, would probably have waited a few more weeks to tell him. But Annie and Jack had only been married nine months; they were practically newly-weds. He'd gone to a dental appointment, but perhaps he was planning to buy his wife a bunch of flowers on the way back to the factory. Or something more prosaic. A saucepan. They were both earning, he very nicely. They'd have been feathering their nest, hoping that the storm clouds over Europe might by a miracle disperse and allow them some more time.

But fate had other plans for them that August lunchtime.

'Should have left it,' Bridie says. I know she means that her father should have walked on and not stopped to pick up the bicycle. But he was probably a naturally tidy soul, like his daughter. And besides, someone might have tripped over it. But picking up the bicycle wouldn't have mattered if he hadn't happened to visit the house in Clara Street days earlier on a misunderstanding. If he hadn't been a young Irishman. If he hadn't been overheard in a works canteen saying that, all things considered, he thought Ireland would be better off as a united independent country. If he hadn't sent the postal order to the uncle . . . Myriad small details adding up to a portrait that was grotesquely inaccurate. My grandfather was a kind and friendly soul. Perhaps he should have been more discerning in his friendships and family loyalties.

A train of small events that brought Jack to the noose and Bridie to the convent. And me to the house on the Thames.

'It wasn't him,' Bridie says. Nuala and I exchange glances. Has she taken in what we tried to explain?

The clouds that have threatened us all morning sprinkle raindrops on us, and the walkways and shops of Coventry turn grey.

'Feck,' Bridie says. Nuala and I grin. Bridie means it as a comment on the unfairness that brought her father to the gallows, and Coventry's city centre to this. Despite the solemnity of the moment, I can't help giggling at the formerly prim Bridie using the word. She must have picked it up years ago from the more outspoken Kathleen.

'Fancy a cup of tea?' I suggest.

Her eyes brighten. For all her life spent in England, an Irishwoman's blood still runs through her veins and no good reason exists for turning down a cup of tea. There's a department store close by. It's a modern building, not the proud new Owen Owen on Broadgate that had been open only a couple of years when the IRA bomb went off, and was still standing until the following year when the Luftwaffe blitzed it. Or there's the museum cafe, where we could also look at some of the exhibits, give ourselves a sense of Coventry before and during the war, if Bridie's up for it. Possibly I could even find somewhere that serves a snack I could eat. I forgot to bring gluten-free food with me. I think again of my grandfather, who might also have had coeliac disease, but was hardly well placed to obtain a diagnosis before they hanged him at Birmingham, even if the cause of the condition was known back in the thirties.

Bridie smiles at me. 'Grand day out with Nuala and with Sara, my daughter.'

I stop at that last word and try not to let too much emotion show on my face. It might confuse her, worry her. But I can't help smiling. Coventry is a Midlands city that has had a lot of its beauty despoiled by man and history, but for me, and perhaps for Bridie, it's taken on the status of a place of pilgrimage. Bridie drops her handbag. A young Asian man picks it up for her with a smile. I like this city.

It all ends at Coventry.

The rain fizzles out. We walk through the steel and concrete that have replaced the Broadgate my grandfather walked down, and I think I feel his breath on my neck. If I turned quickly enough I might just catch a glimpse of a young man in a 1930s suit among the twenty-first-century shoppers, his face friendly, open. Hopeful. It might break my heart, but I might see Jack Brennan on his way to pick up that bicycle. I could tell him to walk on quickly, not to be the kind of person who wouldn't just leave a bicycle on the pavement for others to trip over.

'Come on, sweetheart.' My mother takes my hand, her voice as firm as it was when I was a child and needed guidance. 'Or it'll be another day gone.' She leads me on through the shoppers before I can turn around.

AUTHOR'S NOTE

The 1939 Broadgate bombing really happened. I have deviated from history by creating a fictional character: Jack Brennan. In reality, two men were hanged at Birmingham: Peter Barnes and James Richards. Three others were found not guilty. The identity of the person who left the bicycle with its deadly load in the Coventry street has never been officially made public. The IRA bombing campaign in England in 1939–1940 claimed seven lives and injured around 100 people and seems to have aimed at putting pressure on Britain to withdraw from Northern Ireland, as well as attracting the attention of Nazi Germany in the hope that it might ally itself with the Republican cause.

On 14 October 2015, a memorial stone to the five victims of the 1939 Broadgate bomb was unveiled on Unity Lawn in the grounds of Coventry Cathedral.

◆　◆　◆

This morning, as I start the final stages of proofreading this manuscript, news has come through of 41 people dying the previous night in a gun and bomb attack on Istanbul Ataturk airport. This has followed the killing of 49 people in a gay nightclub in Orlando, Florida, earlier this month. About three months ago, in March 2016, just as I was embarking on the major editing work on this novel, 32 people died in terrorist explosions in Brussels. March 2016 had already seen previous terrorist attacks in Turkey, Pakistan, Nigeria, Ivory Coast and Mali. And that's without listing all the very many atrocities taking place around the world during the 18 months or so it took me to write and complete this novel on terrorism. May all the victims rest in peace.

29 June 2016

BIBLIOGRAPHY

The IRA in general

A Secret History of the IRA
Ed Moloney
Penguin, 2007

Armed Struggle: The History of the IRA
Richard English
Pan Macmillan, 2012

The IRA bombing campaign in England, 1939–1940

The Devil's Deal: The IRA, Nazi Germany and the Double Life of Jim O'Donovan
David O'Donoghue
New Island Books, 2010

Coventry

Hanged at Birmingham

Chapter 25: The Coventry Outrage: Peter Barnes & James Richards
Steve Fielding
The History Press, 2009

Coventry at War
David McGrory
The History Press, 2009

7/7: the London bombings

Into the Darkness: An Account of 7/7
Peter Zimonjic
Vintage, 2008

Life in religious orders

Through the Narrow Gate: A Nun's Story
Karen Armstrong
Flamingo, 1997

I Leap Over the Wall
Monica Baldwin
Robert Hale, 2015

Adoptions in Britain in the seventies and eighties

Half a Million Women
David Howe, Phillida Sawbridge, Diana Hinings
Penguin, 1992

Thanks also to the contributors to the Historic Coventry website,
http://www.historiccoventry.co.uk/

ACKNOWLEDGEMENTS

Special thanks go to Kristina Riggle, Alis Hawkins and Aliya Whitley for their cheering on and suggestions at various stages of writing this book; to Will Atkins for his input on the text; and to my editor Sammia Hamer at Lake Union for her editorial advice, kindness and encouragement. Thanks also to Sana Chebaro, Hatty Stiles and Bekah Graham at Lake Union. A huge amount of gratitude goes to Victoria Pepe for her forensic editing skills, which helped me hone and plait a complex text into a more focused form. Thank you, as well, to Alex Higson and Julia Bruce for applying their eagle eyes to the text. My gratitude to the staff at the History Centre of the Herbert Art Gallery and Museum in Coventry for their help with tracking down original documents relating to the 1939 IRA bomb and the Coventry Blitz. And, as always, heartfelt gratitude to my family: Johnnie, Mungo and Eloise, for bearing with me when the writing became intense, and to members of the Newplace and MNW groups for their ongoing support.

ABOUT THE AUTHOR

Eliza Graham spent biology lessons reading Jean Plaidy novels behind the textbooks, sitting at the back of the classroom. In English and history lessons she sat right at the front, hanging on to every word. At home she read books while getting dressed and cleaning her teeth. During school holidays she visited the public library multiple times a day.

At Oxford University she read English literature on a course that regarded anything post about 1930 as too modern to be included. She retains a love of Victorian novels.

Eliza lives in an ancient village in the Oxfordshire countryside with her family. Her interests (still) mainly revolve around reading, but she also enjoys walking in the downland country around her home.

Find out more about Eliza on her website: www.elizagrahamauthor.com. You can also follow her on Twitter: @Eliza_Graham.